Praise for *Everything Hurts*

"Bill Scheft masterfully gives us a tale full of wisdom and grace. *Everything Hurts* is a story of self-realization, family, the nature of our politics and our pain. He does it all with a razor sharp sense of humor that cuts to the bone."

—Lewis Black, comedian and author of *Me of Little Faith*

"Pain is king and laughter is his fool. . . . The book achieves a subtle poignancy."

—*Chicago Sun-Times*

"I love this fresh, brilliant, and hilarious novel. Bill Scheft has written an original story full of twists and turns that will surprise and delight you. *Everything Hurts* is the ultimate guide to a man's heart, intellect, and spinal column—and once and for all will answer the question 'Why won't my man go to the doctor?'"

—Adriana Trigiani, bestselling author of the Big Stone Gap series and *Very Valentine*

"[Bill Scheft] plays both ends against the middle, satirizing our glib and cynical pop culture in a glib and cynical novel. Phil grows on us despite himself."

—Amanda Heller, *The Boston Globe*

"If you've never felt physical pain or experienced family problems, then this book is not for you. Otherwise, join the fun, family, stand-up comedy, deeply felt angst, frustration, lust, loss, and love of Phil Camp, aka Marty Fleck. In *Everything Hurts*, everything hurts because it's so funny and also because everything moves beyond

the funny bone, past Rush Limbaugh and Jerry Springer and Keats, and straight to the secret closet of your heart. Bill Scheft smokes."
—Clyde Edgerton, author of *The Bible Salesman* and
Walking Across Egypt

"A hysterical journey of self-discovery. . . . Falling-down funny."
—Kurt Rabin, *The Free Lance-Star* (Fredericksburg, VA)

"The writing is swift and breezy but with an underlying message that deals with guilt and pain. Because it's a novel, it's more sit-down comedy than stand-up. . . . Sometimes you laugh only when it hurts."
—Charles Lee Boyd, *The Post and Courier* (Charleston, SC)

"A painfully funny novel."
—*The Daily Beast*

"Scheft skewers physical and emotional pain with a mercilessly comic touch and a bit of poignancy. . . . Phil is a wonderful protagonist, and Scheft's biting wit coexists nicely with the undercurrent of uplift."
—*Publishers Weekly*

"A stylistic cross between Don Rickles and Michael Chabon."
—Ben Kaplan, *The National Post* (Canada)

"A wincingly funny, honest, and sardonic novel."
—*Booklist*

"Like [Woody] Allen, Scheft seems to know his way around the psychiatrist's couch; he has a keen sense of the emotional pathways of depression and of how therapy awkwardly leads people into and out of their worst experiences. . . . Scheft's rendering of family dysfunction is consistently sturdy. Much like Phil's fictitious self-help book: meant as a gag, but with enough smarts to be taken seriously."
—*Kirkus Reviews*

"Clever prose and quirky characters. . . . Just what the doctor ordered."

"Satisfying as it is quirky . . . Scheft knows how to create characters which stay in your head long after you finish the book."

Also by Bill Scheft

THE RINGER

TIME WON'T LET ME

THE BEST OF THE SHOW:
A CLASSIC COLLECTION OF WIT AND WISDOM

Everything Hurts

Bill Scheft

Simon & Schuster Paperbacks

New York   London   Toronto   Sydney

Simon & Schuster Paperbacks
A Division of Simon & Schuster, Inc.
1230 Avenue of the Americas
New York, NY 10020

First Simon & Schuster trade paperback edition April 2010

SIMON & SCHUSTER PAPERBACKS and colophon are registered
trademarks of Simon & Schuster, Inc.

For information about special discounts for bulk purchases,
please contact Simon & Schuster Special Sales at
1-866-506-1949 or business@simonandschuster.com.

The Simon & Schuster Speakers Bureau can bring authors
to your live event. For more information or to book an event,
contact the Simon & Schuster Speakers Bureau at
1-866-248-3049 or visit our website at www.simonspeakers.com.

Designed by C. Linda Dingler

Manufactured in the United States of America

1   3   5   7   9   10   8   6   4   2

The Library of Congress has cataloged the hardcover edition as follows:

Scheft, Bill.
Everything hurts / Bill Scheft.
p.   cm.
1. Journalists—Fiction. I. Title.
PS3619.C345E94 2009
813'.6—dc22

ISBN 978-1-4165-9934-0
ISBN 978-1-4165-9940-1 (pbk)
ISBN 978-1-4391-1016-4 (ebook)

To Adrianne, my love.

Thank you for showing me the artist's way.

Everything Hurts

That inescapable animal walks with me,
Has followed me since the black womb held,
Moves where I move, distorting my gesture,
A caricature, a swollen shadow,
A stupid clown of the spirit's motive . . .

—DELMORE SCHWARTZ

The only time I'm not peeing . . . is when
I'm peeing.

—IRVING COHEN

1

Let's get something straight. Phil Camp had not set out to become a fraud, or, as it turned out, to prevent himself from perpetuating the fraud that he had become. That's just what happened.

Huh?

Man writes book to pay off ex-wife. Book is supposed to be a spoof. World takes book seriously. Man's life changes. Man under whose name book was written, his life changes as well. Ex-wife paid off, but pissed.

A week shy of nine years and seven months ago, on August 10, 1994, Phil was standing at the bottom of Terminal A at Newark Airport, filling out a lost luggage form. He had been on the road for two weeks with the Mets, then Yankees, then Mets and, at thirty-six, was pretty sure he was about to become temporarily obsolete. After two years of inert negotiations between players and owners, Major League Baseball was seven days from its final drop-dead work stoppage date, with little chance of resuming play before next season. As the shell-shocked maintenance worker who walked around the athletic fields at Phil's college used to say, "*No game. Go home.*"

And if Phil's financially bulimic employer, Excelsior Publications, had its way, stay home. For the last six months, Excelsior had been circling his desk, dropping subtlety-filleted reminders that he'd better grab the twelve-weeks-with-pay/six-months-medical-buyout package the newspaper was offering before it was snapped up by someone with less of a past and more of a future.

Phil made it until the Tuesday after Labor Day before he took the buyout. But it had been the kind of coincidence-laden three weeks that happen to other people. Two days after he got home, he did ten minutes on some syndicated radio show called *Bob and Tom* and talked about everything other than baseball, prompting the kind of big, raucous laughs from the hosts they normally bestowed on C-list celebrities. The day after that, some guy who called himself a "book packager," Wayne Beiliner, called and said, "If you ever have an idea for a funny book, call me." The day after that, Continental called and asked if he'd be interested in hearing about his baggage. "I know all about my baggage," said Phil, "but I'm interested in hearing about my luggage." Ten yellow legal pad pages after that, he phoned Wayne Beiliner. "I think I may have something," he said.

When Phil told Wayne Beiliner the title, *Where Can I Stow My Baggage?* the book packager shrieked, "You just made five thousand dollars, pal!" By the time Wayne Beiliner finished reading the ten pages of notes, Phil had made another five thousand dollars.

"How long will it take you to write fifty thousand words?"

Phil's head did the math. His one-thousand-word baseball stories took about an hour. Fifty hours. Forty-hour workweek, but no need to bust his ass. . . .

"Three weeks."

"Take two months," said Wayne Beiliner. "I have to sell this, then get an illustrator."

"You think you can sell this book in two months?"

The book packager packaged a good laugh. "No, pal," he said, "getting the illustrator takes two months. I'll have this sold by Monday."

That Tuesday, the ten-thousand-dollar check arrived by FedEx. It sublet Phil's checking account for the five business days needed for clearing. In that time, he managed two phone calls to his ex-wife, the former Trish Lamphiere, then Trish Camp, now Trish Lamphiere, that were about as civil as the green room at *Jerry Springer.* The transcript from the first call still survives:

TRISH: Hello?
PHIL: Hi, Trish. It's Phil.
TRISH: Yeah, what?
PHIL: I got laid off at the paper.
TRISH: Great.
PHIL: But I have a proposition.
TRISH: Okay, let me sit down. Now, it's going to sound like I'm hanging up, but I'm really just pulling up a chair. *(SFX:* Click, followed by dial tone.)

The second call went to completion. He offered Trish a one-time buyout of ten thousand dollars rather than pay the last twelve months of an alimony agreement. It turned out to be a savings of two grand for him.

"Fine," she had supposedly said, "and sorry about hanging up."

"No problem."

"You're the only one who makes me act like that."

"Yeah," said Phil. "I know."

Their marriage had lasted three years, which apparently is as long as it takes to convince the average woman that you're not kidding when you say you don't want kids. Phil never imagined he would have to bother getting persuasive, because during their four-year courtship, he and Trish had often supped on the shared belief that families were other people's migraine.

But somewhere in between dancing with her little cousin at their wedding reception and unwrapping the fifth Panasonic bread maker, all of that changed for Trish. Throughout the first two years of the marriage, whenever the subject would come up, Phil would say, "Please don't ask me to have children," as if he contained both sets of reproductive organs. Trish laughed, and figured him to be merely gun-shy, and mostly ironic. No otherwise kind man would deprive his wife of such joy, would he? Especially one who often told and retold such vivid stories of his parents' rearing of him and his older brother. Painfully hilarious tales of survival of the fits and starts, but mostly fits. And unexaggerated. The older brother, Jimmy, would stop rolling on the couch to weepingly corroborate every episode. Jimmy, who had two girls and a boy of his own and regretted none. So why not? If Phil could recall and regale and laugh along, why not take a shot at a scarless version of upbringing?

He couldn't have meant it. How can a man say something like *Please don't ask me to have children* and mean it? But he did.

In the end, Year Three, when he was exhausted by the topic, Phil would quote lines from two then-recent movies: (1) "I don't believe in childhood," (*Nuts,* 1987), and (2) "My sister loved New York City because it had nothing to do with her childhood," (*The Prince of Tides,* 1991), which would be followed by Trish saying, "It takes a real deep thinker to have Barbra Streisand as the principal architect of his philosophy," and then *SFX:* <u>Door slam.</u>

Trish was hardly the average woman, clicks and door slams aside. Until her monumental misjudging of Phil's feelings about raising a family, she had made one mistake in her previous forty-three years, an eight-month marriage when she was twenty. The only daughter of Patrick Lamphiere, the liquor store baron of Rumson, Fair Haven, and points south on the Garden State Parkway, Patricia had spent every day of her life but two bathed in the rarefied heir of someone well aware she is in charge and constantly being pursued. Others might have taken that splendidly dealt hand and wiped out the rest of the table on entitlement alone. But with Trish, the appreciation of her lot made her as magnanimous as she was attractive. The kind of magnanimity that comes with almost never losing.

Almost. Phil and Trish had one session with the couples counselor, who said the only way to resolve an impasse over children was to give in to the partner whose feelings are stronger.

"I'll leave you over this," she said.

And Phil Camp, whose carefree path had been well marked with signs that read GIVE IN HERE, got to hear himself say, "I'll miss you, Trish."

"Maybe we should pick this up next week," the counselor had said when his jaw had finished its descent. It got a nice laugh from both of them.

That was the last laugh for a while. The divorce became final in 1992. The three-year, one-thousand-dollar-a-month alimony was a penance Phil wanted to live with. Resolved guilt. He more than understood that a woman does not get that time back, and a man is not allowed to say, "I can't have children" unless he's broke and sterile. And as long as you are the son-in-law of Patrick Lamphiere, your wife will not be liquor-store barren.

Sad time. No winners. Phil would call his brother and say, "Everyone has their baggage, but this will always be my extra suitcase." And so, he gave birth to his first baggage analogy.

Where Can I Stow My Baggage? could have been called *Around the World in 101 Metaphors*. Luckily, that wasn't the title, because the fad-buying public doesn't care for literary-device-of-comparison shopping. Phil Camp, who had always wanted to think of himself as an immensely complicated man, found that his pen-to-page concepts were quite simple. His prose was spare and endearing, and all that crap, but more important, it was accessible. Come on. Who couldn't read chapter 1, "What's My Baggage?" or chapter 2, "How Much Baggage Do I Need?" and not relate to the point where they thought *they* had written the book?

Under each chapter heading came the same subheadings:

Family
Marriage/Relationships
Workplace/School
Secrets/Lies
Archenemies (Shit List)
Potential Enemies (Shit Waiting List)

Apologies Due
Regrets
Expectations
Right Now

The rest of the Contents, laid out in bite-size twelve-page chapters, which borrowed less from the highbrow template of self-help books and more from the browse-worthy tradition of a Sunday supplement, was equally unavoidable.

How Much Baggage Will I Claim?
Does My Baggage Have the Proper Identification?
What Baggage Will I Carry On?
Can I Make My Baggage Fit Over My Head or Under My Seat?
No? Then What Can I Do Without?
Lost Luggage
Matching Luggage
Anything Else to Declare?

The sixty or so illustrations gave the book a good deal more than another dimension. It pushed the page total to 182 and justified the $18.95 cover price. Inked by the talented Jeff Hong (think Bruce McCall before his fee went up), each drawing was realistically peopled by featureless souls with whom a reader could identify but not judge, and propelled by thankfully unsubtle comic imagery the same reader could take or leave, but usually took.

Phil took the entire three months to write *Where Can I Stow My Baggage?* and half of that time was spent shaking his head and asking himself, "Are people going to get that I'm just trying to be funny?" It was a fair question, because some of the jokes were unmistakably jokes *(Of course, if you can make yourself feel better about your family by saying you were switched at birth, go with that . . .)*, and some of the flip comments designed to fill a page *(Someone once defined insanity as doing the same thing over and over again, expecting different results. And I bet that same guy said that line over and over again, expecting everyone would agree with him . . .)* turned out to be accidentally profound.

The following December 1995, *Where Can I Stow My Baggage?* wedged itself into the bookstore checkout sightline of the solace-starved, stocking-stuffing consumer literati. The book's publication date was as fortuitous as its placement. Two years after souls had gorged themselves on chicken soup, two years before the same souls would stop sweating the small stuff while wondering who moved their cheese.

"But it was supposed to be a goof!" Phil said when he found out he would be collecting royalties a day after the book went on sale.

"Hey, what can I tell you?" gushed Wayne Beiliner, who had moved from book packager to agent without touching the ground. "You're a big, fat shining star. They can't get enough of Marty Fleck."

Marty Fleck was listed as the author of *Where Can I Stow My Baggage?* From the beginning, Phil knew he would write the book under another name. That name. Marty Fleck was the shortened version of Marty Fleckman, a less than unknown amateur golfer who had led the 1967 U.S. Open after three rounds. It was the one joke Phil had kept for himself. During his years as a newspaperman, whenever he was having trouble getting in touch with an athlete, politician, or celebrity, Phil would pose as a publicist, Marty Fleck, and leave his number along with some vague message about a fifty-thousand-dollar personal appearance fee for "just showing up at some kid's bar mitzvah on Long Island and waving out of the limousine window." If whoever was taking the message pressed for more information, Phil would say, "Just have Darryl Strawberry (Senator D'Amato, Glenn Close) call me before three or I call my backup, Dwight Gooden (Governor Cuomo, Kathleen Turner). Look, I gotta go. Salman Rushdie needs a suite upgrade." Or something equally brio-saturated. It would crack up the newsroom or Trish, if she was home. And whoever Phil wanted to reach would always call back. Always before three.

Marty Fleck was playful in a way Phil Camp never was, and mercifully shallow. Phil knew he had at least the inch-deep insight that comes from three decades of therapy. But guess what? Inch-deep is as far as most people want to go. If the explanation a person is most comfortable with turns out to be, "Well, that's the hand I was dealt," why dig when you can pack? And if you pack, pack light. And light was where Marty Fleck came in.

Marty Fleck reduced childhood to "Yes or no: My mother wasn't my type." Answer yes, make some room in your baggage. Answer no, make more room. He could admit to being seduced by a thirty-year-old woman when he was seventeen and two chapters later ("Does My Baggage Have the Proper Identification?") confess to the reader that nothing happened, he'd just been trying to impress you.

There are another 180 pages of examples, some less gimmicky than others, but the upshot of all of it was America had a new prophet. Marty Fleck. The media waffled, one day proclaiming him the new Mark Twain, the next day dubbing him the "Dalai Lame-ah," but it waffled on a daily basis and kept the buzz charged through the holidays and beyond.

Meanwhile, the offers started coming in. TV, radio, appearance fees with real money and no waving out of a limo window. Phil told Wayne Beiliner to turn them all down. And six months later, when *Where Can I Stow My Baggage?* was still on the bestseller list and M. Scott Peck, the author of *The Road Less Traveled* and *People of the Lie*, was going out of his way to call Marty Fleck "irrelevant," the offers had quadrupled. Phil's publisher, Duffy Hill Press, was begging him for a sequel, claiming it was the least he owed them for keeping his real name out of it. Phil made the mistake of saying, "Haven't we all made enough money off this nonsense?" and his editor, Rob Wolfmeyer, laughed and said, "Perfect title for the next book, Marty."

Two nights later, during an opening segment called "New Books," David Letterman turned a mocked-up cover toward the camera and said, "Well, advice-maven Marty Fleck is at it again with his latest offering, *Where Do I Stow All These Bags of Cash I Made off This Crap?*

By the time the misinterpretation of *Where Can I Stow My Baggage?* had become the mass interpretation of *Where Can I Stow My Baggage?* Phil Camp felt he had no choice but to continue hiding behind Marty Fleck, while not completely hiding Marty Fleck. So, a year after hardcover hysteria, he ended up accepting one offer. A twice-weekly syndicated newspaper column for, of all bosses, Excelsior Publications, called "Baggage Handling." The plan was to systematically de-guru Marty Fleck and have him emerge as a man with no answers, a man as confused as the thousands of people who had credited him with compartmentalizing their confusion.

The money from the syndication deal was hardly lucrative. Enough to live comfortably in a one-bedroom in Astoria. But the money that kept rolling in, now almost nine friggin' years later, from *Where Can I Stow My Baggage?* kept Phil in the enviable sprawling midtown Manhattan three-bedroom. Four bedrooms, if you counted The Pad on the living-room floor. The Pad was Phil's nickname for the 1 1/4-inch-thick, 7-by-5-foot remnant of a wrestling mat on which he now spent most of his waking and unwaking hours, lying on his back, thanks to this limp. This goddamn limp.

Nine months ago, it showed up, unannounced, over the July 4th weekend. Phil was minding his own business and overnight became a forty-six-year-old man with a limp. And not even a good limp. Not even enough to make people feel sorry for him. No, this was the kind of limp that had others feeling sorry for themselves. The *"Aw, shit. Now we're definitely going to be late"* limp. The *"Great. Now I suppose we're only playing nine holes"* limp. A limp that favors them.

It was no use talking about the pain now. No use talking about something that was always there, but never in the same place in the same way. A pain as impervious to explanation as it was to medication. Over the counter, behind the counter, under the counter, astride the counter. What was the point of discussing this now? Maybe someday, when he might have an answer when someone asked, "What happened to you?" Why walk hobbled among those who could not understand, least of all him? Why talk hobbled? *No game, go home.*

The limp had slowed Phil, but not stopped "Baggage Handling." He would stay in and do the column on the pad. The pad (lowercase) was the correct term for the long Ampad yellow legal tablet he used to write his column. The Pad (uppercase) was, well, we've already met The Pad.

The column was now in its eighth year. Eighth Inexplicable Friggin' Year, as Phil would say to himself. From the beginning, "Baggage Handling" had satisfied those Marty Fleck disciples who now at least knew where to find him. Back then, Phil was sure his services would only be required for maybe a year before some other fraud, more interested in craven self-promotion, came along. But he hadn't really been paying attention. Months before his column had started, a legitimately celebrated journalist, Joe Klein, emerged out of the marketing shadows and fessed up that he was indeed "Anonymous," the author of the hugely successful 1996 roman-à-Clinton novel *Primary Colors.* America's vigorous six-month debate about an author's identity was over. The country immediately returned to its natural literary state, not giving a shit about who should correctly be credited for writing what. This was not the United States of Jeopardy, so, Marty Fleck would be safe. And so would Phil Camp.

The hundred-plus daily papers that still carried his column were never picky about what filled the space as long as Marty Fleck brought customers into the tent. And he did. And he still did, seven-plus years, six hundred-plus installments later. However Phil rambled for the first seven hundred and fifty words mattered little, as long as he saved the last fifty or so to draw a Marty Fleck-type conclusion with the beyond-irony signoff, "Happy Baggage!"

He got more mail now than ever. Eighty percent still began, "Dear Liberal Jew Commie New York Faggot Asshole . . ." but who read that nonsense? As long as they were reading his nonsense.

As a columnist, Marty Fleck took a half-dozen reportorial forms. He would appoint himself someone's publicist (Saddam Hussein, Charlton Heston, Robert Downey, Jr., Sister Souljah) and try to faux earnestly resurrect careers or reputations. He would answer fake letters from imaginary readers. He would give fake answers to real letters from real readers (mostly culled from the 20 percent that began "Dear Marty . . ."). He would interview long-dead people from history. And four times a year, when he was under the weather, he would let his wife, Stacey Fleck, write the column and expose him for the less-than-insightful, flawed handler of baggage that he was.

After Trish, a four-times-a-year wife-in-print was the best Phil could manage. He could have done better. Hell, he was all set to do better. Two years ago, in the winter of 2002, he was about to marry his girlfriend of eighteen months, Amanda Rabinoff. Divorced, Jewish, grown kid out of the house, bright, had her own money, and lower maintenance than a studio in Spanish Harlem. All set. Then, just before the start of the ceremony, somebody called in a bomb scare to Central Synagogue. Five months after 9/11, those kinds of calls still got people's attention. And Amanda Rabinoff—divorced, Jewish, grown kid out of the house, bright, had her own money, and lower maintenance than a George Foreman Grill—took it as a sign and never reopened the discussion about rescheduling. Which wasn't the only thing Amanda Rabinoff never reopened to Phil. So, *No game, go home.* All that because somebody called in a bomb scare.

Yeah, *somebody . . .*

As much as he had succeeded with his goal to not perpetuate the fraud he had become by fading quietly into the Marty Fleck column, after the bomb scare and Amanda's adroit evacuation, Phil could not prevent the onslaught of becoming another stereotype: Self-help guy who couldn't help self. Years before the phenomenon of *Where Can I Stow My Baggage?* and M. Scott Peck calling him "irrelevant," Phil had read a piece on Peck in *Rolling Stone.* Tremendous. Every time M. Scott Peck did something society might frown upon, he said it was part of his research for an upcoming book. So, lighting up a Marlboro red in a crowded elevator? Research for a book about Americans' attitude toward smokers. Taking some eyelash-fluttering coed up to his hotel room after an out-of-town reading and having her take a ride on the cock less traveled? Research for a book about infidelity.

Phil never wanted to be that guy. He never wanted the voice of Marty Fleck in his head, uninvited and unmutable, justifying all his behavior as if it were some kind of promotional campaign. He wouldn't be that guy. He wouldn't be that guy, and alone. He wouldn't be that guy. And by the time, last August, when Phil Camp realized that being someone whose ex-wife calls in a bomb scare at his wedding qualifies you for lifetime membership as That Guy, it was too late. He had already been limping five weeks.

So, to recap: Man writes book to pay off ex-wife. Book is supposed to be a spoof. World takes book seriously. Man's life changes. Man under whose name book was written, his life changes as well. Ex-wife paid off, but pissed. Ex-wife makes phone call on man's second-wedding day. Man's life doesn't change in way he planned. Man's ass hurts. Man limps. Man under whose name book was written, his ass hurts as well.

Boy, it would have been great for Phil if it were all that simple. If the *So, to recap* . . . did indeed recap so. But logic and time got in the way. It made no sense that Phil's ass would wait almost a year and a half after the canceled wedding to voice its displeasure. None. Especially since he had driven out to Rumson a week after the incident to confront Trish. It was Saturday, February 23, 2002. Around 7 P.M. Phil remembered it the way any man remembers the last time he had the kind of sex he thinks about until that memory is usurped by a more vivid, more current, gloriously dirtier version.

She was leaning in the doorway of one of her father's houses when Phil fishtailed into the driveway and slammed the driver's side door so hard he scared himself. Just for a second, then Trish smiled and his anger was redetonated.

"Any calls?" he snarled.

"Good one, Marty," she said. "I know my ex-husband couldn't have come up with anything that clever."

He was now three strides away. But his fury misstepped and in that second, he took too long a look at her. Wow. Can you have that much rage and an erection at the same time and not wind up in a mug book? Well, sure. That's why they call it a raging hard-on.

She wore a soft, expensive, light blue jogging suit she must have tossed on just out of the shower. Must have. Her professionally dickered, computer-mixed blond streaks were still wet. And the southbound zipper on her top more than indicated that underwear hadn't even aspired to afterthought.

They thrashed around naked on the living-room rug where others had only been required to remove their shoes, and Trish's shrieks were so loud, if the house had been anywhere other than Rumson, neighbors would have heard her two acres away. But who has less than two acres in Rumson? Maybe an ex-husband living in a pool house.

And that was the former Trish Camp's sentence for the Class A felony of making a terrorist threat over the phone: Five to seven yelps.

Phil drove away just after nine o'clock that night, pretty sure he was now a solid candidate for a *Jerry Springer* panel "I Slept with My Ex-Wife Rather Than Turn Her In!" Amanda came by his apartment the next day to pick up four liquor boxes and a suitcase worth of weekend sundries. She brought her grown kid (a daughter, as it turned out), a twenty-five-year-old, taller, more angled, darker-haired version of Amanda. Phil had met her for the first time the week prior, just before the alarm went off in the synagogue. On this occasion, their exchange was even briefer. "Well," said Sarah (her name, as it turned out), "it was nice almost getting to know you."

That turned out to be the extent of Phil's punishment. The sting lasted half a second, then Amanda, with no room in the liquor boxes for anything other than closure, laughed and said, "Phil, I'm grateful. And I can tell you are, too. Somebody was doing for us what we couldn't do for ourselves."

Yeah, *somebody.*

So, it couldn't have been that. Couldn't. He hadn't even mentioned Trish to the Irish Shrink until a week ago, just before he was about to go in for the disk surgery. Ass hurting, limping for nine months. This was the answer. Disk surgery. Happy March Madness. Happy Purim.

Oh, he thought he had told the full story before, sometime in the last two years, but he hadn't. It was near the end of the session, and the Irish Shrink had said something like, "Phil, maybe you're limping all these months because you're making the hero's journey . . ." Something like that. But Phil had laughed and said, "Yeah, the hero's journey. How many guys can claim their ex-wife called in a bomb scare to their wedding?"

"Excuse me?" said the Irish Shrink.

"My ex-wife, Trish. Called in a bomb scare at the temple. You know that."

"I know about the bomb scare."

"I told you it was Trish."

"No, you didn't."

"Of course I did."

"Phil, I think I would have remembered a detail like that."

"I know I told you."

"Phil," exhaled the Irish Shrink, "I've noticed over the years that on occasion you confuse things you think you've told me with things you might actually have told someone else. Like your brother."

Phil jumped in between "bro" and "ther." "No way," he said. "I would never tell my brother this. Do you know about my brother? Have you been paying attention?"

"Yes, I have."

"Are you sure I didn't tell you?"

"Yes."

Phil half-snorted, clearly entertained by his own denial. Is that progress? "Well," he said, "it happened two years ago." *My Ex-Wife Called in a Bomb Scare at My Wedding and I Didn't Tell My Therapist for Two Years!!—on the next* Jerry Springer.

"We really should talk about this."

"Fine," Phil said. "When I get out of the hospital."

"When are you going into the hospital?"

"Next week. For disk surgery."

"I thought you were going on vacation next week."

"I am. But I'm spending the vacation getting the disk surgery."

"You didn't tell me you had decided on disk surgery."

"Oh, come on!"

"Phil."

"Okay, I'll give you the Trish thing. But I know I told you about this shit."

"You said 'vacation.'"

"Some vacation."

"Indeed . . . anyway," said the Irish Shrink, which meant the session was over.

2

Some vacation.

They wake him up at 6 A.M., don't feed him, and promise someone will be by with drugs who never shows up? Just what kind of package is this?

There is no button on the phone for "Guest Services" in a semiprivate hospital room. And the closest thing to a concierge was the orderly who gave him directions on how to operate the sink. That guy, who changed the linen in the now-empty bed on the other side of the curtain, was the last person who had to be in here. For every other worker on the eighth-floor, north wing of St. Clare's, attendance in Phil Camp's room was optional. Or elective. Like elective surgery.

The pain had started nine months ago. Innocently enough. In his left gluteus. That's right. Pain in the ass. The ass proper. That's where the pain landed. That's where it pitched Phil Camp. Sometimes it was toothache-sized and sometimes it felt like a retroactive dead-leg slug from a big brother that had missed the front of the thigh and the wind took yonder. And sometimes, Phil thought about unscrewing his left buttock and just leaving it on the side of the Bruckner Expressway, next to the left shoe that leaned up against the shoulder every half mile, like the closing credits of a yard sale from the Koch Administration.

"Anything else?" the cashier would ask at Starbucks or the deli or the newsstand or the cleaners or the place where Phil got his beard trimmed.

"Yes," Phil would say. "A new ass."

Women would always laugh. The odd guy would respond like the odd guy. "Newport?" "*Newsweek?*" "New Age music?" "Decaf?"

Had it really started in his ass, or in the left foot? He'd run up Park Avenue to the reservoir, take a lap-plus around the cinder track, then back down Park. Five and a half miles. Took fifty-one minutes. A year ago, his left foot would go numb thirty-five minutes into the run. Thirty-five minutes on the nose. Dental work numb. He could still run, and the numbness would vanish thirty seconds after he finished running, but what was that? Shoes too tight? Too loose? A subtle reminder from the good folks at Nielsen that he was no longer in the coveted eighteen to thirty-four male demographic, and hadn't been since half-past Poppy Bush?

He had asked his doctor, Ted Wiley, an old college classmate who viewed actual symptoms as the ultimate conversation stopper, about the numb left foot. And his pal told him man was not meant to walk erect and then went on for ten minutes about the female caddies in Japan and the time the two of them had independently picked up roommates the same night on a road trip to Fordham. (An incident that happened once, but was relived in Dr. Ted Wiley's office with the frequency of a prostate examination). So, Phil adopted the vaudevillian medical approach to the problem. His foot became numb when he ran? Don't run.

But the toothache ass, that was tough to ignore. It grabbed his attention and was almost impossible to treat as if there were something more interesting across the room.

And let's face it, how much real treatment are you going to get when the only diagnosis you have is a shoulder shrug and a back-hand wave? When the only cure known to you is a "new ass"? Or "decaf"?

The new-ass line hadn't really applied since Thanksgiving. That's when the limp had upped its ante and the pain had started to move. Ass to lower back to hip to thigh to knee to inner thigh to groin back to ass and, just for laughs, all the way to the ankle and the top of the big toe. And then, for a couple hours at a time, it would be gone. Some kind of unplanned physiological-union job action. No pain. And more important, no pain just long enough for Phil to think it was gone. Yeah, *gone*. Gone like anti-Semitism. Back it came, making all the local stops. And taking on passengers—pinched nerves, muscle weakness, tingling, spasm, and the occasional leg buckle.

Ah, the leg buckle. Is there a more empowering feeling than to be pulling a chair out for a woman at a business lunch and to have your left side opt for the express checkout? No warning, no explanation. Even worse, no explanation from you! Neither Phil Camp, nor Marty Fleck, urban wit, had developed a spinned response to the public leg buckle. The best Phil had come up with is, "Jesus. I'm an old Jew now." Not exactly, *"Anything else, sir?" "Yeah. A new ass."*

Somewhere around the fifteenth buckle. That was when the isolation had begun. No more business lunches. No more face-to-face meetings, social or antisocial. No more gratuitous leaving of the apartment most New Yorkers wouldn't want to leave anyway. He'd do his column on the pad and venture out only when he had an appointment with someone who might get the pain to stop. Or stop moving. Or start moving if moving meant it was going away.

Chiropractors, acupuncturists, acupressurists, massage thera-pists, physical therapists, reflexologists, and something called the Alexander Technique, which had something to do with getting out of a chair as if there were a string attached to a hole in the middle of your head. And it all worked—for about five to fifteen minutes after he left whatever office. After that, it was all up to Phil. To walk and sit and run and bend like any other neurotic forty-six-year-old had become his full-time job.

Phil's part-time job was urinating. Fifteen times a day. Well, that's when he stopped counting. Another good reason not to leave the house. Just last month, he had gone to Ted Wiley about this. His classmate listened, then gave him a specimen cup and said, "I know it's a lot of pressure, but see what you can do." Two minutes later, Phil came back and said, "I could have filled up two more of these and I had gone before I left—forty-five minutes ago."

Dr. Wiley's reaction was sober and learned. "Well, that's not normal," he said. "Hmm. That's a new one."

His doctor's follow-up question was just as incisive: "Have you been anxious lately?"

"No," said Phil. "Not until you asked that question." And then, mouth open, Ted Wiley looked off into space and dropped his shoulders slightly. Good Christ. Can we get the American Medical Association to start fining its members when they ask, "Have you been anxious lately?" Or its rich uncle, "Been under any stress?" Let's just assume here, Manhattan 2004, aw, shit, *anywhere* in 2004, the answer is an all-caps yes, unless the patient has signed some sort of waiver. YES, I'm anxious. YES, I have stress. And now, I'm going to ask the questions, Doc. Question one: How does my anxiety or stress get distilled every twenty minutes into eight ounces of clear amber liquid? Or do I need to see a specialist, like the Sam Adams beer guy?

But why ask? So Dr. Ted Wiley could answer, "You got me"?

Nobody had any answers. Nobody gave a shit. The only people who gave a shit, the only people, were the strangers sitting behind Phil at a movie or a ballgame or a show, when he would awkwardly get up three times in two hours to ruin their view on his way to the john. *"Again?"* they'd murmur. *"Maybe that's why he's limping."* Those people were no longer being disturbed. Not since sometime around the fifteenth leg buckle, when Phil retreated to The Pad with the pad, getting up only to eat and go.

Phil looked at his watch, then cocked his head while he did some math. You know what? He hadn't had to go in almost three hours. Maybe he was getting better. Maybe all he had to do was show up at the hospital and *yeowwwww!* Lightning up the left leg. And a headfirst slide into the toothache ass.

Right. That's why he was here.

Phil pulled his hand from under the sheet and reached around the nightstand. Slowly first, then frantically. Where the fuck was the astronaut pen?

Now, where have we heard about the astronaut pen before? The pen for people who have to write on their backs. Right, that episode of *Seinfeld*, where the old guy at the senior citizen condo in Florida gives Jerry the astronaut pen and then something happens and people are yelling and everything gets resolved in twenty-three minutes. This is not about that, and Phil had not copped the idea for the astronaut pen from the episode of *Seinfeld*. His chiropractor got the idea from *Seinfeld*. Ordered six dozen of them, for his patients who now spent the good part of the day writing upward. In Phil's case, lying on The Pad. Using the pad.

The wrestling mat remnant, The Pad, was that heavy-duty Ensolite foam rubber, coated in thick maroon vulcanized latex. Something like that. He couldn't lie on anything with too much give, otherwise it seemed to conform to the pain. So, a futon was out. He bought the 10-by-5-foot half-mat on the Web for $350 and for an additional $20 had his super trim the length three feet with one of those Al-Qaeda-issue box cutters. Under his head was either of two other Internet purchases: The $69 buckwheat-filled pillow, or the $14.95 "Trakshun" neck cradle, another piece of red-molded foam that looked like either the funniest pair of size 18C tits or a model of Jennifer Lopez's ass at six months. The "Trakshun" neck cradle was supposed to simulate that great massage move where the masseuse digs the tips of six fingers into the occipital ridge at the base of your skull and your head drops like you're part of a magic act. Well, that's what it was supposed to do. What it ended up simulating was your head on Jennifer Lopez's six-month-old ass, which, once you got by the initial wash of creepiness, was not bad, but not really effective.

Now that the limp had established residence, he would scratch out "Baggage Handling" with the astronaut pen to the eight hundred words he needed, then, around 5 P.M., call his neighbor's fifteen-year-old daughter, Elly, to come over and type the column into the body of the e-mail while he dictated it. If he could get the brighter-than-she-should-have-been Elly Vogelbaum to laugh a couple of times, he knew he had something that day.

Up until the twenty-third leg buckle, Phil had done his own typing. Before Elly came aboard, the column was a two-and-a-quarter-person operation. Phil wrote it, polished it, shipped it, took full legal responsibility for it. The quarter-person, Stan Feigensen, an editor at his syndicator, the Excelsior Newspaper Group (an in-the-red subsidiary of Excelsior Publications), called just before deadline and needed maybe three word changes and five minutes being convinced that one could really use Treblinka as a comic reference. And Sandy Collewell sat at her desk in the PR department at Excelsior and handled the hundreds of e-mails and letters that came to any one of the hundred-plus papers that syndicated his column twice a week, 80 percent beginning with some variation on the idiom, *"Dear Liberal Jew Commie New York Faggot Asshole: I took a shit this morning that was funnier . . ."*

Five years ago, the relentlessly estimable *Newsweek* columnist Jonathan Alter had shared insight with Phil when they met at some uptown open-bar nonsense for some fellow brilliant yet misunderstood writer. "When you write a column and you take your shots," said Alter, "you wear a big sign that says KICK ME." Phil had never thought about that when it came to the response from readers. The fact that he never saw 80 percent of his mail helped. In fact, he had forgotten about Alter's words until nine months ago, when the pain began, and he found himself constantly thinking about reaching just above his ass, feeling around for the big sign that said KICK ME.

You know, for all the inattention he was getting, the hospital room could have passed for Phil's apartment. Here he was, alone and on his back. A pad, a Pad, and an astronaut pen away from starting another column, even though he was taking two weeks off from it for the surgery. But don't tell anyone. They just thought it was another vacation. And don't tell anybody, but over the last few months, Phil had become quite fond of *La Vida Hermit.*

I am now one of those guys, he thought, a phrase that occasionally began Phil's thoughts. *I am now one of those guys . . .* I am one of those guys about whom the doorman says, "I think I saw him go out for the paper one night. Late. But that was three years ago, and it was only because the delivery guy was sick."

Or maybe the super says, "He can't leave. He's sick. Couple of workmen brought a dialysis machine up there last summer."

But he's interrupted by the other guy working the front desk: "Nah. That was 'Dial-a-Mattress.' He gets a new bed every three months."

And then the yenta on seven, Mrs. Pritch, Marion Pritch, walks by and says, "You talking about Camp? You're all wrong. He's nuts. Made a ton of money with some government contract or an idiot TV show, lost almost all of it, and now he has a hundred thousand ten-dollar bills stacked in the middle of the floor and he sits on it all day, staring at the door, yelling out some woman's name." And then, whispering for no reason, "It's either the ex-wife or the mother."

That's what they'll be saying about me, his head continued. Lots of stories and theories and "Let me tell you what I heard . . ." And it will end as these things usually end. Some tenant on the twenty-fourth floor will yell at the new porter about cleaning the trash chute and he'll say, "I cleeen three day ago back," and then the tenant will say, "Well, what the hell is that smell?"

But for today, this morning, pity not the solitary man who lays in the hospital with no visitors. He was going to be pain-free. That's what the orthopedist had told him. Took one look at the MRI and said, "The bad news is you need an operation. The good news is after it's over, you'll be pain-free."

David Glindelvoss, orthopedic surgeon and two years behind Phil and Ted Wiley at Columbia, had pointed to the MRI with the reassurance of a TV weatherman in Phoenix giving the forecast.

"You see this?" Dr. Glindelvoss began. "This is your fifth lumbar disk. The L5. You see that goo seeping out of it? Most doctors call it *nucleus pulposus*, or disk material, but I like the term *goo*. More technical. Your disk has slipped ever so slightly out of place and is rubbing against the sciatic nerve, over here. The S1. That's what's causing all the pain from your lower back all the way down your leg. L5-S1 herniated disk. This is textbook stuff. In fact, they couldn't draw it better in a textbook."

Dr. Glindelvoss had then risen to his full five-foot-seven and shone his eyes into Phil's face. "You an athlete?"

"Was. Racquets, that shit," said Phil. "And I ran, when I could run."

"And you're," referring back to his desk, "forty-six?"

"Yes."

"This is the hip of a sixty-year-old man. You're years from a re-placement. But if you ask me . . ."

Phil's eyes had started rolling. Not in disbelief. He was doing a sweep of the room, searching for the person who *had* asked Glindelvoss.

" . . . right now, you gotta fix that disk and relieve the pressure."

"What about another MRI?" Phil asked.

He never got the second MRI. Glindelvoss and Wiley double-teamed him and it was a blur of *"How's Thursday, March ninth?"*

"Okay, I guess."

"Okay, then . . ." and here he was. Alone, on his back, awaiting surgery that was supposed to have been done by now.

Wait a minute. It was the ninth. But it was a Tuesday. Had Glindelvoss screwed up? How can you be a fucking surgeon and get the days of the week mixed up? Jesus, get a fucking calendar that works! Get a fucking bell on your fucking Blackfuckingberry! Get a radio in your Beamer with a big fucking light on the dash that says *Tuesday, the ninth, shithead!* Get a—

Wait a minute. Glindelvoss *had* said Tuesday, the ninth. Whew.
So, where was anybody?

"Hi."

Phil looked over at the door. Standing next to the foot of the empty bed was a man, who looked like anything but hospital staff, with a forty-year-old leather satchel.

"Hi."

"Is Seamus here?"

"Seamus who?"

"Seamus Something. I don't know his last name," the satchel guy said. "He's in my group, and they told me he was in Room 8-32."

"I've been here since last night," Phil said, "and that bed has been empty—8-32 North, South, East, or West?"

"Shit. This is North, right?"

"Right."

"Shit."

Phil sat up, rather easily for someone in constant pain. He was excited about the company, rather strange for someone still smitten with isolation. "You're going to have a hard time finding this guy if you don't know his last name. I can't believe you got by security without knowing the name of a patient. Especially with that bag."

Satchel Man smiled and sat on the empty bed. He definitely shouldn't have smiled. Big-time smoker. "They know me. I'm here every week for my group."

"What's the group?"

"Nic Fitters."

Bingo. "Trying to stop smoking, eh?" Phil asked.

"Nah," matching-satchel-and-teeth said, "the others are. The idea is we meet every week in a hospital, we sit around and tell stories, and don't smoke for an hour, then they take us to see someone. I just come here for the stories. I can go for two hours if I have to. And if I get squirrelly, I pop some of the gum."

"They let you chew nicotine gum in the group?"

"Nah," he reached into the satchel, "I put 'em in a Chiclets box." He shook the box and damn if didn't sound like Chiclets.

Phil laughed and stuck out his hand. "I'm Phil Camp."

The guy shook a piece of nicotine gum into Phil's hand. "Lenny Millman," he said.

"Hello, Lenny Millman." Hello, indeed. Phil never used anybody's full name unless he was fond of them. The only one who merited that honor lately was Elly Vogelbaum from across the hall. *Hello, Elly Vogelbaum.* But Phil loved this guy. A column walks into a hospital room. The teeth, the bag, the group—Nic Fitters, for Christ sake!—the Chiclets box. And the rest of the outfit. He had to be close to sixty, but wearing the same leather vest, plaid shirt, jeans, and sandals getup he threw on forty years ago to make the late show downtown at Folk City. The wire-rimmed glasses with the adhesive tape on the corner that he'd been meaning to get fixed since Skylab. The thin curly gray hair that was vigorously toweled in the morning and then abandoned like a latch-key kid.

And wait a minute . . . on one of the belt loops. Was that a Che button?

Phil knew in another ten minutes, he'd have two columns' worth from this guy. And if, oh, if he could just get him to turn that leather satchel over onto the empty bed and emcee its contents, this could be 8,000 words banged out in four days and the summer off.

"What are you in for?" asked Lenny. Great. He was staying.

"Back surgery."

"Bullshit!" Lenny jumped up, like he'd been given a posthypnotic suggestion to yell "bullshit!" and jump up every time he heard the phrase "back surgery."

"What?"

"Please," he negotiated. "Tell me you have some bone disease. Don't tell me you're in here for a herniated disk."

"I am in for a herniated disk. It's pressing against my sciat—"

"AAAAAAhhhh, stop! Whatever you're going to tell me is crap."

Phil laughed. This guy was so much more entertaining than the dialogue he created for the people in his building.

"Do you want to see the MRI?" he said halfheartedly.

Lenny Millman started going through his bag. *Oh, boy.* "Save it," he began. "I know all about it. Pain up and down the leg. Starts in the lower back. Down the tush. Every so often to the groin?"

"Right."

"I've been in this play. Bob, is it?"

"Phil."

"There's nothing wrong with you, Phil."

Lenny Millman's head disappeared into the satchel. Phil tried to appreciate the effort, but he was biting the inside of his lip to keep from laughing further. "Lenny," he squeaked. "You're a pisser. You've made my day, and I'd love you to—"

"Ah!" said Lenny as he emerged with a well-worn, dog-eared-into-deafness paperback. "Usually, I carry a spare, but I'll have to give you my copy."

He tossed the book onto Phil's lap. *The Power of "Ow!" How the Mind Gives the Body Pain.* By Dr. Samuel Abrun.

"I think I've heard of this guy."

"You should have heard of him," Lenny said. "The world should have heard of him. But you know, with the true visionaries, you have to get to the people one at a time. Sometimes they don't make it into the consciousness until after they're gone."

"Uh-huh." Phil was reading the blurbs on the back flap. Another bestselling healer, an actress who couldn't walk, and—Good Christ— that conservative radio asshole, Jim McManus, who seemed to shit on Phil's column with the regularity of someone on a diuretic.

"You know Van Gogh only sold like two paintings before he died."

Phil was absorbed in reading the testimonial from Jim McManus:

The last thing I want to do is blow my reputation as a hard-line, new-science skeptic, and enemy of anything that smacks of psycho-babble pablum for the emerging race of feeling-based effeminates. So all I will say is this: I tried everything for my back, including doing my radio show lying on a mat in the studio. Nothing, abso-lutely nothing, worked until I read The Power of "Ow!" *I have been out of pain for five years. Dr. Abrun is a genius. And only a genius can spot another genius.*

"Phil?"

"What?"

"Were you listening to me?" said Lenny.

"Yeah. Van Gogh."

"No, that was before. I told you to read the first thirty pages, and if your pain doesn't go away, feel free to get the fake surgery. I gotta go."

"Really?" Phil started to consider the thought that he might have to give the book back to Lenny Millman. A thought that had been bothering him since he had read the phrase *"doing my radio show lying on a mat."* "You can't stay?"

"Nah. I gotta find Seamus."

Reluctantly, Phil began the process of handing over *The Power of "Ow!"* "Where can I get this?"

Lenny was on his feet, banging a pack of Marlboros against his palm and then waving Phil off with the same free hand. Screw finding Seamus. Lenny had realized in the time it would take to sit quietly and wait for Phil to read the thirty pages, he would lose the opportunity to fit in a quick men's room smoke on 8-North before resuming his search for Seamus. Seamus Somebody. "Keep it."

"But it's your copy."

"Then get it back to me."

"When?"

"When you get out of here."

"I'll tell you what," Phil said as Lenny's palm pack-banging and back-pedaling sped up. "Go outside. Go nuts. Have yourself four cigarettes. Then come back. I'll be done and you can get your book back. I can't keep your personal copy, with all your margin notes." He turned the book toward Lenny and pointed at the all-red, felt-tip caps: "GODDAMN RIGHT!"

"Yeah. Okay. I can usually hang out on the bench in front of the ambulance drop for a while."

"Great. Nicely done, Lenny Millman."

"For you, Bob, I'll do it."

A half hour later, Lenny hadn't shown. Twenty minutes after that, still no Lenny, and Phil was well into the second chapter of *The Power of "Ow!"*

Phil found Lenny in front of St. Clare's. By then it was ten-thirty. Phil closed the door of the cab before the guy behind the admissions desk could ask him if he had been processed out. Other than leaving a paper towel on his pillow with the astronaut pen–inscribed phrase, "Uh, never mind, Dr. Glindelvoss," no.

So, no.

3

"**Yes, a** question over here."

A man who looked as if he sneaked out of work asked, "I read your book and got seventy percent better immediately. It's been a month. How come I can't get that last thirty percent?"

"It's very simple," said Dr. Samuel Abrun. "If you still have some pain, you still have work to do."

"What work?"

"The homework!" he boomed. "Yes, young lady?"

A housewife, obviously delighted to be called "young lady." "Dr. Abrun, when my back acts up, I talk to my brain, like you said, and it goes away. But for the last two weeks my left pinkie is numb all the time. Is that the same thing, APS?"

"Of course it is," he squealed, "you should be thrilled about your pinkie! You brain is listening. Consider it a gift. This is a gift! Or," he chuckled, "you can ignore it and really piss your brain off. That works, too.

"I can't see. Is that a hand in the back there?"

He wasn't lying. He really couldn't see. Samuel Abrun, for all his stature among the thousands he had saved, stood only five-foot-four. He gave a little self-effacing jump because he knew even if it didn't help, it would get a nice laugh. It did help. No one in the back was raising their hand. Just a college kid putting away his cell phone. And it did get a nice laugh.

"So, everything is APS?" blurted a man, who was not called on. "Every pain? Everything that goes wrong in my body?"

"Of course not." said Dr. Abrun. "Not everything. Not cancer. Not AIDS. Not hepatitis. Many ailments are not psychogenic."

"But how can I tell?"

"You call me and I'll tell you."

"I call you," the man who was not called on mimicked, "and you'll tell me. Over the phone."

"Yes. Why not? It happens every day. Been happening for the last fifteen years. Somebody called me yesterday and asked if the wart on his foot that he's had for two years was APS."

"That was me," Phil mumbled.

Dr. Abrun twinkled, his natural state. "I didn't see you hiding over there on the side, Mr. Camp."

This was the third lecture by Dr. Abrun that Phil had attended. Dr. Abrun gave the same two-hour lecture every Wednesday night, 6 to 8 P.M., on the physical and psychological manifestations of APS, Acute Psychogenic Syndrome, the foundation for *The Power of "Ow!"*

Cute name, *The Power of "Ow!"* Way too cute. For two decades, patients had been shuffling or clip-clopping into Samuel Abrun's office in a variety of pretzel shapes. For the first few years, he handed them an eighty-page three-holed splay-clipped thesis called "How the Mind Gives the Body Pain." Simple, unsexy, and unbound. By the time his work was commercial book length, Dr. Abrun had probably been sideswiped by some marketing mischief ferrier from his publishing house and forced to jettison his original title in favor of the parody line. Had to be what happened. And it was probably the last time Samuel Abrun would let himself be talked out of anything.

"I'll say it again," he said. "The brain will not be denied!" *The Brain Will Not Be Denied*. Not a bad title for the next book.

If he had his choice, everyone who read his book would be out of pain. Unfortunately, that only happened about 40 percent of the time. So, Dr. Abrun had to deliver what he wrote in person. And if he'd had his choice there, the talks would have been forty seconds long. He would have thanked everyone for coming and said, *"Look, most structural abnormalities are a natural part of the aging process. They do not cause pain. When your conscious mind is threatened by the rage, hurt, or sadness, but especially rage, in your unconscious mind, the brain distracts you by creating mild oxygen deprivation to any number of areas. Back, legs, shoulders, neck. Just a little, say ten percent. But that's more than enough to cause pain, sometimes constant, excruciating pain. The pain is real, but the source is not the body. It is the brain's desperate attempt to ward off rage from reaching your consciousness. And the brain will not be denied. But . . . in the same way the brain caused your pain, it can make it go away.*

"Disregard the physical symptoms, reject previous diagnoses, acknowledge the psychological source, accept this diagnosis, APS, experience the psychological connection, and eventually you will be pain-free." And then he'd add, *"And don't take this wrong, but I hope this is the last time I see any of you."* Which is the way he ended the two-hour lectures. That line he'd keep.

Funny thing about people. They'd rather be lectured. They'd rather be convinced. Unfortunately, Dr. Abrun was not in the convincing business. You either accepted his diagnosis, or you moved along to the doctors uptown with the transparent nail polish and the unnecessary surgery. Not bothering to convince people really cut down on the overhead. Dr. Abrun was ridiculously cheap. You bought and read *The Power of "Ow!"* for $14.95. The book was your potential ticket of admission into Dr. Abrun's program. The only way you were admitted is if you were examined by Samuel Abrun himself and told by Samuel Abrun himself that you indeed had Acute Psychogenic Syndrome. And here's where it got tricky: You had to accept that diagnosis. If you had any doubts, come back another day when you didn't. Dr. Abrun was not in the convincing business, and believed that where there was doubt, there was pain. The type of pain that sent most people scurrying to orthopedists, chiropractors, all the way to the operating room. And Abrun rarely said this because of its inherent contradiction, but he believed the chief characteristic of Acute Psychogenic Syndrome was denial of Acute Psychogenic Syndrome.

But . . . if you read *The Power of "Ow!"* and developed a kink in your neck from nodding at all the points you related to, if you concluded that there indeed was nothing physically wrong, that your brain was capable of inflicting such atrocities on your person, then you wrote your first and last check for five-hundred dollars (70 percent covered by the insurance companies Samuel Abrun believed were part of the problem) and could attend as many lectures and Abrun-led group sessions with fellow APS sufferers as you wished.

"Missed you in the group last week, Mr. Camp."

"I had a thing," articulated Phil.

Abrun smiled. "We didn't have any good talkers like you." He turned. "Yes, sir. I don't recognize you. Have I seen you?"

"No," said a beefy type. "I came with my buddy from work. Dr. Samuels, I had disk surgery six years ago and it was a huge success. No pain. Now my orthopedist says I have a meniscus tear . . ."

"Achhh! That's because doctors treat X-rays rather than patients!" (Samuel Abrun, Dr. Samuel Abrun, said "doctors" the way whatever party out of power says "this administration.") "That disk surgery was utter garbage. Completely unnecessary. A placebo. And the placebo worked, until your brain found a substitute location for your APS."

"My what?"

The twenty other people in the small lecture room groaned.

Dr. Abrun's twinkliness vanished. "This is a lecture, not a recruitment drive! Read the book! Accept the diagnosis! Do the homework! Or join the epidemic of thousands getting unnecessary surgery every year!" He took a deep breath. "Okay, Slide Number Thirty-three: Sources of rage, emotional pain, and sadness. . . ."

Sources of rage? Phil thought. *How about that guy who just spoke?*

• • •

In the forty-eight hours after Phil walked out of the hospital, he finished reading *The Power of "Ow!"* (including all the bullshit small-type appendixes), wrote two columns about Lenny Millman ("Benny Mullman"), did forty-five minutes on the NordicTrack. (Fifty, if you count the time it took to remove all the clothes hanging on it) and got laid for the first time in nine and a half months (same woman as before, friend of a friend, who rolled off him and while looking for her cigarettes said, "So, what, see you in 2005?")

And on the third day, the Lord said, "Let there be light spasming." And there was. And it was discouraging.

Phil started trying to call Dr. Abrun on Day 4. It took an hour. Lying on The Pad, he left one message, then spent the next fifty-eight minutes punching Redial, hoping for an actual person. He hadn't done that since he tried to get Mets playoff tickets in 1985, the year before they were actually worth anything. No, that was wrong. He had been punching the Redial button six months ago. A vain attempt to reach that call-in radio prick, Jim McManus. Don't worry. The irony that McManus's blurb on the back of *The Power of "Ow!"* proved to be the catapulting impetus that led to his early checkout of St. Claire's did not escape Phil. In fact, it enraged him. And that rage was quite conscious. So there.

"Hello?" a real woman said.

"Thank God. Can I speak with Dr. Abrun?"

"Have you read his book?"

"Devoured it."

The woman cleared her throat. "What does Dr. Abrun list as the six basic needs of humans?"

There was a quiz?!? This cat Abrun wasn't lying about screening patients. "Uh, uh, to be taken care of," Phil began, "to be immortal, to be liked, uh uh . . ." Shit. This was like trying to come up with a name for the bouncer looking through the door slot at the after-hours joint before he'd let you in to lose your ass at blackjack.

"That's okay," the woman said. "That's enough. Hang on. The doctor will be right with you."

"To be perfect!" Phil yelled just after the Hold button clicked.

In the four minutes they spent on the phone, Samuel Abrun answered Phil's answers with "Well, you know that's crap" three times before telling Phil to read his book at least twice more before they met the following week. The initial consultation was much longer, livelier, with a minimum of prodding and the word "crap" now embellished by the idiom "conventional medicine." (As in, *"Well, you know that's that conventional medicine crap."*)

The whole visit defied convention, except for the fact that it took place in a typical doctor's office, in an established Manhattan hospital, where they must have known that the guy behind the door, Dr. Samuel Abrun, was telling anyone he let in to disregard how the rest of the building made its business. However, there were a couple of moments bookending the forty-five minutes that aspired to be nonsequiturs. The first came when Abrun asked Phil to describe areas where he had pain. When he said "the groin" (third on a list of seven), Abrun leaped out of his chair, wildly shook Phil's hand and said, "You just said the magic word! I don't need to see the MRI! I don't even have to examine you! But . . . you paid for the time . . ."

The other came at what turned out to be the end of the consultation. "How was your relationship with your father?" Dr. Abrun asked.

In the pantheon of loaded questions, this was Zeus or Jupiter, depending on where Phil kept his pantheon. *How was your relationship with your father?* Got a minute?

Phil was ready to go. He'd tell the caddying story at age twelve and then say, "Your witness." Had it all loaded up. But somewhere on the way out of his mouth, a lump materialized in his throat that no X-ray would locate, but that was anything but benign.

"Well," Phil gulped, "you're talking about a man—"

"That's all I need," said Dr. Abrun as he stood up and shook Phil's hand for the second time since the magic word was "groin." "Mr. Camp, I am not a psychotherapist, treating emotional symptoms. I am a physical doctor who has identified the psychological cause of physical disorders. But," he twinkled, "you don't have to be a shrink to know that anyone who begins a sentence about their father with, 'Well, you're talking about a man . . . ' has, well, what's that goddamn word I hate?"

"Issues?" said Phil.

"You're a writer?"

"Yes."

"I knew it! Well, the homework should be duck soup for you."

"Homework?" said Phil.

Abrun handed Phil a five-page pamphlet. "Read this. Basically, you make a list of all the traumatic events of your childhood, all your personality defects, and all the current pressures that might enrage you. Then you write an essay on each item. Every day. We try to bombard the unconscious with conscious anger and bring the rage to the surface. You don't have to express your rage. You don't even have to feel it. Just acknowledge it. That's what the homework does. The brain is no longer threatened by the rage, abandons its strategy, and the pain goes away."

I think, Phil thought, *I'd rather have the bullshit surgery.*

"And if that doesn't work," Abrun reached up to slap Phil on the shoulder and lead him out, "we send you to one of my psycho-therapists."

"I have a shrink," Phil said.

"Is he analytical?"

"What do you mean?"

"Are you seeing him to stop smoking or because you're a klep-tomaniac?"

"No."

"Then he's analytical. Tell him to read the book. He'll know what to do."

"So, he has homework, too."

Abrun gave Phil another stretched slap. "You're a good talker. Have Ginny sign you up for one of my groups. They meet at four-thirty, five, and seven-thirty on Tuesday. And I lecture on the book every Wednesday, 6 to 8 P.M. She'll give you directions. It's in this building somewhere. Next to some idiot recommending surgery."

• • •

"But why now?"

Samuel Abrun smiled. He usually got that question earlier in the lecture. Got it every Wednesday.

"I thought we might make it to the end before somebody asked that question," he said. "But if we had, it would have been a first. You got the pain now because your unconscious is a reservoir that can only hold so much hurt, sadness, rage, and other primitive feelings. When the reservoir is full, the rage tries to escape and let the conscious mind know. But the brain is too threatened. As I've said, the unconscious part of your mind is not a nice guy. It is an angry, unreasonable little child. The brain does not want these feelings to reach the conscious. The conscious mind is too intellectual for the childish, primitive mind. So, the brain creates pain. Of course, we are unaware this process is going on. All we know is one morning you can't bend over without feeling as if you've been stabbed and a month later it's not getting any better."

"It's not stabbing, it's more like lightning."

"We'll talk about it in the group, Mr. Rivington, but your timing is perfect." Abrun waved and the slide projector clicked to a crude illustration of what looked like a leak in a basement. "Here is the reservoir of rage . . ."

Phil looked at his list of childhood traumas, personality defects, and current life pressures. Forty-one items. He started to make an arrow next to item Number 1: Diarrhea—1959. He felt a stab in the lower back. No, not a stab. More like lightning. He dropped from 70 percent better back to 40.

Good Christ, Phil thought. *The pain of recounting each item on this list will kill me. On the bright side, I'd be dead and really not need the unnecessary surgery.*

Then, in the same instant, another, more moving notion: What must it be like to be one of those guys, to have written a book that really, actually, helps?

4

Phil reread the first chapter of *The Power of "Ow!"* and got his body to a state where he could sit up in a chair at his desk. He pushed the astronaut pen aside, grabbed the pad, and began writing the first APS essay.

> Diarrhea—1959
> When I was thirty, my mother told me that when I was a year old . . .

No way. Too painful. No way. Not ready.
Phil stopped, grabbed the astronaut pen, lay back down on The Pad, and wrote the essay the only way he could.

Baggage Handling
by Marty Fleck

RUNS FOR YOUR LIFE

Dear Mr. Fleck,

When I was a year old, I was hospitalized for diarrhea. I almost died from dehydration. My mom and dad did not take me to the hospital because they were having a party that night. So, I think the housekeeper took me. I don't know. I only found out about this when I was thirty. It has taken me sixteen years to write you. Where does all this go?

> *Sincerely,*
> *Phil Camp*
> *(please withhold name)*

Ladies and gentlemen, I am not thrilled. We could have had a good old time with diarrhea, and trying to work up some hilarious wordplay with "binding," "fiber," and "the runs." But this is clearly a man who is in pain. And can you blame him? He is reaching out to old Marty Fleck. Not for advice. Not at all. He wants Marty Fleck to get angry for him. He wants Marty Fleck to summon the deep rage within. Now, we all know I have contacts, I have juice, but I do not have *rage* on my speed dial. My car service, yes. On the speed dial. My bookie, yes. Doris Kearns Goodwin (for baseball chat only), yes. Conservative radio gasbag Jim McManus, yes. My mother, yes. But not rage. (Although, we could call my mom and maybe get a twofer here. . . .)

No, I cannot simply summon this man's fury. My philosophy, now in its tenth year of gestation, is built on self-recognition and awareness. This would go against everything I have tried to impart to you, my readers. Not only that, there's no money in it.

That said, I will try. *(Note: Please excuse whatever changes may occur in tense or voice. Or vernacular.)*

What kind of a parent lets their one-year-old kid find his way to the hospital rather than cut a cocktail party short? Just how good were the fucking hors d'oeuvres, Mom? (And remember, you can't spell hors d'oeuvres without "w-h-o-r-e," kind of.)

Are you kidding me? Are you fucking kidding me? The housekeeper? He's a year old. He's probably so dehydrated he's translucent. This sounds like a job for someone who came to this country with a suitcase full of flies from postwar Europe. Just how drunk was everybody that night? And where was Dad? Oh, right. Late 1950s, you weren't allowed to bother Dad with anything that had to do with his children after 6 P.M. I'm sure this was a law somewhere. Shit, the Vatican moved quicker to change. Vatican II, Dad zero.

Wait a minute? Isn't that Dad in deep conversation with the wife of the new couple from two streets over? Let him just knock back his sixth scotch and take off his jacket before he demonstrates the correct move to hit that low-lining hooded four-iron and knock the ball out of the rough. Does the young wife of the new couple from two streets over want to try? Well, she hasn't really played much, but okay, if Dad stands behind and watches. Hmmm. Well, I think I hear a baby, but okay. Wait, let me turn up the phonograph. Okay, now we're ready. Just get your hips moving. . . . That's it, Doris . . .

So, Mom, this one's on you. Your son may be

dying. He's crying. What other possible solution could there be, you know, other than making sure the door to the nursery was closed tight? Just what fucking level of narcissism are we dealing with?

Infants. What timing, huh? They're always screeching at night. There's always excrement involved. FOR GOD SAKES, KID, WE HAVE COMPANY! Shitty timing. That must have been where they got that phrase.

Just our luck. Bridey, the housekeeper, is out getting ice, and the baby's dehydrated. Irony.

See to your child, you solipsistic pricks! No wonder he still feels like a piece of shit. That's all he was at a year old.

You should be fucking ashamed. Marty Fleck will never forgive you.

(*End of summoning rage*)

Okay, now where does this go? If you have a section "Crap that is none of my business but that I feel anyway"—there. If not, create that compartment. You may be here awhile. And remember, parents know not what they do, except when it comes to throwing a kickass cocktail party. Happy Baggage!!!

Phil looked at the second entry on his list of forty-one traumas.

Caddying for Dad—1971.

They weren't chronological and he still wasn't ready. And so . . .

Baggage Handling
by Marty Fleck

TOTE THIS!!!

(The following is a transcript of a recent broadcast on KMRT, the official Voice-in-Head radio station of Marty Fleck:)

"Hello again, everybody. This is your old pal, Marty Fleck, with another installment of 'F***ed-Up Fathers.' My guest today is Phil Camp."

"I thought we weren't going to use my name."

"Right. Sorry. Okay, Mr. Donatelli . . ."

"Christ, forget it. It's too late. Might as well blow my anonymity. It may help."

"Great! Now, you have a story for us?"

"Yes."

"About your father?"

"Yes."

"And it's f***ed-up?"

"I think so."

"Great! I'll be over here, trying not to judge."

"When I was twelve, my brother Jimmy, my stepbrother Jimmy and I were caddying for my father and his friend, Arnie Pearl. Neither of us had ever caddied before, and we were running around, not really knowing what to do. The bags were heavy and we couldn't follow the balls all the time and the clubs always ended up with some of my dad's in Mr. Pearl's bag and vice versa.

"Jimmy was caddying for Mr. Pearl. Mr. Pearl didn't give a shit. He'd laugh and say, 'Well, I guess I have to hit my six-iron here. It'll be good practice.' Jimmy took Mr. Pearl because he had the heavier bag and Jimmy was bigger than me. Still is. And he was kind of big and dopey anyway, so people didn't expect much of him. Still don't.

"So, I wound up caddying for my dad. And he was on me the whole day. Just barking and yelling and a lot of 'What are you doing?' . . . 'No!' . . . 'Do you have any idea what you're doing?' and . . . 'Jesus, *think!*' At one point I said, 'You know, I never did this before,' and he said, 'What's that supposed to mean?' But it stopped him from yelling at me for the next hole or two."

"Was your father always this critical?"

"Only when he was paying attention."

"Ouch."

"That's a little condescending, Marty."

"Sorry, Phil. Go on."

"One time, Jimmy and I were raking leaves in the backyard and we were trying to get every single leaf, even under the bushes, so Dad wouldn't have anything to say. We were almost picking them up one at a time. He walked out after we'd been at it three hours and all he said was, 'Geez, you're working so hard and you're getting so little accomplished.'"

"Whoa. Gut punch."

"What is it with you, Fleck? Do you think that's empathetic at all?"

"I apologize. Just trying to add some color."

"I think we're fine with the color."

"Please. Go on."

"Now, we're walking up the sixteenth fairway. My shoulder is killing me from the leather strap digging in. And it's hot and we had spent too long looking for my dad's ball in the woods and when we finally found it, he took a bad swing and topped the ball. It dribbled into the fairway. I clenched my teeth and kept my head down and did not look at Jimmy, who I knew was laughing. I might have coughed.

"All I was thinking about was getting through the next two holes and buying a Coke with my money at the caddy shack. That I knew how to do. My dad hit a wedge onto the green and I said, 'Nice shot.' And he said, 'Tell me. How much does a "B" caddy make?' B caddies were the lowest level of caddy.

"Three bucks for eighteen holes, I said. 'But you can pay me what you think I'm worth.'

"He began to walk ahead of me toward the green. 'If I paid you what you were worth,' he said, 'you'd be paying me.'"

"That sounds pretty f***ed-up."

"Wait, Marty. I'm not finished."

"Sorry, Phil."

"So, he doesn't pay me after four hours lugging his bag around. Okay, fine. Point taken. But then, when we get home, he makes me and Jimmy write letters to Arnie Pearl apologizing for how much we sucked, and makes Jimmy send back the five bucks Arnie had paid him."

"Wow. That is totally f***ed-up."

"It's as if my dad was saying, 'You know, it's not enough that I'm not proud of my children. . . . I need to let the world know. I need to get something in writing.'"

"That's great. Can I use that?"

"Be my guest."

"Did your stepbrother ever get the money back from Mr. Pearl?"

"Yeah. How'd you know?"

"Of course I'd know."

"Oh, right."

"Well, that's all the time we have today. Join us next time for 'F***ed-Up Fathers.' And remember, Dads are just like everybody else, except more so. This is Marty Fleck. Happy Baggage!!!"

"Can I read you the essay I wrote for Abrun's program?"

"I'd rather you not read in here."

"It's pretty entertaining. I wrote it as a column."

"I'm sure it's entertaining. You're always entertaining, Phil." The Irish Shrink laughed to himself, as if he was remembering some crack of Phil's from a previous session. In fact, their first confrontation, their only real confrontation in six years of working together, had come over Phil's ability to entertain. At the end of maybe the eighth session, the Irish Shrink had said, "I have to watch it with you. You tell such good stories, I can forget why you're here." Phil had actually called his therapist's machine two hours later and said, "Hey, guess what? The $125 I pay you every week? That's now my fucking cover charge!"

Paddy O'Reagan, Dr. Patrick O'Reagan, had called back quickly and apologized and said they were doing good work. Phil had been in therapy since the first days of the Reagan Administration. (The phonetic irony of Ronald Reagan, as opposed to Patrick O'Reagan, was not lost on Phil. The joke Phil told himself, and only himself, was that the president's real name was O'Reagan, and when he became an actor, he had dropped the "O," turned it into a zero, and earmarked that as money to fight AIDS.) In the ensuing twenty-four years, Phil had broken in half a dozen guys, but they had all been fellow Jews who took him as far as they could. So, nowhere. But Patrick O'Reagan, the Irish Shrink, was stamped out on a different psychotherapist assembly line. For one thing, he called back. For another, he apologized. For another, he spoke about the process and previous studies that had bearing on whatever they were discussing in session. For another, and stop the clock on this, he shared from his own experience when the situation warranted. "I don't mean to interrupt you, Phil, but something like this happened to me . . ." And it would invariably be *nothing* like this, but damn if the feelings he spoke of didn't match with Phil's, right up to the DNA. Not that feelings have DNA, but the metaphoric point is Paddy O'Reagan was free enough to occasionally operate in a room without walls. And Phil recognized and appreciated the space.

Yeah, the Irish Shrink was okay. And not threatened by all the recent demands placed on Phil by Dr. Samuel Abrun. Demands that more than inferred that more digging was necessary, more dots had to be connected. And if the Irish Shrink wasn't up to it, well, maybe one of Samuel Abrun's hand-picked therapists could pull the APS out of Phil like a casino illusionist yanks razor blades out of his mouth on a fishing line.

"Come on," said Phil. "Let me read it. It's the story about when my mom made us change our names."

"What?"

"Jesus, I know I told you about *that*. A couple of times."

"Ah, Phil . . ."

"Yeesh . . ." Phil cleared his throat. "*Cute story. When I was twelve my brother and I . . .*"

"Phil, I told you I didn't want you to read it."

Phil started to lunge the three sheets of typed heavyweight bond toward the Irish Shrink. "Any chance you'd read it?"

Paddy O'Reagan laughed and grabbed the pages. "Sure," he said. And that's why Phil called him the Irish Shrink. What self-respecting couch jockey would pass up the chance to have a patient recount a painful story from age twelve? "But after I finish reading, you tell it anyway."

And that's why he was the Irish Shrink.

"Tell you what, Doc. When you're done, I'll be happy to answer any of your questions." And that's why Phil was in his third decade of therapy.

The Irish Shrink laughed again, and turned the pages over on his lap. "Go."

"So, my brother and I now kind of know how to caddy, but my parents don't want us caddying at their club. Didn't like how it looked. I guess it looked like they weren't doing well enough so their kids had to work in front of people they were trying to impress at the club. Whatever that shame masquerading as pride is called. Oh yeah, being Jewish.

"Okay, so they make us caddy at Burnwood, the other Jewish club three miles away in the next town over. But it's the same dilemma. What if someone figures out who we are? We had only lived in the area a year, but they didn't want some member saying 'Camp . . . Camp . . . Are you Harry's and Shirley's kids?'

"So, my mom tells us we have to use the name McCammon. Jim and Phil McCammon. That way we can caddy at Burnwood and 'be safe.' Her words. 'You'll be safe. It's better.'

"Oh yeah, it was better. None of the caddies knew us. They were the same age but went to the public school. And none of them were Jewish. Everything was 'kike this,' and 'kike that.' They called the club BurnJews, which was as clever as it got. And they called us the Polack Brothers because we wore white athletic socks. This is 1971, when no kid wore white socks on his own. And they were all bigger than us. Jimmy was three years older than me and, at the time, was maybe two inches taller and two pounds heavier. He got much bigger later on.

"The big problem was Jimmy had trouble remembering the fake name. He knew we were McSomething. So, he'd end up saying McKay or McCoy or McManus before I would correct him."

"Heh-heh. That's great."

Phil gave the Irish Shrink a "don't make me read my essay" look.

"At any rate," he continued, "one day Jimmy is caddying in the foursome ahead of me. The course was crowded. So, I keep catching up to him on the green, or at the tee. A guy in his foursome asks him what his name was, and Jim says, 'Jimmy Camp.' Completely forgets. Well, the guy goes nuts. 'Harry's and Shirley's kid? I'm Lester Heimmerman, your cousin!'

"Two holes later, the guy sees me talking to Jimmy. He says, 'What's your name, son?' I'm ready. 'Phil McCammon,' I say. He looks shocked. 'Jesus,' he says, 'you look like a Camp.'

"For the next few holes, he keeps looking back at me. I try and look away, but I can feel him. Finally, at the turn, the ninth, he's getting hot dogs for the other players in his group. My group wants to play through. We walk by and he sees me and Jimmy laugh. Sometimes, you know, all we had to do was look at each other and we'd start. So, Lester says, 'Are you sure you two aren't brothers?' Jim says, 'Yes' and I say 'No.' Like he's Moe and I'm Shemp. 'Are you sure?' says Lester Heimmerman. Now, Jimmy says, 'No,' and I say, 'Yes.' So now, it's a lame sitcom. Lester gives us a big wink, which we were dumb enough to think meant he wouldn't tell anybody.

"The next day, the club pro, Dane Riddles, this big blond from Georgia, comes over to the caddies' bench and asks to see us. The other caddies love this. They go apeshit. 'Uh, oh. Polack Brothers in trouble. Don't sweat through those white socks. . . . ' They didn't say that, but if they hadn't been complete morons they might have thought of something like that.

"Okay, so Dane Riddles—who we later found out couldn't play at all. You know, 77-79, that sort of thing, but I'm sure he was fucking a few of the wives—Dane Riddles takes us aside and says, 'Look, I don't give a shit what your name is, I can't have you taking work away from these other fellas when your parents can afford to be members. But, if you want a job, you can come here at five-thirty every night and clean up the driving range. I'll pay you a dollar twenty-five an hour. Take it or leave it.'

"We took it. It kept us away from the other caddies and we made a little money. A real little. We had to pick up range balls in the rough of the driving range and under the trees using shag bags, these handheld metal and canvas things that allowed you to pick up one ball at a time without bending. Like a vacuum cleaner without the vacuum."

Phil stood up to give a brief demonstration of the shag-bag technique for the Irish Shrink. Phil waddled briefly around the office, arms at his sides, punching the ground, like he was auditioning for a spot on a dance line in a Chaplin revue. Paddy O'Reagan picked it up right away.

"When the bags were filled—they each could hold about fifty balls—you'd unzip them and dump them in the hopper of the cart that cleaned up the range fairway. It was driven by this guy Scully. Mouth breather. So, two hours of this . . ." He completed the demonstration. "And it always took close to two hours. And we never got more than a dollar twenty-five. Dane Riddles or his assistant, Billy Clemens, another big Southern Jew hater, would say, 'No, boys. That's one-twinny-fahve uh day.' The only time they paid us more was when the cart broke down and we had to do the entire range by hand. Three hours. I think we got five bucks between us. No, four.

"So, we do this for about four weeks. Six nights a week. A buck twinny-fahve. My dad was all over me about what a sap I was for doing it."

"Not Jim?"

"Nah. He was always on me. I was three years younger, yet I should know better. That kind of shit. All the time. *'What are you, some kind of sap?'* I know I told you that. So, we do this for four weeks, and one night, as Dane Riddles is paying us, he says, 'Ah'm puttin' you boys on notice.' We don't know what this is. We think it means he's going to put a notice up about what a swell job we're doing. We say, 'Great!' He says, 'No, I'm giving you boys two more weeks. We've lost thirty-six hundred range balls in the last month. Now, ah'm not sayin' you boys stole them, but we're missing thirty-six hundred range balls. And we'd like to know where dey wint.'

"Jimmy and I look at each other, and start to laugh. Thirty-six hundred balls. Come on. Then Billy Clemens comes out from the back of the shop and says, 'Go ahead and laugh, but we could make you pay fer them balls. See how funny yo daddy thanks it is when he has to write a fitteen-hunnart-dollar check. We know he got it, boys.'

"We get home that night, and I tell my mom the whole story. Thirty-six hundred balls and I do the Dane Riddles and Billy Clemens impressions. She laughs and says, 'You have to tell your father.' I say, 'Why can't Jimmy tell him?' And she says, 'Because you'll tell it better.' So, this is the last thing I want to do. This is the If-I-paid-you-what-you-were-worth-you'd-be-paying-me guy. But I do it. And I get him on a good night. He's mad. He knows we didn't steal the balls and he knows they just want to get rid of us. He tells me to call Dane Riddles the next day, around the time we're supposed to be there, tell him we're quitting. I never thought to ask him to call Dane Riddles. I never asked him for anything. Not worth it.

"No, that's not right. I didn't ask him because I thought of a great thing to say. I called at 6:05 P.M. and Dane Riddles answered. I said, 'This is Phil McCammon. My brother and I are quitting. We've been working there a month, and to lose thirty-six hundred balls we'd have to be stealing one hundred twenty balls a day, or one every thirty seconds. Ask Scully if he ever saw us take a ball. You know we didn't do it. We can't prove it. We don't need the two-week notice. We're not coming back.'

"I was shaking and was getting ready to hang up, when Dane Riddles said, 'Tell you what. Make you a deal. I won't tell your cousin Lester Heimmerman about the stolen balls, and you can get the hell out of here and change your name back.' And that's when I realized I was still using the fake name. Still protecting them."

The Irish Shrink cleaned his glasses with a Kleenex, then used it to blow his nose. Paddy could always be counted on to find something in one of Phil's stories he had either not meant to include or if he did, considered incidental. "McManus," said the therapist. "Isn't that the name your brother uses?"

"Yeah, Jim McManus. And that's not the name he uses. That's his name. And he's my stepbrother."

"Technically, he's your half brother."

"Well, I didn't know that expression until I started watching the soaps last fall. So throw me in semantics prison."

"Ha-*hah!* Sorry."

"So, we're going to do fucking nothing about my mother making us change our names? You don't think this is the, you'll pardon the wordplay, mother lode of dysfunction?"

The Irish Shrink held up a finger. The "I'll be right with you" finger. But he wouldn't be right with Phil. "I notice," Paddy O'Reagan said instead, "that sometimes you refer to Jim as your brother and sometimes as your stepbrother. Is it to save time?"

"I don't know. I didn't find out we had different fathers until I was nineteen and he got married. So before then, brother. After that, stepbrother. No, actually, I didn't start calling him my stepbrother until he reinvented himself. Started drinking that conservative Kool-Aid and got on the radio."

Phil had a feeling he had just told the Irish Shrink at least two things he thought he had told him in the past but in actuality was just blurting out for the first time. He waited for the Irish Shrink to correct him, but he got nothing. So, he used the awkward silence to try and remember exactly when Jimmy Camp, brother, became Jimmy McManus, stepbrother, before becoming Jim McManus, conservative radio gasbag. The only words that came into his head were not his own:

> . . . *I tried everything for my back, including doing my radio show lying on a mat in the studio. Nothing, absolutely nothing, worked until I read* The Power of "Ow!" *I have been out of pain for five years. Dr. Abrun is a genius. And only a genius can spot another genius.*

The end of the blurb on the back of Abrun's book, attributed to "Jim McManus, radio personality." Phil swore he hadn't said that out loud.

"What?" said the Irish Shrink.

"What?"

"You just said, 'Jim McManus, radio personality.'"

"So?"

The Irish Shrink smiled. "Don't you think it's, let's say, interesting, that in your recounting of this episode, of all the names you say your brother mistook for your fake name, one of them is the name that actually turns out to be his real name?"

"What?"

"McManus."

"What?"

"You said he could never remember McCammon, so he would say McKay or McCoy or McManus. . . ."

"Oh, for Christ sake."

"And it sounds like your dad really stood up for you."

"Is this that shrink thing where you say something deliberately to get me angry at you?"

"No."

"Well, it didn't work."

"I'm delighted to hear that."

Phil didn't hear that. *I have been out of pain for five years . . .* was banging around in his head. His edition of the book was at least three years old. Had it been over four years since they had stopped talking? Had to be. His brother hadn't been in pain the last time he saw him. And neither had Phil, until his brother had thrown him against the wall. Four years? Really? Maybe more? Okay, it's March 2004. *Where Can I Stow My Baggage?* came out in December 1995 and he'd been doing the column since 1997 and they met the one time after that in the studio. . . . The math he was attempting started shooting migraine pellets.

"I have to figure this out," Phil said, and as he stood to leave, his right leg, the good leg, buckled, and he went down on one knee like a basketball sub getting ready to report in.

"I understand," said the Irish Shrink. With the help of the couch arm, Phil pushed himself back up to the full and upright position he had longed for seconds ago. Just how much of this shit was inside him?

"Say," the Irish Shrink added, "isn't that your good leg that just gave?"

5

Phil decided to forego the M31 bus that went down Broadway and up Fifty-seventh Street. He would walk straight from the Irish Shrink to the CBS Broadcast Center on Fifty-seventh and Tenth Avenue. Normally, this was a half hour walk. But "normally" was an adverb that had not existed for ten months. Even though he was getting better (Current reading: 65 percent), it took about five blocks for Phil's left buttock to become the cement mixer and his left leg the funnel. The limp would begin, gingerly at first, and then Manhattan would pass in slow motion, a series of unpainted speed bumps. Abrun said to ignore the pain. *Change your relationship with it.* Sometimes, the best relationship Phil could manage while walking was a steady mumbled unbalanced chant of "*Fuck-You . . . fuckYou . . . fuckYou . . . fuckYou . . .* " So, the half-hour trip would take an hour. The fact that he now had to allow so much more time to get anywhere, and then tack on another ten minutes just to be safe—that hurt more than any twinge. Sure it did. But right now, this awareness that something important had just happened during his session with the Irish Shrink, something he needed to act on, was rare. As fleeting as a pain-free moment.

So, beard dropletted with sweat, bone-weary, allergy-filled, and whatever other emotions could fit into a space too small to let him alone, Phil arrived where he had to be, Fifty-seventh and Tenth, and with enough of a cushion to compose himself before facing his brother. The same brother he had not spoken to in almost five years. But now he was pain-addled curious enough to find out what particular nuggets of Samuel Abrun wisdom had helped Jim so much that he would want to blurb *The Power of "Ow!"* And more important, would he want to share them with Phil?

Jim McManus made time work for him. He taped his syndicated radio show, *Jim McManus: Stand By for Truth*, on a seven-minute delay. That way, he could walk out the front entrance of the CBS Broadcast Center at noon sharp, while his audience was still listening to the ersatz religiosity of his good-byes. Did anybody out there in Neo-Con Nation know he was Jewish? Okay, know that his mother was Jewish? Mom's a Jew—that's pretty much the end of the argument. You talk about faith-based. When Mom's a Jew, that's where your faith is based. That's the ink-stamping of one's hand by the guy at the door to B.B. King's House of Worship. Did they know that? Of course not. Why screw up *Stand By for Truth* with something so niggling, so inconsequential, as the truth?

Why indeed? Jim McManus did not believe for a moment he was being deceitful about who he was. Why should he? *He* was the one who had been deceived, so all bets were off. All beliefs, too. So, go ahead. You want to call the guy with the Jewish Mother and the liberal upbringing who, starting at twenty-two, became a Christian, then a radio host, then a Conservative, then a Christian Conservative, then a Christian Conservative radio host, you want to call that a reinvention? Go ahead. Knock your judgmental selves out. Jim McManus called it his path. Unlighted before that December in 1977, when he told his parents he was going to marry his girlfriend of three years, Mickey Loretta, and they said, "That's wonderful! Say, you might want to tell your real father, Bob McManus. Here's his address in Maryland." Say what?

As much as this sort of news doubled him over, there was relief. The last person Jim would want to quote was Marty Fleck, but it was like the line in his book about being switched at birth. At last, this explained everything! Jim McManus was the literal definition of preconception. He had been dropped at the screen door of a man whose fully formed outlook he did not understand, respect, or aspire to. And now, he no longer had to.

The lie he would forgive. He could forgive his mother, Shirley, because at twenty-two, he understood what someone might do for their child. The guy she married, Harry Camp, the man who had raised, no, underwritten and devalued him, he could forgive as well. But still be free to resent. But pray for. Forgiveness, understanding, resentment, and prayer. Come on. He had to be a Christian!

All of which should explain the ensuing lineage of his political sensibility. Jimmy Camp, Democrat begat Jimmy Camp, Libertarian begat Jimmy McManus, Independent begat Jim McManus, conservative begat Jim McManus, radio genius.

He had added the seven-minute delay last June, after his popularity soared and he grew tired of signing autographs and posing for pictures with midday fanatics holding up signs that read "Damn Right!!!" . . . "I'm a Jim Rat!" . . . "McManus from Heaven" . . . and wordplay much less subtle. And it might have worked, except his PR people told everyone about the delay, so the disposable cameras, video phones, and placards showed up in front of the Broadcast Center that much earlier.

Jim had been a radio lifer since college, doing any job on any local station that would keep him. It took a dozen years for his topical views to congeal, and another six for an audience to catch up to them on the dial. (It might have happened faster if he hadn't been sidetracked by a two-year addiction to painkillers.) Since the early nineties, he had been a semisuccessful on-air personality. If there is such a talk-radio creature as a palatable blowhard, it was Jim McManus. He was one of the first to call the Republicans "smug," and that had attracted liberals and moderates who saw him as a voice of almost-reason in a forest of Limbaughs. Yet he could and would offset that voice by sticking syllable by syllabus to the black-and-white script about "family values." And he beat that family-values drum until his own twenty-two-year, three-child marriage fell apart. Which was around the same time his listenership fell off, and McManus bounced around in various time slots when he didn't quite have the second-term taste for Bill Clinton's blood that his colleagues loved to quaff. (Although he did love the rumor about Clinton smuggling in cocaine to a remote airstrip in Mena, Arkansas. What recovering addict wouldn't?) Programmers always found a place for him, and his followers always found that place. Wherever McManus wound up, the casual or rabid listener could be assured that he was not privy to a fixed fight. Jim McManus took calls on both sides of any issue and had been known on a couple of occasions to be swayed by a cogent point, which should have been enough to get him booted out of the conservative radio hosts' union. The occasional well-placed rash of fairness was one consistent trait of a McManus radio show. The other three were his evil, gurgling chuckle, his set-your-clock-by references to himself as a genius, and his twice-weekly beyond-gratuitous eviscerations of the column "Baggage Handling" by Marty Fleck. Just when you thought it might be personal, Jim McManus would tell you it wasn't personal, call himself a genius, gurgle up a laugh, and be fair with the next caller.

Eleven months ago, May 2003, the doors to this self-contained broadcasting ecosystem would be flung open wide. Coast-to-coast wide. When one caller, Kenny from Madison, wondered aloud why President Bush, in the middle of questions about his service in the Alabama National Guard, had the arrogance to put on a pilot's costume and land on an aircraft carrier in front of a White House-funded banner that read "Mission Accomplished," Jim McManus held his cough button for three seconds before yelling, "He's the commander in chief. He can wear whatever the hell he wants!"

Okay, sure it sounds a little on the level of "I know you are, but what am I?" at first, but oh, how the conservatives lapped it up. In the endless search for the simple heartlanded message, the seemingly irrefutable point where refutation = sedition, *"He's the com-*

mander in chief. He can wear whatever the hell he wants!" was right up there with *"If you don't support the war, you're not supporting the troops."* Not only that, and even more important, it changed the subject.

Jim McManus became a hero and a darling and whatever other unelected titles the fair and balanced media were handing out for a limited run. During the traditional Arbitron wasteland of summer, McManus's ratings doubled. He was moved in several top markets to the nine to noon slot. Pre-Limbaugh! All of a sudden, he was taking fewer calls from regular listeners because his producer was furiously punching up on the monitor *"Tom DeLay—Line 3—Wants to Chat!"* It was heady and exhilarating and whatever other epithets were bestowed when overnight the world knew what someone living in the darkness of radio air looked like and claimed him as their property.

One thing did not change. However many Rumsfelds, Reeds, or Romneys were backslapped into an offering of *Stand By for Truth*, there was always time for a few minutes at the top of the show twice a week to slam Marty Fleck. Always. And as Jim McManus hung around as an increasingly sought-out voice, so did the unconscious hardening of mainstream thought: That Marty Fleck and his column were not to be read, but watched. And scorned.

Phil looked a good twenty feet west, to the spot where their last conversation had ended. The last third of the outside front wall of the CBS Broadcast Center, where Phil had thudded scapula-first. He had come to the studio to ask his brother why he felt the need to turn Marty Fleck into a bi-weekly nom de-pummel. Was it just envy? Could it be that simple? It wasn't like Jim McManus hadn't built his own fully funded cottage industry of self-empowerment. Or were his feelings about the sanctity of the family and premarital sex and chemical abstinence and all the ideals he held so dear since, since when, since what seemed like twenty minutes ago, were they that real that when he came across a legitimate fraud in his own family he had to speak out, even if speaking out meant not admitting that he knew Marty Fleck, and how he knew Marty Fleck?

Nah.

Even Jim said so right up front when they had last spoken, almost five years ago. "Philly, come on. You know the business. It's Big-Time Wrestling. You think I mean it?"

"Yes," Phil had said. "I think you do. I've known you my whole life and I think you do."

"Well, whether I mean it or not, it's Big-Time Wrestling. You want to attack me, go ahead."

"I don't want to attack you. You're my brother."

"Correction," Jim said. "We share the same mother."

Phil had burst out laughing at that line, then quickly realized his half brother meant it. Around the age of seventeen, Jim had gotten big. Quarterback to tight-end big. The "Big-Time Wrestling" smile left his normally salesman face and he raked his thick brown hair like he had somewhere to go. Anywhere else.

"I gotta go," he said. "You want to be a big-shot columnist and treat the world as the frivolous playground for your self-conscious whimsy, fine. But be prepared to take your hits from people who believe what they do is important and that it's a serious time."

"This from a guy who left an AIDS fund-raising auction to do blow in the ladies' room," Phil had said, with great whimsy.

"That was eighteen *fucking years* ago!"

"Well, what happened?"

"That guy got clean," Jim huffed.

"I know that," said Phil. "But 'that guy' loved me. I meant what happened to him?"

Phil's memory of the rest of the conversation was murky. Murky as Shit Creek. Jim had made some remark about having to be responsible and Phil might have snapped back about all the times he had taken care of his older brother, not just the one summer when they were thirteen and sixteen. How far Phil carried that point, and its corresponding guilt, was unclear, but it did not sway Jim McManus, who at that moment was not exactly standing by for truth.

And then Phil made some inquiry, well-meaning he could swear, about his brother's recent divorce. Didn't mention Mickey, the ex-wife, even though he'd liked her. All he said were words to the effect of "Are you getting any support from Mom or Jamie?" Jamie, Jim's oldest daughter, was then twenty-one.

That's when his tight end of a half brother had grabbed Phil by his belt and the back of his neck and thrown him against the wall.

Phil turned back from the spot on the wall toward the entrance in time to see Jim McManus emerge. Dressed in the same outfit that clad every promotional photo—gray year-round wool pants, starched white buttondown broadcloth shirt under a navy lambswool sweater, red felt-tip pen tucked into the right ear—he had a meaty handshake for the eight or nine well-wishers who were still sleeping peacefully at the three-quarter pole of George W. Bush's first term. He looked a little heavier (a pound a year?), his hair still enviously brown. Eyes less hooded. Or maybe that was Phil projecting. Jim playfully grabbed a woman's portable camera and took a picture of her and her girlfriend. He was clearly more accessible. Or again, maybe that was Phil hoping.

He signed his last autograph, tucked the red Flair back in his ear, and turned east. Phil pushed himself off the side of the Broadcast Center and took two halting steps toward him. He was not tentative. Halting was now his regular gait.

"Marty Fleck," said Jim, "as I live and breathe righteously."

Jim McManus tried lamely to stifle a smile. The brothers attached in a convincing hug.

"Five years, Phil?"

"Something like that," Phil said. "I see they repaired the side of the Broadcast Center, where I landed."

"Yeah, that. I, uh, apologize. Me and Mickey back then. Divorce, you know, shit. Things were said. Well, you know how it is. Before they settle down to become ex-wives."

Phil considered telling Jim about Trish calling in the bomb scare to his wedding, but by the time his mind got to the word "scare," he had already decided it would be less dangerous for his brother to get a hold of uranium than that little nugget. So, he just puffed an exhale and replied, "Yeah, before they settle down."

"Speaking of settling down," Jim grinned, "I'm thinking about laying off Marty Fleck."

"That would be great, Jimmy."

"I figure it's been six years, my work is done."

"Seven and a quarter," said Phil.

"Really? Well, maybe we keep going to eight. Make it two full terms."

Again, Phil had a phrase ready. Actually, not a phrase. More like a well-latched epithet train, *fuckinelitistAndoverJesusfreakhalfacowboy-fascistmoron* . . . Instead, he took a trait he normally avoided. The winking humility of Clark Kent. Or Bruce Wayne. Or Nathan Zuckerman. "Well," Phil Camp spoke, "I can't speak for Marty Fleck, but I know he'd appreciate it."

"Anyway, I'm thinking about it. You're kinda done anyway."

"Why? You know something?"

"What? You didn't hear?!?" Jim McManus pop-eyed before smiling. He could still tease like a big brother. "Nah. What would I know?"

"That's kind of why I'm here."

"Philly, I gotta go. I told you I'd think about it."

"I came about something else."

"What?"

"I got what you had. APS."

"No shit. Right leg?"

"Left. Starts at the ass."

"Yeah, that's it. Have you read Abrun?"

"A million times. I've seen him. Heard the lectures. Been to the group. Bought the T-shirt. I love the guy, and I believe all of it, but I can't shake this."

Jim McManus brightened as though his radio producer had told him James Dobson was on hold. "You want to get some coffee?"

"Love to."

They began to walk toward Ninth Avenue. McManus hung a few feet back. "Nice hitch there, hoss."

"Fuckin' sucks. Can't believe this pain."

"How long have you had it? Month? Six weeks?"

"Almost ten months ago it started."

Phil walked a few more feet, figured his brother would have caught up to him, but stopped when he heard only his distinct clip-clop. He turned around. Jim had his hands on his knees, staring at the Hudson, ready to sprint in the opposite direction.

"Hey, Jim!"

"Ten months?" His brother screamed at Eleventh Avenue. "Ten fucking months!" He wheeled, then pranced toward Phil.

Phil scratched his beard and laughed. "What? Is that too long? Did I break your record?"

"You know what, little half brother? Fuck you."

"What?"

"I can't believe I almost fell for this shit again."

"Jim, you're scaring me. What happened in the last ten seconds?"

"How about the last ten months?"

"Again, what?" pleaded Phil.

"You're dragging around a bad leg and there's nothing wrong with you? You have Acute Psychogenic Syndrome? Pain caused by unconscious rage?"

"Yeah."

"And the pain started ten months ago?"

"Yeah." It was the only answer to give, but Phil was pretty sure it was wrong.

"Shit . . . taxi!" Jim corkscrewed his right index finger, normally the universal signal to a waiter for another round, but the cabdriver heading toward Eleventh knew it meant to make the midday U-turn on Fifty-seventh. He dropped his tight-end shoulders and calmed down as only a man leaving a confrontation can. He squeezed Phil's shoulder. Hard.

"Big fucking mystery," Jim McManus summarized. "You have pain. You became a grandfather and you're furious."

"I what?"

"Ten months ago." He opened the door to the cab. "But don't worry. You'll have no responsibility. Nothing is required of you.

Nothing's changed." And then, to the cabdriver: "Just go. I'll tell you where."

Phil leaned into the window. "Jimmy, Jesus. Why would you say something like that? What's wrong with you?"

"There's nothing wrong with me, you duplicitous piece of repressed shit. I'm not the one who's limping. Hey, Achmed, *go!*"

The yellow Crown Vic with sideswipe accents pulled away, and Phil thought about doing the corkscrew gesture himself and backing it up with the film noir fiat, *Follow that cab!* Didn't have it in him. A few seconds later, an unhailed one pulled up anyway. He gingered himself in, bad leg first, felt a twinge and a half, and grunted as he yanked the door closed.

"Prick bastard fucking liar," Phil mumbled.

"Okay?" said the driver.

"Yeah," said Phil. "I just need a new ass."

"Astor Place?"

His brother was right. Nothing had changed.

6

"Well, I played golf over the weekend. I walked all eighteen holes and shot a 116."

"That's terrific, Mr. Breeden."

"Dr. Abrun. I'm a five handicap. I haven't shot a 116 since I was twelve."

"Not important. Do you see what Allan, Mr. Breeden, did? He told his APS to go to hell. A month ago, you couldn't get out of bed."

"I guess so."

"Celebrate every victory."

Samuel Abrun never went around the room in any specific order. God forbid he be conventional, even in a small group. He tilted his glasses down and fixed his nearsighted gaze at the man next to Phil.

"Here's a man who does not want to talk. Mr. Honickman, tell us what brought you here."

The well-dressed sixty-year-old, who was clearly here on time only after lying to his secretary, began: "Six months ago, I started to feel numb around my tailbone."

"Coccyx."

"Yes. Oh, I'd love it to be just that now, but it's gotten worse. I couldn't sit comfortably, and whenever I got up, it was like a knife going through my rect—, my rear end. I went to an orthopedist and he recommended a month of no exercise, rest, and anti-inflammatories. Nothing. So, then he gave me a steroid injection. He said if that didn't work, I'd have to have the tip of my tailbone removed."

"Of course he did."

"The injection gave me relief for about a day. The pain came back, but the idea of having a piece of bone removed didn't, well, that didn't sound right. I had a client in the office and he gave me your book. That was two weeks ago. Now I'm here."

"And we're glad you're here," said Dr. Abrun. "Now, what happened six months ago?"

"Nothing. A year ago, my son took over our accounting firm . . ." A combination of snickers, coughs, and tongues smacking teeth caromed around the conference room. Honickman smiled and held up his hand. "It's not like that," he said. "He's a good kid. Kid—he's thirty-five. He was virtually running the place for the last year anyway. I'm proud of him."

"I'm sure you are," Abrun said.

Even though his mind was still nine blocks west, gridlocked between "grand" and "father," Phil mouthed the next question along with Dr. Abrun. "What was your relationship with your father like?"

"Great."

"Great?"

"Yeah, great. He was very supportive. I was lucky. I always did well in school. I excelled at sports and academics. I was the first one in my family to go to college. He was very proud of me."

"But whose idea was that?"

"What?"

"To excel and be a great student and go to college?"

"Well, mine."

Phil involuntarily shook his head. Abrun caught him. "That's right, Phil. Shake your head." Abrun jerked a finger his way. "He's heard me say this a thousand times. *You* didn't come up with the idea of excelling. *You* didn't come out of your mother's womb and say, 'I think I'll be the first person in my family to attend college.' That pressure was imposed on you. We want to be good. We want approval. This. Is. Basic . . . Stuff." Abrun would sometimes talk hesitantly, as if awaiting the arrival of a word other than "stuff." Never happened. Didn't matter.

"I am not a psychotherapist or a psychiatrist," he disclaimed, "but as proud as you are of your son, it must be infuriating to turn your business over to him. It cannot—"

Phil leaped in "—sit well with you."

Big laugh from Abrun. "Yes!" Then laughter from the rest of the group, anxious to belong.

Samuel Abrun went on to shower the room with his standard glaze about the unconscious, that bigger-than-real life factory outlet that is heated and cooled by devouring an irrational mix of approval/pleasure/comfort/immortality . . . and rage. But it was all white noise to Phil. He had gotten his big laugh, his approval from the author of *The Power of "Ow!"* and he felt as if he could fly.

And the best part of flying? No limp.

Why is it all about approval? And why, when one becomes convinced it is all about approval, does it immediately become about something else?

"Nice to see you without the walker this week, Bernice."

"Thank you, Dr. Abrun."

"But what's with the cast?"

"I tripped over my cat and broke my arm."

"I'm sorry."

"I think I might have been drinking."

"You think?"

"Anyway," Bernice said, "no pain in my leg for a week now. It's a miracle."

"No it isn't," laughed Abrun.

"Why?"

"Anyone want to answer why?"

Phil and the woman who never said anything mumbled in unison. *Because she has a real injury, she's distracted from her APS.*

Abrun clapped his hands once and pointed at Phil. "My alter ego," he said.

Two other women, one a regular, one new, asked what to do about husbands who thought *The Power of "Ow!"* was bullshit, and an orthodox Jew with a yarmulke bobby-pinned to his scalp and his mother sewn against his sleeve (*"Look at him! He read your book twice and he's no better! All he does is sleep . . ."*) asked if he could call Dr. Abrun and talk about something private.

"Mrs. Nishwitz," Abrun said to the mother, "I told you, you can only come to the lectures. Not the group."

"I thought you were talking to someone else."

"And, Akiva, the private, ah, stuff, you need to talk about with, which one of my people are you seeing, Dr. Jilson?"

"That's right," nodded the yarmulke.

"Well, you need to speak with him."

"I thought," said Mrs. Nishwitz to the room, "he was talking to someone else."

"I'm fine," Akiva said.

Abrun smiled. "And Phil," he blindsided, "while we still have time. What's new?"

"Nothing," Phil said. "Sixty-seventy percent, same as two weeks ago. But I'm not discouraged. Still doing the reading and the writing."

"You are *not* seeing one of my therapists."

"That is correct."

Again, the smile. "My alter ego betrayeth me." Big laugh from the room. Almost everyone. Except her. The woman who never said anything.

"Good for you," she said to Phil.

A month now, three group sessions, and until just now—the mumble and "Good for you"—nothing. Nothing that would be considered the spoken word. As everyone got up to leave and thank Dr. Abrun, she would occasionally stop on her way out, take a small notebook out of her pocket and write a line or two.

Whatever she was writing couldn't be any better than the line Phil had for her. He'd wanted to linger after her as she was jotting and, in his best stage whisper, say, "If you need any help, I know how to spell 'lunatics.'" That was the plan. And by "plan," we mean the fantasy of repartee initiation Phil envisioned as he lay on The Pad after each Abrun group session and jerked off.

What was wrong with her? Nothing that he could see. She was slacks, T-shirt, and L.L. Bean car-coat crisp. Two pieces of jewelry and makeup if she felt like it. Every twenty minutes or so (not that he was keeping track), she would readjust whatever was clipping or securing whatever precinct of a vast county of dark hair. Dark. If there isn't already a shade at the colorist called "Fuck It—More Black," there should be, and this would be it. The right hand made all readjustments. The left was buried just over the ear, holding up what had to be, had to be, a smart head, that spent the entire hour staring at Samuel Abrun in various arrays of skepticism.

What was wrong with her?

Hell, what was wrong with him? And what was with that friggin' "grandfather" crack?

The session before this, as they filed out and Phil once again didn't use the "lunatics" line, he had heard Abrun meekly call after her, "Janet, they're going to need to hear from you." She had waved the readjusting right hand behind her head, and Abrun probably would have said more, but the high tide of thanks rose too quickly. As always happened at the end of the group meetings, a receiving line/papal audience attempted to break out, as one Abrun patient after another was desperate to corner the elfin genius and in thirty seconds of face time, try to turn him into their own personal healer. Or, short of that, a proud father.

Phil was usually right there, but he was sidetracked by now having a name to put with the silent face. Janet. *Janet, they're going to need to hear from you.*

And now, one week later, they had heard from her. Or, at least Phil had. "Good for you," she had said.

Good for you. What was wrong with her? Other than nothing.

"Janet!"

She was waiting at the slow elevator when he tried to catch up to her. The only thing slower was how long it took him to reach her. The elevator arrived and the door opened. He waved, expecting her to get inside and disappear.

"See you next time."

She shrugged and waved at whoever was inside, then turned back toward him. Phil quickened his hobble, as if a stage manager at the Labor Day Telethon was rushing him out in front of the scrim before Jerry Lewis got the big check from Hickory Farms. Sixty to seventy percent, as Phil had told Abrun, meant the pain was manageable, unless he decided to speed up the limp. Didn't need to here. The woman, Janet, waited.

"No next time," she smiled. "This is it for me. The last group. I am not allowed in anymore if I don't talk. And I ain't talking."

"You spoke today. You said, *Good for you,* to me, for which I was trying to thank you."

"For which you're welcome," she said, smiled again and resummoned the elevator. What was wrong with her?

"I just thought it was interest—"

She turned back and squinted. "Look, it was just refreshing to see someone not fall for his manipulative bullshit for a change." She was hitting the down button like it was a video poker machine. She looked back down the hall. Dr. Abrun was walking cautiously, trying not to stumble into the members of the group backpedaling in front of him.

"Shit, here he comes," she said. "Can you do stairs?"

"Sure." Phil wasn't lying. Down was easier than up. You go downstairs the right way, you can make a limp work for you. That said, he had a three-flight limit. "Sure," he said, "but I have a three-flight limit."

"Great. Come on. I'll buy you coffee and a Vicodin."

• • •

She took a bite of her scallopine and didn't finish chewing. "If you can make it through the rest of this meal without using any combination of the words 'Sam Abrun,' 'genius,' 'visionary' or 'cutting edge' in the same sentence, I'll give you a blow job in the cab uptown."

"I've been out of the dating scene for a while," said Phil, "but that's quite an offer."

"I'll let you know when this is a date," she said. "As for the offer, I wouldn't have made it if I thought I'd have to pay up."

They were way past "I'll buy you coffee," and had been for the better part of two hours. They had had a cup of coffee, but then that place got crowded with much louder, much much younger people, and they both knew and liked the place two doors down. Café du Kips Bay. Phil was usually extroverted out by the end of a group session, so he never realized all the post-spew critiquing one could do, if one wasn't so anxious to get back to one's apartment and isolate. Samuel Abrun, along with his book, his program, and those who sat attentively in its audience, was like some moving sculpture whose impact was as simple as it was elusive. It had all the answers and none, depending on how firm the soil on which your acceptance stood. It inspired intimate conversation and confusion among strangers who could only agree on one thing: This little man who kept saying, "If you still have pain, you still have work to do," was a friggin gen—

"You still haven't told me why you were there."

"You mean," Janet said, "what's wrong with me?"

"Yeah."

She speared some salad. "Does it matter? According to Dr. Abrun, it's all APS. If there's too much garlic in this dressing and I get heartburn, that's an APS equivalent and I am enraged about something or at someone."

"Maybe the salad chef?"

"That's my point. Why is everything that isn't a disease something else, and always the same thing?" She pushed her Fuck It—More Black hair behind her ear and finished her salad slowly, thinking Phil would be into next week chewing on that last riddle of a remark.

"Look, Janet-san," he bowed. "I don't give a shit what is wrong with you, especially since it gives me more time to talk about what's wrong with me. But why would you show up every other week to the group and not say anything and not respond to a guy you obviously have questionable respect for and who doesn't treat anyone unless they accept his diagnosis? Were you mandated by a judge who had unnecessary disk surgery?"

She leaned in after the waiter cleared the plates. "I was one of his first patients. I was a diver in high school. On my way to a scholarship. And toward the end of my junior year, I hit my head on the board. Traumatic, but it turned out to be a couple of stitches. No damage. X-rays and tests up and down the pike. I stopped diving for a year on the advice of my coaches and parents. Just as the year is up, I begin to develop all kinds of neck and shoulder problems. Incredible pain. Everywhere. Some days I couldn't get out of bed. This goes on for six months. I almost have to drop out of college, where I am *not* on a diving scholarship. Desperate, I decide to see Sam Abrun, who gives me thirty pages of stapled paper to read, homework, and the name of a physical therapist who is sensitive to his theories. In two months, I am completely pain-free."

"Wow."

"I know, a miracle." She squinted at Phil. "Shit. I owe myself head."

Phil behaved. "Now," he asked instead, "why wouldn't you want to share that with the group?"

"Because twenty-plus years of research and experience tells me that it is not so simple. The pain goes away, but comes up elsewhere. It's like that Whack-a-Mole game in the arcade. He doesn't tell you that. He doesn't tell you that this is a life's work. He says, 'The brain will not be denied.' The brain will *never* be denied. It was installed at birth. None of us, least of all Sam Friggin' Abrun, knows the size and depth of the unconscious."

He wanted to ask her why she was the only one he'd heard call Abrun "Sam." But he opted to try and continue to make it a conversation. "Dr. Abrun says the unconscious is timeless."

She exhaled. "That's pat. That helps contain his theory. Just like his harping on rage. It's all rage. You can't feel it, but it's all rage. That's shoddy. It's superficial. He knows there's more, but people would rather be told about how furious they don't know they are. It's primitive. It's sexy."

Her eyes blackened to punctuate her last point. *Okay, you got me,* Phil thought. *Rage is sexy. But an angry woman with a salad fork may not be.* Again, good sense had the final edit. "He talks about sadness and shame," he said.

"Only to cover his ass. There is much more sadness . . ."—her voice caught—"much more than he lets on. But that is too painful. The sadness may have come first. Before the rage. And isn't fear at the base of all anger or rage?"

He wanted to say, "You sound angry. What are you afraid of?" Instead, he tried not to look at the check.

"I know I sound angry," she half-smirked as she grabbed the check. "I got this. Business."

(Business?) "Janet—"

"Forget it, Phil. Let me finish. Believe me, I know what Sam Abrun's contribution is. The millions of people who never read the book who could have been helped. But I don't like neat packages. I don't like the relegation of sadness to an afterthought. That is where the healing is, I believe. We have butted heads on this more than a few times, and I thought maybe if he bent a little, I could be one of his therapists. But I watch him, I hear him, and I know he'd rather talk about rage. He'd rather confront a reservoir of anger than tears. Because . . ."—her voice caught again—"he is his own shitty APS patient. Resistant. He'd rather be liked. And people like a little guy who smiles and treats rage like a bully."

Phil went to pat her free hand, and she held up the check like he was trying to beat her out of the treat. He ignored the independent single gal semaphore and patted her hand anyway. She smiled.

"You're lucky I didn't order a drink," said Janet. "After a couple, I tend to get a little strident."

They walked outside and Phil made some sort of JV elegist remark about how the seasons must have changed while they were deciding against ordering dessert. Janet gave him a look that said nothing but, "Nice try."

"All right," he said. "So we agree that this was business. And the next time is a date." She shook his hand with the right pump of fake sincerity. "And we agree that the man is a genius, a visionary, and on the cutting edge."

"Sorry," she fake-frowned, "the offer expired when I took the check."

The fake-frown was returned. "Damn. Okay, then, where's my Vicodin?"

She took a pad out of her purse and scribbled on a piece of paper, as if she were writing him a fake prescription. Funny. She ripped it off with a flourish and pressed it into his hand.

"I can get my own cab," she said.

She waved and flagged one down. Must have. Phil was too busy looking at the paper in his hand. Real script. Real name. Janet Abrun-Fitzgerald, MD.

7

It took Phil about an hour after he had walked home from Café du Kips Bay to realize he had walked home. That's when his upper leg began to stiffen and the area from his left ankle to foot felt like it had been replaced with one of those disobedient fourth shopping cart wheels. So, Phil's thought process went something like this: *Shit, the leg again . . . Well, I did just walk two miles home . . . Shit, I walked two miles home!* That was another less than charming feature of Abrun's Acute Psychogenic Syndrome: It didn't occur to you that you had been out of pain until you were in pain again. Of course, it could also be a more than charming feature of Abrun's daughter.

Ten-twenty. Maybe the Knicks had temporarily gotten over sucking and taken somebody to overtime.

Shit, the column!

Usually, Phil was home from the APS group session by seven and would check in across the hall with Elly Vogelbaum to make sure she had proofed and e-mailed the Wednesday piece. For the last month, as he hovered tantalizingly around the 70 percent-better threshold,

Phil had progressed to where he could not only write with the pad on The Pad, but then do forty-five minutes standing up typing it into his computer. But he loved seeing his neighbor's daughter, loved getting his live laughs (which were, now that he thought about it, accompanied by no pain), so her duties had recently been altered to proofing and shipping via e-mail as an attached document.

He rang the peephole bell of Apartment 24D, and Wendy Vogelbaum muted *Dog, the Bounty Hunter* (damn, *Dog, the Bounty Hunter* was on), shuffled on the parquet floor, and the door was jerked open with a WD-40-deprived yelp.

At some point, Wendy Vogelbaum must have been her daughter's mother, but there's nothing like a piece-of-shit ex-husband and a decade of being a legal system piñata to stonewash one's genetics down to raw matter.

"Oh great," Wendy greeted, "a man."

"Sorry."

"Phil, do you have any idea what time it is?"

Phil smelled the question and wanted to say, "Three hours before last call," but he still had some restraint left in him from dinner.

"Wendy, I'm sorry. I know it's late. I got back an hour ago and I wanted to know if Elly had come by to ship my column."

Elly appeared behind her mother, smiling, in a two-year-old soccer uniform that now served as pajamas. Her long brown hair was in a ponytail. "Sure I did," she beamed. "Around five. I'm not the screw-up."

"Thanks, Elly Vogelbaum."

"Later, dog." She scooted back into her room to catch the end of the bounty hunt.

Phil smiled. "She won't let me pay her," he said to Wendy.

"She's learned not to expect anything when men promise money."

"Okay, bad subject," he said, wincing.

"Always is," she said. Wendy Vogelbaum could metafork any utterance back to her divorce. Especially after nine o'clock, when she'd start her nightly bottle of Zinfandel.

"Have I told you lately what a good job you did with her?"

"Bad subject," she said.

In that half-second of vulnerability, Phil leaped lightly. "Wendy, do I have to become a fag for you to like me any of the time?" Nothing. "Okay, I guess that's a yes. I'll start to work on it. Good night."

Before Wendy could close the door, Elly was back. "Weird column today, Phil," she called after him. "I didn't know they let you curse."

Phil's next thought, *Curse?* was drowned out by the snapping of a Multi-Lock deadbolt. Halfway across the hall, the same thought screamed *Curse!!!* and he ran the last ten yards like a man who had nothing physically wrong with him, which he was, but with APS—shit, we have no time for this.

He staccato-poked the Back icon on his browser and found the column Elly had dutifully attached. He squinted as he slowly scrolled up to the top of the piece, but his cold sweat and nausea were way ahead of him. He just wanted to make sure.

Baggage Handling
by Marty Fleck

THE NON-GENTILE CYCLE

Years ago, I went to the famous comedy club Catch a Rising Star on the Upper East Side of Manhattan. I used to go there all the time in the late seventies-early eighties, when it was a thing to do. And before everybody became a stand-up comic, including the super in my building and two different women who washed my hair at the salon on Seventy-ninth and Lexington.

On this night, the emcee was working the audience between acts. You know, "What's your name?" "Where ya from?" The emcee, who I had seen before, was named Larry, and was one of my favorite acts at the club. Very quick. Okay, so he's working the crowd and he keeps getting interrupted by a loud guy up front. Larry kept burying the guy, death by a thousand cuts, and the audience loved it. But then, the loud guy up front thought he was part of the act. Larry started introducing the next comic, and this idiot said something like, "You mean me? Am I the next comic?"

Well, the audience groaned. They'd had enough. And I'll never forget the next exchange.

> LARRY: Let me ask you something. Are you Jewish?
>
> GUY UP FRONT: Yes.
>
> LARRY: Well, congratulations. You're the reason we've been kicked out of every country we've ever been in . . .

Screams, applause, and here comes the next act.

Let me make two points. First, Larry was Jewish, which made it all right. And funny. I laughed, and I remember the line all these years later.

Second, and this is critical: Fuck you, all of you fucking Jew haters. I have had to eat your shit my entire life. I've changed my name and sung your hymns and been thrown into cesspools, real and figurative.

I've heard you snicker and snigger and ask where my beanie was and call my most sacred holiday Halloween. I watched you try to wipe the pulverized concrete of The Towers off your clothes and years after 9/11, you still look at me as if to say, "You people happy now? You ruined my suit."

I've read your "evidence" that the only Holocaust was the miniseries with Fritz Weaver, and then, on the same page, read the inevitable disclaimer that even if there was, get over it, it's been sixty years, and look who wound up with all the money anyway.

Well, here it is. I forgive you. Just like Jesus would have. Jesus, the Jew you let in. You think I don't know you support Israel because you want to round us up all in one place and then flick a switch? Just like it says in Ecclesiastics or Revelation or Kikebegone or whatever the genocidal loophole you found in the New Testament. The New and Improved Testament. I know it, and I still forgive you. I have no problem with you. Today. (Although, that may change later on, when I talk about Shit Creek. . . .)

My problem is with the biggest Jew hater I know. Perhaps you have heard of him. Fellow by the name of Marty Fleck.

Marty Fleck found out at an early age that just mentioning the word "Jew" gets a laugh. His grandfather, a steerage-ferried Austrian Hebe, had a favorite joke that went something like this: *Guy goes to hell. Shortly after he gets there, he finds himself in a giant room, standing up to his neck in shit. He turns to the guy next to him and says, "This is hell? This ain't so bad." And the guy next to him says, "Wait till the Jews come by in their speedboats. . . ."*

Years later, Marty Fleck hit upon another revelation . . . and not the one about getting all the Jews in one place. He realized that the sound of laughter after you said "Jew" was the same whether the person was laughing because he related to a fellow sufferer or laughing because he just loved the sound of "Jew." What is that sound? The sound of something always derogatory. Always. *What can*

you tell us about our next contestant? / Well, Bob,
he's a Jew . . .

Armed with that insight, Marty Fleck continued.
He never wrote it in a column, until now. Why?
Because he's a fucking coward. He didn't have to
write it by then. He was a rich J———, yeah, one
of those. But he continued saying it, thinking it,
laughing when he heard it. And it worked. Why?
Because he's a fucking coward and because he
hated himself way before everybody else, even
before he started getting a hundred pieces of mail
every month that begin, *Dear Jew . . .*

So, look at him now. Hobbling around like an
old man. With a self-inflicted wound. Hey, it'll get
you out of the service, you fucking coward.

Keep limping, Marty. Keep limping, Jew. You'll
never be able to drive the speedboat. That enough
baggage for you, you fucking fraud?

Honest mistake. Perfect length—790 words, just like one of his columns. Same font, too. Sitting there, in the computer, just waiting to
be sent. Phil had banged it out an hour before leaving for Dr. Abrun's
group, trying to jog the unconscious rage into present time, which
was as close as he got to jogging these days. He had liked this one.
Good and angry and self-loathing. He thought about printing it out
for the Irish Shrink, decided against it, then saw he was running late,
and left it up on his screen. Didn't save it, didn't hide it in the deep
cranny of hard drive with the other Abrun essays, in a file obtusely
marked "Butt Talk." So, why would Elly Vogelbaum think it was anything other than that day's column? Sitting there, 790 words, double-
spaced 11-point Arial. She didn't. She sent it. Honest mistake.

Which now raised the question: How many of the hundred-plus
daily newspapers would run this honest mistake? The remnants of
his meal-that-wasn't-a-date at Café du Kips Bay coalesced into a
carb-based geode of terror. The syndication side of Excelsior Publi-

cations was not one that fussed too much with oversight. The night editor, harmless Stan Feigensen, usually pencil-whipped Phil's stuff on through. Phil heard from Stan twice a year, the day before he went on vacation and the day he came back.

Nah. It was out there. The Marty Fleck meltdown, Diasporama 2004 was out there. Phil checked his e-mail.

Sender	Subject
Seth James	Where the fuck are you?
Seth James	Where the fuck are you?
Seth James	Where the fuck are you?
Seth James	Where the fuck are you?
Seth James	Where the fuck are you?
Seth James	Where the fuck are you?
Seth James	Where the fuck are you?
Seth James	Where the fuck are you?
Seth James	Where the fuck are you?
Seth James	Where the fuck are you?
Sandy Collewell	RE: Where the fuck are you?
Seth James	Where the fuck are you?
Seth James	Where the fuck are you?

Seth James was Stan Feigensen's backup on the night desk. He was easily excitable and as Phil liked to say, not feckless, but dangerously low on feck. Sandy Collewell worked in the PR department at Excelsior, was the one who kept track of the "*Dear Jew*" letters, and his only friend there. And the fact that she remained his only friend after they had slept together twice last year and agreed it was a bad idea right up there with New York getting the 2012 Olympics said volumes about one or both of their characters.

He read Sandy's e-mail first. Given its position in the stream of "Where the fuck are you?" and the fact there was no second message from her, Phil hoped she might be able to do what six people in public relations could actually do—keep the public out of the relations, and leave no fingerprints.

He double-clicked on Sandy Collewell.

SETH—PHIL KNEW STAN WAS ON VACATION AND WANTED TO FUCK
WITH YOU. CAN'T BELIEVE YOU FELL FOR IT. IF YOU SENT THIS OUT,
IT'S GONNA BE YOUR ASS. HE DID THIS SIX YEARS AGO WITH CAP
KONSTANTAKIS. SAME COLUMN, TOO.
SANDY C

Wow. He would call her tomorrow and offer her steaks, whitewall
tires, another shot at his cock. She had saved his ass. His toothache
ass. He could not leave an incriminating cyber response. But he had
to respond. He hit "reply" and let her know how grateful he was
with lowercase ambiguity.

. . . and that's why you're you . . .

The twelve e-mails from Seth James, sent every twenty or so minutes
starting at seven-fifteen, were a dizzying graph of mild annoyance,
hysteria, chagrin, anger, renewed hysteria, bargaining, paranoia,
and bravadoed denial. It was fascinating to read the most recent
one first on down, as e-mail chains go. Like hitting the Rewind button on Elisabeth Kubler-Ross's stages of grieving. From now on,
Seth James's new nickname would be Ross Kubler.

It replaced his old nickname, Dangerously Low on Feck.

7:48 *SANDY COLLEWELL JUST WROTE ME. V-FUNNY. HILARIOUS. NICE*
GOING. YOU GOT ME. BRAVO. NOW, WHERE'S YOUR COPY? IF I DON'T
HEAR FROM YOU IN THEN NEXT TEN MINUTES, I'M RUNNING THE OLD
COLUMN ON ST. PATRICK'S DAY.
SETH

Eleven-eighteen now. Phil gave it a good ten seconds of thought,
then hit "reply."

SETH
JUST GOT IN. NEW?
PC/MF

Phil was halfway through his second cup of coffee the next morning when he looked at his feet and remembered his left sock. He hadn't forgotten to put it on, he just hadn't remembered putting it on. But there it was, the white, all-cotton crew-length, six-pair-for-five-dollars street fair special, snug on his foot and ready for whatever borderline athleticism the day held. Snug on his foot like it was nothing. And it had been nothing. Which was something.

In the world of sciatica, APS, or whatever the hell had burrowed itself in Phil for the last ten months, putting on his left sock was the epicenter of exasperation. He would sit on the edge of his bed, mumble, "Okay, here goes," inhale deeply, and then watch himself try to raise his life mask of a left leg to the absolute minimum angle at which his lowering upper torso could awkwardly throw the top of the sock over the foot and hope to feebly lasso the big toe. It would take at least three attempts (the first two were usually weak tosses as Phil tried to rock himself out of inertia as he thanked God no one was there to watch), but once he had the toe, the lunge-worthy momentum was there and he was able to yank the sock over the four other toes and around the foot, over the heel, and four or so inches above the ankle, crew-length permitting.

By the time he had stopped panting and thought about reaching for his sweatpants, Phil would invariably point two open palms at his socked right foot, earlier sheathed, and slipped on in a flutter with the deft of a three-card monte dealer, then stare to his left, as if to say, "Why can't you be more like your brother?"

The point is, none of that had happened this morning. No effort. No awkwardness. No lunge. No panting. Mostly, no pain. Hey, Phil mused, maybe now we're at 80 to 85 percent.

Mostly? Maybe? This called for a test. He turned on the radio. Just in time for the fife and drum sting and the union voiceover guy.

"Welcome back, America, to Jim McManus: Stand By for Truth . . ."

"You're listening to the Jim McManus Show, nine-to-noon five days a week. I'm Jim McManus, I'm an American, and I fight evil wherever I see it."

Good Christ, thought Phil, that's new. He heard the rustling of a newspaper over the radio microphone.

"Now, if you know me, and I think you do, you know I don't waste time with daily newspapers. I have no need for the liberal media lying to me about my leaders in order to promote their seditious agenda for a society where, if they had their way, Mary and Joseph would have stopped by the Bethlehem Abortion Clinic on Christmas Eve. And it would have been open!"

More rustling.

"Sorry, I have a problem with traitors. I'm funny that way. Grab a shyster and sue me. Now, normally I have no use for the daily newspapers, but I couldn't help but notice a piece in the *News* this morning by my favorite syndicated column-nast, Marty Fleck. Perhaps you have heard me talk about him before. I've mentioned him from time to time, okay, twice weekly, and many of my listeners wonder how I could be so fixated on one writer when there are so many more utterly heinous, contemptible scribes out there. I love you, too, Maureen. And you, too, Frank. And I haven't forgotten you, Jonathan Alter, my little *Newsweek* puppet. But I don't mention them because (a) I don't read them and (b) Why should I give them any further promotion than the liberal media machine already gives them? Why should I defile the pure goodness of my loyal listeners?

"So, I stick with Marty Fleck, who is that rare troika of untalented, harmless, and harmful. His message is much more subtle. Take nothing seriously. Blame the family. Make fun of God, your leaders, or God, your leader."

I'm glad we had that little chat the other day, Phil thought.

McManus chuckled. "You know what we should do? Let's get the environmentalists involved. The ones that say we don't care. We don't care? Do they have any idea how many trees are wasted in the name of 'Baggage Handling' by Marty Fleck? Where is that demonstration? Where is that e-mail petition? Where is that Howard Dean psycho screeching screed—"

His rant was curtailed as self-satisfying laughter gurgled into hacking cough. A cough-faw. *New bit*, thought Phil. *Good for you, bro. So, so glad we had that chat.*

The radio host rallied as only a demagogue can. "For some reason," McManus cleared his throat, "the *News* chose to run a previous column by Marty Fleck. His salute to St. Patrick's Day from five years ago. I will excuse the third-rate open-miker jokes about green vomit, the disastrous puns like Erin Go Wonderbragh and the stillborn wordplay on the phrase IRA . . ."

IRA . . . Hey, good one . . .

"And I will, defender of free speech that I am, overlook the fact that it's friggin' April . . ."

"Why?" Phil asked his radio. "That's a legitimate complaint, Jimmy." And then, quietly to himself, "Uh-oh."

"But," McManus stridented, "I will not stand for a reprise of his vicious and depraved parody of *Angela's Ashes*, in which he talks about his poverty-stricken childhood in the suburbs, where he and his brother were forced to eat regular Kraft Macaroni and Cheese, and not the deluxe style, and I quote, *'where the processed cheese came in a can.'* Ladies and gentlemen, you don't have to be Sherlock Holmes to deduce the inference in the phrase *'came in a can.'*"

"For the love of God," Phil yelped.

"And just in case you missed it, he ends the stereotypic muddle by jamming a rainbow flag atop this pile of God-hating excrement. And I quote, *'Yes, for one day, everybody is Irish. Except gay people in New York City. I'm going to the parade. And if I hear one marching band play one Broadway show tune, I'm going to call the authorities. Now, if I can only find a cop . . .'*"

"So, let me see if I have this, you'll pardon the expression, straight. The Irish are denied the right to assemble and freedom of choice, but the media-ruling Jews and their fruit brethren are permitted full access to ridicule? Just as long as I am clear on this.

"Marty Fleck is not the shallow-end humorist he appears to be. He is a rapacious, soulless manipulator, bent on choking off the windpipe of the just with his relentless fluff-coated bile. In the next twenty-four hours, I expect, no, demand, fifty thousand e-mails to Excelsior Publications calling for the immediate dismissal of Marty Fleck and whoever authorized the reprinting of that March nineteen ninety-nine column. Marty Fleck and his 'Baggage Handling' column are evil masquerading as entertainment. The word pictures he paints are hardly innocent. I don't have to remind you people—Hitler started as a painter . . .

"Okay, let's turn our attention to something more uplifting. Here's Terry Dixon with an update from Iraq . . ."

Phil was trying to google his long-term memory to figure out if, indeed, he was the first Jew to be compared to Hitler by his own brother (with the reverted Irish name) when his answering machine beeped.

"Phil, if you're screening, pick up, it's Sandy."

He turned the radio off. "Sandy, my hero. Things quiet enough for you?"

"I don't know. How'd it go with Turner?"

Phil smirked at the receiver. Turner Billings was the executive editorial director of the Excelsior Newspaper Group, a capital-hemorrhaging division of Excelsior Publications. Phil spoke with him every nine months, whether he needed to or not.

"I haven't heard from him. Why would he call me? The column never went out, right? You took care of it, right?"

"Right," said Sandy. "I don't get it, either, but he called me an hour ago for your number. As far as I know, everybody cooperated and the piece never left the newsroom. Nobody there talks to Turner. They all hate him. Like you."

Turner Billings, a thirty-year veteran of the magazine business, had come over to Excelsior three years earlier after doing everything but carrying the bag of lime in burying *Talk* and *Brill's Content* within twenty-four months of one another. He had built his reputation in magazine design and marketing, so it made perfect sense to put him in charge of editorial content at a newspaper chain. He was an ideal dinner guest, forever between marriages, perpetually charming, the kind of man who was always being mistaken for somebody famous, or taller. And yet, with all his considerable survival-strewn gifts, he was totally free of the burden of a sense of humor. Turner Billings never got 'Baggage Handling' by Marty Fleck, and would only acknowledge its appeal under oath. The every-nine-month phone call almost always amounted to Billings suggesting that Phil devote a column to the size of women's handbags or why men are so secretive about manicures. "I think you could make some great comedic hay with that," he'd bluster. Phil would jut his jaw and come back with "Let me noodle that." And that would be it for another nine months.

"This is just a coincidence. He probably wants me to work at a Starbucks for a day and do a four-part series."

His phone beeped.

"That's him," said Phil. "I'll call you back. Dinner sometime?"

"Jesus," Sandy said.

Despite the Excelsior Publications exchange on his caller ID, it was not Turner Billings on the other line. It was a young woman who introduced herself as Lorraine Corrano.

"What kind of name is that?" asked Phil.

"Corrano?" she up-spoke. "Colombian?"

"Let's go with that," Phil said. "I don't think we've spoken before. I hope this is a reminder about getting a flu shot." He looked out the window. April.

"Uh, please hold for Turner Billings?"

Phil began to pace around his living room with the cordless phone. He did not notice he was walking perfectly.

"Phil?"

"Hello, Turner."

"This is so weird. I was just going to call you."

"You did call me."

"I did? Weird . . ."

"Okay," said Phil. "You first."

"Okay. We're letting you go. Your contract is up in two months. You'll be paid in full, so you can stop writing immediately."

"Is this about the whole thing last night with Seth James? Did he make a complaint?"

"What is a Seth James?" Billings dismissed, "and what does it have to complain about?"

"Well, is this about the last column?"

"The St. Patrick's Day column? Hell no. I liked it. I actually laughed."

"Well then," said Phil, "why?"

Turner Billings was ready. "Because we're done."

"I'll be honest, Turner. I never saw this coming. Marty Fleck has been a big feature of this chain, your chain, for almost eight years, and at my salary, I'm a goddamn bargain. Even you'd admit that. I always thought it would end when I wanted it to end."

Again, Billings was ready. "Hey, life is wide."

What did that mean? Fuck it, Phil thought, I'll ask. "What does that mean?"

"Gotta go, Phil. Talk to Joan if you need anything."

"You mean Lorraine?"

"Who? Oh. Yeah."

The line clicked, and Phil yelled "Life is wide? What the fuck does that mean?" into the dead receiver. And then he realized Turner Billings had answered him. It meant, *Gotta go, Phil.*

And Phil might have congratulated himself for figuring it out, might have, if he hadn't been distracted by his left leg giving way and his body following lurchingly floorward.

8

It **had** been, as bouts of hysterical paralysis go, a productive four hours on the floor for Phil. From just after 10:15 A.M. to just after 2:15 P.M. with The Pad but twenty feet away, the only things in motion on Phil were his tearducts, larynx, and memory. Big, big, big racking sobs. Like an eight-year-old trying to imitate a Paris police siren. He turned himself inside out with weeping, and that set of emotional calisthenics exhausted him into a deep hour of sleep. Only to wake up, unable to budge, and think, "Well, *it's just me now. How did this happen? I guess I'm not done . . .*" That was enough for another round of dry, heaving wails, and when his eyes shut tight (Oh yeah, the eyelids worked, too), an image appeared of himself throwing a shovelful of laptop computers into what must have been a grave. Marty Fleck's grave. *Well, it's just me now. . . .*

The cordless phone was near enough to his head, but Phil's fall had cracked the battery loose from its housing. The only thing in the whole apartment that had literally fallen apart.

By hour three, Phil began to own up to what had transpired

with Turner Billings. An ego-based version, but a version nonetheless. He reran the fantasy press-release statement in his head. As if people would miss Marty Fleck. They would, but not enough to demand a statement. "I am Buffalo Bill," he thought, referring not to the nineteenth-century Wild West showman but the underappreciated Dabney Coleman situation comedy of the early eighties. "I should never have been on the air in the first place, but I was. I had a good run, but not everyone got me. It ended before I wanted it to, which bothers me, but not nearly as much as not seeing the end coming."

He reran the sound bite until it was drowned out by tears, then sleep. Again. He woke around one-thirty when he dreamed his leg twitched.

Just after two-fifteen, the doorbell rang, followed by impatient, youthful pounding.

"Phil, are you mad at me?" Elly Vogelbaum.

"No!"

"I think you are."

"No! I mean no. Please. Elly. Please."

"Are you crying?" she asked.

"No!" he said too loud.

The most impressive fifteen-year-old girl on the East Side of anywhere started to cry.

"Why won't you open the door?"

"I'm not decent."

"Bullshit, Phil."

Bullshit, Phil. That got him to his feet. Although he never realized it until he felt himself hugging his neighbor's daughter and thought, "Hey, look who's on his feet . . ."

Around four, after he and Elly had split a pint and a half of D'Agostino's peppermint candy ice cream, Phil put the battery back in his phone and made a call.

"I lost my gig," he said.

"Who knew you had a gig?" said Janet.

"Heh."

"Let me ask you: Would you have made this call, this *next-day call*, if you hadn't lost your job?"

"Sure," he lied.

"Good answer." She laughed. "Sixty-seven West Eighty-fourth. Number ten."

During her forty-seven years on the planet, Janet Abrun-Fitzgerald, MD, had been on one blind date. One. It happened six months after her divorce became final. She was set up by one of the nurses at the hospital. Some tall, cute guy, a researcher at ABC News, who lived in the nurse's building in the East Eighties. They met for dinner at some Mexican place in his neighborhood. None of this is important. None of this is useful. The only essential piece of information needed about the evening is this: Just after the waiter took their order, the guy excused himself and went a block up the street to a Laundromat to move his clothes into a dryer. Up until then, Janet's biggest concern had been trying not to drink too much on the date. How silly. As the Irish Shrink says, we always worry about the wrong thing. By the time the tall, cute ABC News researcher returned, he had two entrées all to himself. But he'd have to order another giant margarita.

The next day, just after her hangover began to idle, Janet ordered a vibrator online and upgraded to every premium cable channel. That was the last decision she intended to make concerning companionship. From now on, the only thing she would go back for more of would be D batteries.

And it was a solid decision, as decisions aimed at nothing other than vapid self-protection go. Two years now. There had been no looking back, no looking forward, and, except for mislaid books in her apartment, no looking around. And there had been no fellow therapist to ask Janet, "How's that working out for you?" And if there had been, she would have replied, "How's that derivative, pap-based line of questioning working out for you?"

Janet Abrun-Fitzgerald kept her hyphen and the force field that came with it. She had her patients and she had her laughs. When you're treating a thirty-five-year-old Internet billionaire who, mid-session, pulls out a trial-size bottle of Purell hand sanitizer to clean the jumbo economy-size bottle of Purell hand sanitizer that he uses to clean his hands; really, who needs a fella?

The point is—which everyone knows is what people say when there is no point—if you take a beaker and pour in equal amounts of experience from being an ex-wife, a recalcitrant daughter, a periodic alcoholic, and the smartest girl in any room, stir, pop it in a template, and chill, you will wind up with someone destined to spend the rest of her life alone, surrounded by books and a D battery or two.

Alone. Unless you stop and allow the rest of your life to resume the next day.

"You want to hop out?" she said. "I've got to pee."

"This may take a while. I'm on the wrong side of your bed."

"What?"

"If I was on the right side, I could just plant my right foot and swing the bad leg around," Phil explained. "But this way, I have to kind of shimmy out toward the front end. I can't move this leg without the other foot flat on the floor first."

"Oh please," said Janet Abrun-Fitzgerald, "you were moving that left leg fine about five minutes ago."

"Yeah, well, I was distracted."

Janet elbowed his rib. "So was I. About three times."

Phil squeezed her elbow. "Never underestimate the sexual potency of a forty-six-year-old man who just got fired."

"Phil, seriously. I gotta go."

"I'd like to help you." He giggled. "You're a nice girl. A little easy. But me getting out of this bed is not going to happen swiftly."

"Well, what if you rolled over on your stomach? That way, your right leg would be closest to the edge."

Phil nodded his head without looking at her, trying to visualize the never-before attempted maneuver. "Hey, I guess Dad isn't the only genius in the family."

"Fuck you."

"And don't think I didn't appreciate it."

Phil started rocking counterclockwise to get the necessary momentum going for the flop to the stomach. Janet watched in vague horror, like a hernia patient who had woken up in the detox ward by mistake.

"Oh, for Christ sake."

She grabbed Phil by the right shoulder, stopping him just long enough for her to fling her side of the covers off and roll/crawl over him and off the bed with only one "Ow!" between them. She sprang back, did a little faux dismount, with both feet touching softly and her type-A hardened mid-forties body a lovely bouncing postscript. Then Janet Abrun-Fitzgerald curtsied, said, "Or, that . . . ," and bounced off to the john.

Phil looked around, and saw what he had gotten himself into, foreign apartmentwise. Janet Abrun-Fitzgerald had clearly made the decision when she dropped the husband but kept his name to create a living space in which her work was unavoidable. There was nothing one could do in this good-sized two-bedroom with dining alcove, nothing that did not require first moving a stack of books or papers. Twice the night before, Janet had attempted the never-fail seductive bit of falling back on her bed as she was unbuttoning her blouse. Both times, the move had to be suspended when she was stabbed in the small of her back by a medical journal she had failed to clear away. In various stages of undress, they spent a good ten minutes evacuating all reading matter from the bedroom. Phil didn't have the heart to break it to the poor girl that, as a rule, men, especially Jewish men, were not fans of any foreplay that involved lifting. But he would let that go. He would let just about anything go for this former stranger who had been the only person he had thought to call after Turner Billings had bagged Marty Fleck.

Phil was sure he heard the thud of a resituated textbook shortly before Janet opened her bathroom door and emerged. She was in a green terry-cloth robe, which offset the black-black hair in a way that surprised him. A good way. Accidentally regal. She had combed her hair straight back and put on a little makeup. She strode purposefully toward his side of the bed.

"Now, let's see . . ." She pulled the covers back. "This is the problem leg?" She cupped her hand under his left ankle, and felt the entire side of his body tense.

"Shh . . ."

He relaxed long enough for her to gently drop his leg off the side of the mattress, leaving just wide enough a port of entry for her to superfluously push her hair behind her ears and descend mouth-first on that part of Phil's body which was neither unsuspecting nor affected by Acute Psychogenic Syndrome. After a dozen or so thrusts from Janet's disappearing lip gloss, he felt his left leg release itself and his sock-fearing toes touch the floor. This. This was a woman out to prove a point. Well, point taken.

And, oh, it would have been so great if Phil's bliss could have avoided being derailed by a foot cramp. That's right. Nothing says a man being pleasured quite like that same man saying, "Ee-yah! Cramp! Problem! Get! Move! Out! Hah!"

Janet shuffled to the side on her knees with a quickness Phil might have appreciated if he hadn't been leaping off the bed and stamping his foot. The left foot. At the bottom of the left leg.

"Not exactly the result I was hoping for," she said.

Phil stopped stamping. "Are you kidding? That's the best I've moved in months."

"Let's celebrate."

"Do you have anything to drink?"

"No," said Janet. "Will a joint do?"

"Sure. It's been a while." Phil secretly marveled at how easily he was bending looking for his underpants. "Geez. Like five years."

"Me, too. It's been a while. Like three days."

The joint led to some surprisingly good late-night Chinese delivery, for the Upper West Side. They had meant to go out when Phil came over. But they stayed in, and were just getting around to eating.

"Why no booze in the house?"

"My ex-husband grew up in Queens. Galen Fitzgerald," she impressively accented. "Working-class Irish-Catholic family. You know the drill. He was the first one who didn't become a fireman. Between all the people he knew who went down in the Towers and all the relatives I was treating who survived, we didn't stand a chance. Not a fucking chance."

"Sorry."

"Wait," she said. "It gets funny. We split up, and I start hitting the bars. That's not right. I had already been hitting the bars a bit before the Towers. Just couldn't go right home after work. When we split up, there was no reason to go home. So, I started closing a few places. I knew it was not smart, but I decided as long as I didn't drink during the day and as long I took a cab and I woke up in my own bed the next morning, I was okay."

"You're right," said Phil. "Funny."

"And then, one morning, I woke up in my own bed . . . next to a cabdriver."

Phil tried not to bulge his eyes. "Muslim cabdriver?"

"I don't know," Janet said. "I didn't feel like having a discussion about religion."

"So, that's why no booze in the house?"

"Perhaps."

Phil looked at his wrist as if there should be a watch there. "Shit! I gotta move my cab!"

He got to see Janet laugh for the first time, and he paid attention. She looked shocked initially, then threw back her head and gave four stout *hahahs! Hahahs* accompanied by three hand claps, then a wipe of her eyes. Then a giant smile. Another first. Not the pre–blow job *This is the problem leg?* smile. Much bigger. Much more worth pursuing.

She cinched the green terry-cloth robe, then reached down and began patting his left knee, at first as if she were still responding appreciatively to the "my cab!" line. But she wasn't. "This? This here . . ." she patted, "is not about losing a gig."

Phil sat up in his chair. "Are you open for business?"

She recinched the robe, and grabbed a pair of glasses off the breakfast table. "Contacts still out . . . Okay," Janet said. "Let's have it."

Phil stopped to marvel at this woman who, in the space of two slight moves, had transformed herself, her presence, and their oncoming dialogue. He might have continued to stare if he hadn't been prodded to speak by a fortuitous throb from his left buttock.

"Okay then," he began. "Two days ago, I went to see my brother, Jim McManus."

"The radio guy?"

"The radio genius."

"The radio jag-off," said Janet. "Sorry. That's the last time for me."

"We agree," Phil said. "We hadn't spoken in five years, and I went to see him after I noticed he had given Abrun's book, your father's book, *The Power of "Ow!"* a blurb. I had no idea he had ever suffered from APS, and I figured, I hoped, he might be able to help me. Give me a little insight. I mean, not only had he come out the other side of this ass/leg shit, but he was there. We grew up with virtually the same parents."

"Virtually?"

"He had a different father. McManus. Whom he didn't find out about until, Jesus, he was, I don't know, twenty-one?"

"Uh-huh."

"Well, the conversation starts out okay. Fine, in fact. The last time I had seen him, he threw me against the wall. Divorce shit. This time, he starts by telling me he's going to stop trashing my column, which he's done almost since the day I got it. *That* I didn't expect. That's what I had gone to see him about the last time."

"The time he threw you against the wall."

"Yeah. This time, I went to talk to him about Abrun. I said, 'I have what you had. APS.' He was lying on a mat, like me, but for years. He asked if I had seen your dad. I said I had read him, seen him, heard him, done the writing, yakked in the group sessions . . ."

Janet smiled and touched the side of her glasses.

"Well," he smiled, "somebody had to talk . . ."

"Continue," she said almost sternly.

"Jimmy asked me how long I'd had the pain for. I said ten months. He goes nuts. Starts pacing. Grabs my shoulder. I thought he's going to launch me against the wall again. He stops and hails a cab. Tells me the pain started ten months ago because ten months ago I became a grandfather and I'm furious. How fucked up is this?"

"Wait a minute. You're a grandfather?"

"What?"

"I thought you have no children." Suddenly, Janet felt the overwhelming need for a therapy interregnum. The glasses were dashed, the left hand gripped Phil's good knee, and she became the post-coital babe who might have been lied to. "Didn't you tell me you had no kids? You said something like, 'Nah. There's no money in it.' Okay, I had a couple glasses of wine, but I think I would have remembered that tidbit. I remembered, *Any kids, Phil?* *Nah. There's no money in it.* That's your line, isn't it? Hey, if that is a line, what kind of a piece of—"

"Janet!" Phil grabbed her knee-gripping wrist. "I don't! No kids! I have spent my whole life in pursuit of no children. I don't know what else to say to convince you, so I won't say anything else." He stood, still just T-shirted and underweared, and saw the rest of his clothes in a pile next to the chair. "I probably should go."

Janet put her glasses back on, lowered her head, and with it, her voice a few decibels. "Then what is your brother talking about?"

"I have no idea what he's talking about." He found his socks quickly and sat back down. Uh-oh, the socks . . .

"Then the only question left is what happened ten months ago?"

"Dr. Abrun, your father, asked me that. And I told him I couldn't think of anything."

He leaned down to face the dreaded left sock. He felt her kiss the top of his head. "This I know," said Janet Abrun-Fitzgerald. "It will come to you."

Phil's eyes squeezed tight and the back of his jaw seared in a retroactive stab of root canal-ian distress. A pain so distracting, he slipped the left sock on in a half-blink.

"Yes. It. Will," he said through clenched teeth, like someone who had just finished Lesson Number 2 with a ventriloquist. He mumbled "thanks" and dressed in silence. It wasn't until Phil raised his head that he realized Janet had left to give him some privacy.

He had to get home. She knew. He'd call her. She knew that, too.

9

It *was* just after one in the morning when Phil got home. The box that he needed was wedged under his desk behind a metal file cabinet in a crawl space big enough to fit an antisocial terrier, or an eager, limber, fifteen-year-old girl.

Elly Vogelbaum would not be awake across the hall for another six hours. He could wait. The only thing in the box was confirmation of his memory, amplification of his confusion, and the possible resurrection of the id-based cold-cock to the jaw he had experienced in Janet's apartment.

The box was a cache of save-worthy cards and letters Phil had received since he had moved into midtown Manhattan after college in 1981. The family and friends greatest hits collection. Not the *"Dear Liberal Jew Fag"* anthology. That was kept in Sandy Collewell's public relations office at Excelsior. This reinforced, lidded black cardboard carton contained mostly thank-you notes, congratulations, and birthday cards.

Phil Camp had turned forty-six the first week of July. A little over nine months ago. Nine months ago. Not ten. Nine. Rest assured, he had tried to make the connection, but birthdays had never been a problem. If getting older was an issue, why would Phil have willingly walked around for the last two years with a neatly trimmed gray beard that did little else but add years? Besides, by the time he celebrated his birthday, the toothache ass was already in its third or fourth week. He had to cancel a squash lesson, which was a first, but life was good. Phil Camp was alone and free, and Marty Fleck (who still shaved) was around to digest and deflect all flack and flack by-products.

The actual acknowledgment of this last birthday was subdued, even by Phil's standards. Sandy Collewell took him out to dinner at the California Pizza Kitchen, which turned out to be less a milestone tribute and more a begrudging affirmation that they had made the right decision to stop having sex. The old two-dick limit. She did use her Excelsior corporate Visa to spring for the meal (a Thai chicken pizza, jambalaya pasta, and four beers), which made up for her showing up without a card. In fact, Phil received a grand total of three birthday cards: A photo of Elly in her soccer uniform slipped under his door, a bad cartoon/appointment reminder from his new chiropractor, and a belated piece of characteristic wryness from his former sister-in-law.

The worst aspect about Phil's long, unexplained estrangement from his brother was his diminished relationship with Jim McManus's wife, now ex-wife, Mickey. Yes, Mickey McManus. No wonder she had kept the name after the divorce. You don't want to give up a film-noir handle like that. *Mickey McManus, Intrepid Reporter. Mickey McManus, Union Firebrand. Mickey McManus, Broad in a Hurry.*

The real Mickey McManus was none of those. She had raised three children effortlessly, as if she had perused the brochure on feminism but wasn't crazy about the dues schedule. Well-read and well-shopped, she took care of herself in those occasionally quick-gaping slots where she wasn't taking care of everyone else. As a suburban wife and mother, she was as flawless as a showroom-floor minivan. Always available with baked goods or to do an extra shift of volunteer work, both served with whatever room tone was required, austere decorum all the way to the unfettered naughtiness of a bridge club on nitrous oxide.

And funny. Funny like someone who did hair for mobsters' girlfriends or who, in a crowded restaurant, would have loudly told Donald Trump, "Keep it down!" She understood that her life with Jim McManus was about giving up whatever identity was necessary in exchange for the freedom of taking nothing personally, and to do that until the three kids were out of the house.

And then, as these things happen, someone came between Mickey and Jim McManus. Another man. Fella by the name of Bill Clinton.

When Michelle Loretta was eight years old, she came home from school to find her Negro (at the time) housekeeper, Annie C., sobbing. President Kennedy had been shot. "We all done now, Mickey," Annie C. gulped. Mickey spent the next four hours blinking at the television until her mother came home and turned it off. That was the last day she was interested in politics for almost thirty years.

She might have taken some notice, mustered some curiosity, if there had been room for her views. But by the time she left her Nixon-apologizing Jersey home and arrived at Boston University, both sides seemed fully staffed. Three days into Orientation Week, she asked a tall sophomore for directions to Eastern Mountain Sports. "Let me walk you there," said Jimmy Camp. And that was just about the last day she was interested in being at anybody else's side for almost twenty years. Just about.

From the outset, they were more spokesman and sidearm than boyfriend and girlfriend. Again, that was fine with Mickey. If you're going to sing backup, you might as well get behind Sting. Jim was always magnetic, even as the needle on his ideological compass was pulled irrevocably right. Through name changes and job changes and prescription refills, he remained steadfastly handsome and charismatic. But, let's not kid ourselves. As devoted and passionate and endearingly flawed as he was, Jim McManus was no match for Bill Clinton.

Bill and Mickey's first and only meeting took place at some bipartisan charity—some cause with some combination of the words "Concerned," "Healing," "Beyond," "Power," "Action," "Change," "Millennium," and "Now"—just before the 1996 Democratic National Coronation. Mickey, forever blonde, slim, and icebreakingly flirtatious, made the mistake of getting in the receiving line without her husband. Clinton did his signature move, or thang, well documented by any woman who has met him (lesbians included), where he shakes the female hand, and does not let go as he begins his next conversation. For that few seconds, there is a connection. Elusive to describe, but you wouldn't be wrong using some combination of the words "Concerned," "Healing," "Beyond," "Power," "Action," "Change," and "Now."

Not "Millennium," though. That was still four years away. By then the marriage was over. Between Mickey's reregistering as an Independent before the 1996 election and the Clintons' move to five-miles-down-the-friggin'-road Chappaqua in November 1999, that was all the betrayal Jim McManus could conjure and all the unrequited paranoia Mickey would stand. The divorce was a year of name-calling and heel-dragging, followed by eight months of name-dragging and heel-calling, all at an hourly rate. The kids were relieved. The oldest girl, Jamie, was already out of the house, and along with her parents' help, let the others, Ron (18) and Nancy (17), know that this was the only solution.

Though their phone conversations pretty much ended, Mickey and Phil kept in touch by mail as they always had, exchanging a couple of missives a year. After the bomb scare at his wedding, Phil received a Hazmat suit in the mail with the card, *Hope you're still a 41 reg. M.* When he knew their divorce was final, Phil sent Mickey a tabloid photo of Prince Charles, captioned, "I hear he's looking. Know any nice guys?"

HAPPY BIRTHDAY, GRANDPA!

He did not remember the vague transgenerational art festooning the front-leaf or the Hallmark Hall of Lame poetry on the inside flap of this year's card from Mickey McManus. But "Happy Birthday, Grandpa!" he did remember. He remembered laughing once, then again, when he noticed the halfhearted line through "Grandpa" and "Phil" penciled in underneath. Funny. She was always funny.

The fact the card had come a week late was a bit surprising. Mickey had never been flaky when it came to birthdays. Naughty, but not flaky. Years ago, early, early eighties years ago (this was re-occurring to him just now, in the predawn stillness of his living room, waiting for Elly Vogelbaum to wake up across the hall), he had asked Mickey if she wanted anything in particular for her birthday. "Hmm. I could always use gardening tools," she said. "Oh yeah. And sperm." At the time, she and Jim were in the middle of a three-year fertility fallow. That ended soon enough with the arrivals of Ron and Nancy a year apart. "Guess who picked the names?" she had cracked.

Oh yeah. And sperm.

Phil jumped up from the couch and went to his front closet. His golf bag leaned against the back wall, unused since last June. He grabbed his one-iron and quick-hopped over to his office. He could no longer wait for Elly to wake up.

He made sure the bottom drawer of the left filing cabinet was locked. He slipped the head of the one-iron in the drawer handle, grabbed the recently regripped top of the shaft, and yanked. All he needed was to move the cabinet out a foot or two. And if he ruined the one-iron, big fucking deal. The last time he'd spanked a decent one-iron was, well, never. *(Old joke: Two guys are playing golf. It starts to pour, then thunder, then lightning. One player sits in the cart, the safest place in a thunder-and-lightning storm because of the rubber tires. The other guy grabs his one-iron and stands in the middle of the fairway, holding the club in the air. The first player yells, "Jackie, what are you, crazy? You'll be struck by lightning." And the other guy smiles and says, "No way. Not even God can hit a one-iron . . .")*

After three unconvincing tugs, Phil was back in the closet, digging a golf glove out of the side pocket of his bag. When he returned, he reached down to grab the one-iron, then thought well enough to turn around so that his right leg, the good one, would be in back and he could plant it securely. With those two moves, Phil had created leverage where there had been delusion. He yanked and felt the file cabinet lurch, then furrow . . . six inches, a foot, a foot and a half . . . *CRACK!* The file cabinet was now out far enough from the desk and wall, and the former one-iron/now forty-inch steel-shafted, rubber-gripped pointer would serve Phil well in coaxing the lidded black box out of its hutch.

Mickey's card lay on top, just above Elly's soccer photo. It was almost as he remembered, except she had doubled the joke.

Happy Birthday, Grandpa!

PHIL !

GRANDPA !

I mean PHIL . . .

Phil threw the box off his lap, and lay down on his couch. He closed his eyes and heard the conversation with the Irish Shrink.

It was like the time I slept with my brother's girlfriend before they were married.

You never told me that.

No, I'm pretty sure I did.

I think I would have remembered that, Phil.

What about the possibility that I told you and you forgot?

What about the possibility that you never told me, and you forgot?

He woke up to Elly banging on his door. Shit. He had left her a note to come by.

"Forget it, Elly. I figured out how to do it."

"This isn't the thing where you're mad at me, is it, Phil?"

He laughed. "Nah, not at all. Not dressed. Naked."

"Ick," Elly summarized.

Phil doubled the joke. "I love you, too."

She giggled and ran back across the hall, and Phil stared at the birthday card to see if the handwriting on the second "grandpa" was sure. Yeah, sure. The only thing Phil knew about handwriting was what an old man in Central Park with a cap and a Xeroxed Graphology Expert certificate had told him one afternoon a million years ago. About his handwriting.

He had walked by the old man with a cap a few times, waiting to convince himself that he was stuck in enough of a crossroad to seek the counsel of a man whose entire office—two chairs, a table and an easel—could be folded in under a minute. Phil Camp was four years in Manhattan, an Ivy League grad answering phones 6 p.m. to 2 a.m. for the sports department at the AP. Pre-Trish, pre-Marty Fleck, post-*"Oh yeah. And sperm."* There were too many conversations with his mom and his brother that eventually beat around to, "So . . . what *else* are you thinking of doing?" That kind of crossroad.

The entire handwriting analysis took five minutes. Five bucks. Which works out to sixty dollars an hour, but then again, we are talking about analysis here. Phil signed his name and wrote the first three lines of his favorite poem by Keats: *When I have fears that I may cease to be / Before my pen has gleaned my teeming brain / Before high-pile'd books in charact'ry . . .*

The old man with the hat and Xeroxed Graphology Expert certificate grunted. "You are an egotist with low self-esteem," he began. "You are greedy, no, stingy. Look at the way your signature is scribbled, then stops. You won't let anybody get close. No intimacy. Maybe you don't want anybody close because they'll see how stingy you are." Then the old man started chuckling.

"Why are you laughing?" Phil had asked.

"Because I'm telling you things about you that aren't good. I figured I'd try to lighten the mood. So you'll pay me. I'm afraid you won't pay me. Because, you know . . ."

"I'm stingy?"

"Yes!" Another chuckle. Phil's memory of the rest of the time after that exchange was less clear. Something about being a negotiator, no, manipulator, and hanging onto the past. And one more "stingy." Phil had paid the guy with his last five dollars and walked the two miles uptown to his tub-in-the-kitchen apartment. *Well,* he had thought, *that went well.*

So really now, lying on his couch, what did he know about judging another's handwriting? About the veracity with which one writes "Grandpa?"

He tried to finish the Keats poem in his head.

Before high-pile'd books in charact'ry,
Hold like rich garners the full-ripened grain;
When I behold, upon the night's starred face,
Huge cloudy symbols of a high romance,
And think that I may never live to trace,
Their shadows, with the magic hand of chance;
And when I feel, fair creature of an hour,
That I shall never look upon thee more,
Never have relish in the faery . . .

He heard a voice say, "Phil, quit stalling." At first, he thought it might be Keats. Then, maybe Keats doing an impression of him. Then, he knew it was him. He was stalling. Had been since he got home. Phil rose off the couch, went to the bathroom, and washed his face, a ritual he always performed just before he wrote. He was headed for the dining-room table, but his ass and leg had other ideas. Bad pain. Lightning, led and followed by the dull rumble of joint-to-joint ache. Pre-Abrun. Pre-Lenny Millman. The days of Zero Percent Better. He grabbed the astronaut pen, the pad, and lay on The Pad. Deliberately, for the first time in nine years, he wrote as Phil Camp.

When I was nineteen, I slept with my older brother's
girlfriend. They had been going out for three years. He
had graduated from Boston University, was working for a
radio station in Rochester, and she was a senior at BU. I
was a sophomore at Columbia and home for Christmas.

We were all home. Things seemed a little tense between them. There was a lot of "Well, why don't you visit me?"/"Well, why don't *you* visit *me?*"

I had had the kind of freshman year just about everyone has—shitty, thinking about transferring anywhere—and the misery had spilled over into the following fall and winter. The misery took one form: Perpetual failure with women. I had used the retardation of attending an all-boys prep school as an excuse, but my brother Jimmy had gone to the same school and from age sixteen, had never been anything less than a ladies' man.

The pattern was the same. I'd make a decision about a girl, then go after her. At first, she might be charmed, but it never lasted to the second date. When you see a guy coming straight at you, with zero confidence, that's something.

One night, the three of us were supposed to go out with some BU friend of Mickey's. I still remember her name. Mary Cronin. Supposedly very cute. Like Mickey. An hour before the big date, Mary calls up, cancels. Then Mickey and Jimmy start arguing. Same shit. I'm pissed off. I leave and walk a mile in the snow into town and spend the next eight hours getting blind drunk at Buster's, a bar I had played softball for the summer before. I sat in the back room, with my back to the door, drinking Molsons and feeling sorry for myself.

I staggered home and got in around two. I had puked a couple times on the way back, so I knew I would be able to fall right to sleep. I had just gotten into bed, in my underwear, when I heard a knock at the door. It was Mickey. She walked in, and sat down on the floor next to the bed, crying. She was wearing a white thermal undershirt, one of Jimmy's, socks, and panties. I patted her head, told her I was sorry, but I had had a rough night, too. She got up like she was going to leave, but sat next to me and said,

"It's all over." She began to cry again. I didn't want to
look at her, so I looked down, right into her shirt. I saw
her tits for the first time and got hard. I tried to move
away but she put her hand on my cock. That was it. We
started kissing. I was drunk. She might have been drinking as well. I can't remember. I remember I didn't give a
shit. Didn't give a shit. And neither did Mickey. I'm sure
he had cheated on her, which made me not give a shit
even more. And I was angry at my brother. Just another
guy who could get girls, make 'em cry, then get 'em back,
or get more girls. I was surprised they had stayed together
this long. Big Family Values piece of hypocritical shit.
Fuck him. Fuck him. Why should I take care of him again?
When did he take care of me? Where was he at Shit Creek?

The sex was strange. I had only slept with one other
girl, so I didn't have much to compare it to. For all the
kissing and touching, I had trouble staying hard. I had
trouble staying inside her. I think I came. Yeah, I came.
I'm not sure. The few times I've thought about it, I like to
think about the beginning rather than the end, because at
the end, she was weird, getting dressed quickly and trying
not to cry, and I felt like shit again.

The next day, I was wicked hungover. I didn't come
downstairs until noon, and they had already driven into
Boston together. Mom said they had gone to Firestone
and Parson to look at rings. I laughed, and Mom asked
me what was so funny. Man, did I want to tell her. Dinner
comes, they're not back. Me, Mom, and Dad are watching the Bruins game. I'm the only one who's worried.
Around nine-thirty, the phone rings. They're in Maryland.
They just got married. My parents start hugging, but not
because of that. My mom is thrilled we don't have to set
foot inside a church, my dad is overjoyed he doesn't have
to pay for a reception. The Bruins won, and they waited
until after the game to tell me that Jimmy's birth father,

Bob McManus, lives in Maryland. Big secret. Big secret I finally was let in on. Jimmy was now Jim McManus. He and Mickey were Mr. and Mrs. McManus. What!?! Seriously, what the fuck?

I left the next morning. I told Mom I had to take the train back to New York and research a paper before my anthropology final. I got drunk in the bar car and picked up some secretary, who blew me in the bathroom. That. That I told people about.

Jamie was born the following October. Almost ten months later. Dead ringer for Mickey.

Shit. I'm going have to write about Shit Creek. Shit.

Phil rolled onto his side and sobbed hard face-first into The Pad for a good thirty seconds. Then, he rolled back and grabbed the bottle of half-water-half-grape Gatorade. He drank down the last couple of swallows, then pulled his underwear down, attached the open bottle to his prick, and nearly filled it. If anyone had been watching, they would know this wasn't the first time such an arrangement had been negotiated on The Pad. The difference was that this time, it was not motivated by the normal combination of symptoms plus sloth. It was motivated by Phil not wanting to get to a knee, stand up, then collapse-lunge for his desk chair, and hear the voice of the Irish Shrink say, *"Say, wasn't that your good leg that just gave?"* again.

10

Hey, I finally stumbled upon something pretty crucial that I forgot
to tell you about. I guess I just buried this way down deep. The unconscious. Or whatever is behind the unconscious. Maybe it's the unconscious, then employee parking, then this. Okay, here it is: I slept
with my brother's girlfriend the night before they were married."

"Oh no," said the Irish Shrink. "You told me that."

"Are you sure?"

"Yes. I remember things like that, Phil."

Phil rubbed his eyes with both hands while continuing to talk.
"I'm sure you do," he said, "but what about the possibility that another patient told you the same type of thing and you're confusing
him with me. I mean, come on. I ain't the first guy who came in
here and slept with his brother's wife."

"No, you're not. But it wasn't somebody else. It was you."

"How can you be sure?"

"It happened in one of our first sessions, six years ago—nineteen
ninety-eight. I can show you my notes."

"Nah. Screw it. Shit . . ."

"I thought you'd be happy." The Irish Shrink laughed. "Usually, it's the other way around, where you assume—"

"I know," Phil finished. "I assume I've already told you and I haven't. Like the bomb scare at the wedding . . . right? Wasn't that the last time? Wasn't that one of those things like that?" He stared hard and waited for the nod. Yes. Continue.

Silence. Eyebrow flex. Go ahead, Phil.

"Did we ever talk about it?"

"About what?"

"About me sleeping with Jimmy's fiancée?"

"Not much. You dismissed it. You said you were both drunk."

"Why didn't you pursue it?"

"Why didn't I pursue it?" The Irish Shrink turned his head sideways and, thumbing the accordion folder part of his brain, asked himself the question a few times. *Why didn't I pursue it . . . Why didn't I pursue it . . .* He turned back. "I guess I must have been having an off-day."

Paddy O'Reagan had said that to Phil before. And where it had first infuriated Phil, the *What the fuck am I paying you for?* brand of wrath, now he knew it was the Irish Shrink's way of saying it had not been the time to peruse a particular snapshot from the past. That it would come up again, when it was supposed to, like now, or not at all. Still trim from age-defying pursuits like hundred-mile bike races and *not* going for tenure at Columbia, the sixty-eight-year-old white-haired psycho-deacon raised a finger, bounced up and nimbled over to his desk, pulled open a drawer, and grabbed a good-sized Pentaflex file, before bounding back to his overstuffed chair. Paddy O'Reagan always followed the "having an off-day" remark with an almost Britannican account of what had happened during the session(s) in question, going to the notes only if he had to. Even throwing in a little of his own personal history to set the perspective. Actually, yes, giving the patient access to his thought process, even at the risk of embarrassment. And that's why he was the Irish Shrink.

"Phil," he began, "at the time, you and I were just getting started here. We were feeling each other out. Circling the ring, I like to call it. You came in one day with a specific dilemma. You told me your brother and his wife were having problems and heading for a divorce. You wanted to know whether it was okay to have dinner with your brother's wife. You were confused as to your motives." He pushed the file off his lap to an end table. "I remember this especially because at the time, I was thinking about reenrolling in a ballroom dance class, but without my wife, who had taken it with me for the previous six months and hated it. So, your use of the word 'motives' hooked me."

"I knew you were an amateur bike racer," Phil said, "but ballroom dancing?"

"Yeah. Ever try it? Tremendous workout. And," he leaned in, "they never have enough men." The Irish Shrink leaned back, uprighting himself. "Let's not get sidetracked. You said you were confused about your motives because even though you had been friends with your brother's wife, ah, her name was Millie?"

"Mickey."

"Mickey . . . Mickey for years, and had many meals together, a brother and sister-in-law who always got along, with nothing in the way, suddenly you found yourself thinking, thinking about the one time you two had slept together." When he got going, the Irish Shrink would speak in choppy, comma-filled bursts, like a talking, cantering horse. Mr. Continuing Ed. "Even though you were both drunk, as you mentioned to me then, even though you yourself had not thought about the incident previously, as you mentioned then, which was strange, you were thinking about it now. As if somehow, what had happened between your brother and his wife had something to do with you. So, you said, 'Am I being a concerned brother-in-law, or a piece of shit? Is there anything in this for me?' That is my recollection. Words to that effect. Does that sound like it?"

"Ah, yeah."

"And do you remember what I said?"

"I do now," Phil said. "You said, 'With the opposite sex, memories are always better than attempted resolution.'"

He gave a closed-mouth, arched eyebrow "Wow!", grabbed the Pentaflex folder, shuffled some pages, and jabbed his indexing finger at the bottom of page 11 or 12. "Hah! That is what I said! I have to remember that. Give me a second."

Here was another decoded riff from the Irish Shrink. *"Give me a second"* meant *"I need to find something on which to write this so I can remember to put it where I won't forget it. This may take a while."* And it always did. But Paddy O'Reagan scurrying around, looking for the right piece of paper like a woman who knows she does not have the appropriate vessel to hold the flowers you just gave her, was a merciful break, featuring the other flawed human in the room.

"Okay, Phil. Give that to me again."

"Memories are always better—"

"Slower . . ."

Phil's cadence slowed to the remedial condescension level of Al Gore in the first 2000 Presidential Debate. "Mem-o-ries arrrrrre all-ways bet-ter *than* ah-temp-ted rezz-oh-LOO-shun."

"Got it," beamed the Irish Shrink. "Can't believe I came up with that. I must have copped it from somebody."

"That's terrific," Phil said. "We've spent as much time on a story I've told you as we would have had I never told you."

"Well, it's not what you're willing to talk about in therapy, it's what you're willing to not talk about."

"What?"

The Irish Shrink slapped his knee. "Now, that line I got off some overnight guy I heard on the radio. What do you call your brother? A radio airbag?"

"Gasbag."

"Yeah. That's what this guy was. Arnie, I think. Or Artie. Does that sound right?"

Phil shook his bad leg violently in the direction of his therapist. "Hey, Patty," which he never called him. "Can we focus?" Which he never asked.

"Sure."

"All right," muttered Phil, readjusting himself amid clenched teeth. "Shit. I gotta take a piss."

It took two minutes for Phil to go and come back and only twenty seconds for him to tell the Irish Shrink that his former sister-in-law and his half brother had taken turns ten months apart, first teasing, then accusing him of becoming a grandfather to the child of a girl he assumed was still his niece.

"So, congratulations."

"For what?"

"You're a grandfather."

"I don't know that!"

"So then, what is everybody talking about?"

"You sound like Janet," Phil huffed.

"Who's Janet?"

Janet was one of those subjects Phil was not willing to talk about in therapy—for a million reasons, divided evenly between self-protection, superstition, and the off-chance that the Irish Shrink might be so human as to have been threatened that Phil had discussed any of this with another therapist, let alone the erection-provoking kind.

"What I'm saying," Phil was saying, "is I know nothing except what has been told to me, first in jest, then in anger. I don't know whether Mickey told Jim about us when they were pissing on each other during the divorce, or before that. I know my brother never threw me up against a wall before his divorce. I know in all these years Jamie never reached out to me in any way other than as a niece."

"Why is this coming up now?"

"Who the fuck knows? But I need some answers."

"Why is it so important to have answers?"

Phil squinted derisively. "You really don't mean that, do you?" he said. "You're just doing that shrink thing where you want me to hear myself say why it's important to have the answers."

"That shrink thing? Well, now I'm hurt," smiled Dr. O'Reagan. "I thought I was the Irish Shrink. I thought I didn't do things like that. Like a shrink would do. That's why you liked me."

"How did you know I called you the Irish Shrink?"

"I heard you on your cell phone in the waiting room a couple of times. 'I'm at the Irish Shrink.' 'I'm seeing my guy. My help. The Irish Shrink.'"

"Sorry."

"Don't be. I always thought it was a compliment."

"It was meant to be," said Phil.

"And I thought it was funny."

"Good."

"Good."

Phil exhaled. "I have to have another conversation with my brother."

"Don't you mean your half brother?"

"Yeah."

"And don't you mean a confrontation?"

"Yeah," Phil said. "No," he said. "No. Yeah," he decided.

The Irish Shrink tapped Phil on his good knee. "What's the big fear?"

Phil rummaged through all the fears that didn't fit and found the right one in the middle of the rack. "I'm afraid I'm going to get talked into something."

"Talked into something," his therapist mused.

"You're doing that shit again."

"You're right," the Irish Shrink said. "Let's see what that would look like."

"What *what* would look like? I am nobody's grandfather! I am nobody's fucking father! I made up my mind ye—"

The Irish Shrink jumped up. "Save it, Phil. Let's do this for real. . . ."

Another code. *Let's do this for real* meant it was time for them to stage the impending confrontation. They had done this twice before, both times when Phil had been worried about being talked into something. Once three years ago when Sandy Collewell had given him the heads-up that the then-new-guy, Turner Billings, was about to approach him to do a weekly version of "Baggage Handling" for the Excelsior website, and for no additional money. The other was just over a year ago, when Amanda, his almost second wife, tried to get him to phone in to a meeting of her daughter's book club as Marty Fleck. (To put this in historical context, the request from Amanda came a year after their wedding had been jettisoned by Trish's phoned-in bomb scare, and a year before Phil got around to mentioning the incident to the Irish Shrink.)

On both occasions, the Irish Shrink had stretched the notion of "doing this for real" to the stress-test limits of that phrase's irony. Just before igniting the shakedown "confrontation," he had said, "Now, who am I again?" and Phil had exasperated, "You're Turner Billings, the executive editorial director of the Excelsior Newspaper Group" or "You're Amanda Rabinoff. We were supposed to get married a year ago." They were the last lines Phil delivered with any assurance.

Paddy O'Reagan, on the other hand, took the overused idiom "role playing" by the ankles and shook the blood to its point. After Phil told him who he was, he bowed his kindly white head and squeezed the bridge of his nose for a full-launch count of ten. And when his head rerose, he was the most stomach-pit-threatening personification of just what Phil needed to face: The bullshit-fueled, narcissist-driven, *I just came up with a brilliant idea for you* figurehead of a corporate superior; or the otherwise codependency-bypassed, *I know the Batman secret identity thing, but do this and I'll never ask another favor* ex-fiancée-target. Either way, it was a transformation that left Phil flailing in its button-pushing undertow. After thirty seconds of relentless portrayal, the Irish Shrink stopped, became himself briefly, and said, both times, "You need to be as committed dramatically, but as unattached emotionally as the people you're talking to. It's a game for them. They're committed only to the conversation, not the emotions."

"Well, what the fuck am I supposed to say?" Phil asked both times. And with that, the kindly white head of the Irish Shrink rebowed, the bridge of his nose was regripped, and Paddy O'Reagan reemerged, this time as if a big director had told a casting agent, *"Look, you know Phil Camp? I need a much more confident version of Phil Camp. Confident, with a kind of believable sincerity. You know the type, 'Love to do it, can't.' Completely engaging as he disengages. Very personal. 'You know me. You know I love you. If I could do it, you know I would. But I can't. It kills me, but I can't.' That type of thing. That's what I need. And I need him now. Not next week. Not tomorrow. Not an hour from now. NOW. . . ."*

And out the impersonation came. Uncanny. Unapologetic. Unassailable as a trance. Both times, Phil sat there and got to hear himself as he might never be. Oh, he'd be able to retell the story, chapter 1 in *The Legend of the Irish Shrink*, and do the head bows and bridge squeezes and reemergence as either side of the confrontation, concluding with a dead-on impression of Paddy O'Reagan's Phil Camp. But unlike the Irish Shrink, Phil was playing for laughs. One time, during a rare midweek extrovert lunch, Phil did the entire in-session Turner Billings sequence for a friend who worked at NBC, and when the guy stopped wiping his eyes, he said, "If you can work up three more characters like that, I can get you an *SNL* audition with Lorne Michaels."

Phil never worked up the other characters. And his access to the therapy-enhanced role of Phil Camp faded in a neurogenerated mist of psychosomatic special effects: Tingling, numbness, spasm, throb, ache, limp . . .

So here we were again. Another confrontation. This time with Jimmy, arguably the most important man in his life. But who wants to argue? This time with a member of his family. This time with his past.

"Okay, who am I again?"

"You're Jim McManus. My half brother."

"The radio guy."

"Yes," Phil hissed.

Down went the head. Up went the fingers to squeeze the bridge of the nose. And back came what moments ago was the Irish Shrink and now was something else. *What-have-you-done-*

with-my-therapist? something else. In the time it took him to pick his head up, Paddy O'Reagan had gained twenty pounds by throwing his shoulders back, and darkened his thin white hair by shifting into a shadow thrown by some closed blinds. His right cheek was hoisted and tucked under his eye, and the tension to hold it bounced his face into a semipermanent cocked smile. He leaned back in his chair, and put on another five inches and ten pounds. The light now hit him where his heart would have been.

The Irish Shrink let Phil take it all in, just long enough for Phil to try and make his initial recoil look like he'd meant to lean back as well.

"Philly," he basso-profundoed, "what can I do you for?"

"Ah, ah, ah, Jim? . . ." Phil tried to start, but his head was screaming *How the hell does this guy know he used to call me Philly?*

"You're on. . . ." His cheek snickered, like it was in on the gratuitous radio crack.

"Jim, I want to apologize for what hap—"

"Fuck you."

"Fuck you."

"Fuck me? Who's saying that, my brother or Marty Fleck?"

"You're not my brother."

"I'm afraid I am."

Phil looked away. Anywhere else. "Dr. O'Reagan, I can't do this."

"Who's Dr. O'Reagan?"

"Give me a break."

"Give you a break? Give *you* a break? Give you a fucking break, you candy-ass liberal cocksucking hypocrite. You traitorous, irresponsible, disloyal piece of shit. Just how much more of a break would you like me to give you? You're alive, aren't you?"

Phil laughed. "With all due respect. I don't think—"

"Respect? What the fuck do you know about respect, Grandpa?"

"I'm not the fucking grandfather."

"Well, we'll see."

"What does that mean?"

"What do you think it means, Philly?"

"So, what's he going to do," Phil snorted, a noise that was returned with a stare. "I mean, what are you going to do, Jim? Run DNA tests? Ruin three, no, *four* people's lives, whether it comes up me or not? Is that your plan? Is that the way you take care of people you love? Is that your version of family?"

"That's my God's version of family. And what do you know about taking care of anyone?"

"I know a shitload more than you," Phil sputtered as his eyes blackened and filled. "I know a Shit Creek load more than you." He grabbed a *Daily News* and pushed off the arm of the couch to a staggered stance. He stamped his left foot, the twelve-thousandth quixotic attempt to get blood to circulate his pain anywhere else. "You, and your God," he mumbled and hiccup-gaited for the door.

"Shit Creek?"

Phil turned around and stopped, which was slightly less excruciating than stopping and turning around. "Yeah, what?"

The shoulders and right cheek went down simultaneously. The chair came forward and the sun shone again on his kindly white head. The Irish Shrink had returned. "Phil," he said calmly, "this is good. This is good. But we need to take a break for a second. Sit down."

As Phil started to sit down, he looked at his watch, saw there was still time in the session. Too much time. Way too much time. Way too much time, except for now, when he looked back up and saw his therapist staring at the ceiling with his eyes closed.

Phil sprang to his feet, unaided. "You're fired."

The Irish Shrink opened his eyes, his hair now darkened by the shadow of an overhanging patient.

"You want to give me some room?"

"Oh." Phil stepped back maybe three inches, like a second-grader. "Sorry I woke you."

"I wasn't asleep."

"Well, you can drop off now. I'm out of here."

The Irish Shrink stood up. He was taller than Phil. Maybe three inches. How about that? "Phil, I need to know if Shit Creek is an expression."

"You're fired. You haven't been paying attention."

"I can't help you if—"

"No, you can't." He reached up maybe three inches with both hands and shoved the Irish Shrink by the shoulders into his chair, which careened back but did not topple over. Paddy O'Reagan, amateur bike racer, called upon his muscle-memoried sense of balance to jerk himself and the chair forward into a hunch over a pair of imaginary handlebars.

The Irish Shrink closed his eyes and tried to catch his breath. It took a few seconds, and he was almost there, when his eyes were snapped open and his breath resnatched away by the sound of an office door slamming shut. His.

11

In the ensuing two weeks, there were so many letters, e-mails, and phone messages over the cancellation of "Baggage Handling," that Excelsior Publications had to respond. Sandy Collewell, Phil's one corporate champion, had convinced Turner Billings that the best thing would be to let Phil write a final, valedictory column. It would be good PR for Excelsior. The only good PR they would get.

Baggage Handling

By Marty Fleck

CHECKING OUT

(Publishers Note: After almost eight years and 762 columns, Excelsior Publications has decided to discontinue "Baggage Handling." It is a sad day when economic realities force newspapers to make tough choices, a day which now occurs with alarming frequency. Sadder still would be to let such a mainstay

of the Excelsior family leave without saying good-bye.
Good luck, Marty! Happy Baggage. . . .)

Dear Marty Fleck Fans and Toleraters:
  By the time you read this, I will be somewhere,
Uruguay perhaps, where Excelsior cannot extradite
me for stealing over $500,000 in Post-it notes and
selling them to local villagers as clothing. Do not try
to look for me. Marty Fleck no longer exists. Instead,
please enjoy this final column, written by my wife,
Stacey.

Before I begin, I need to explain two things to you about my husband. Thing One: After nine years together (seven married, two dating/fooling around), I know very little about him. Thing Two: The one thing I do know is, he's nuts. Who goes to South America and doesn't say good-bye? I walked into the kitchen this morning, there's a Post-it on the coffeemaker. This is all it says: *I might have gone to Uruguay. Would you be a pal and write my last column? You know they'd love to hear from you. MF* "MF" is right. . . .

In the past, Marty let me write a couple columns a year, when he was sick or I felt he needed to be put in his place as the bit of a hypocrite he can be sometimes. You know, self-help guru, guru thyself. Other than that Post-it note, he has been pretty good lately. He hasn't been well, which I'll explain later, but he has been good. So, this being the last column, I thought I would tell you how he felt about writing "Baggage Handling" for almost the last eight years. Or at least all that he told me. As far as feelings go, Marty expressed them on a need-to-know basis. And like I said, I don't know much. Luckily, I only have to fill another five hundred words or so.

We met a year before he started doing the column. *Where Can I Stow My Baggage?* was still a huge bestseller, but he refused to go out in public and promote it. A woman in my building, Elly Vogelbaum, set us up. I will always be grateful to Elly. On the first date, Marty said we could talk for five minutes about his book, no more, and that was all. I said "What book?" and he said, "I love you," and that was that.

I bought the book the next day (had to go to three stores!), read it, loved it, laughed my ass off, and around the fifth date—at the Randall's Island driving range—I said, "Don't take this the wrong way, but are you embarrassed that people think you know something?" And he said, "You have no idea."

And I think that's why he wound up writing the column. It was the best way to demonstrate that he had no answers, but that people still paid attention to what he had to say. In other words, he never took any of it seriously, any of it. He wrote the book because he was out of work and a guy paid him ten grand. The whole baggage thing was a metaphor that had spun out of control, and he needed to let people know if he knew that they should, too.

But, and this is key, as long the audience was still there, he felt an obligation to entertain. And that's what the column was always about. "My twice-a-week goof," Marty would call it. Any insight, any wisdom, was coincidental. Twice a week, just after he would ship the column, Marty would always say out loud, to himself, or me if I was around,

"Geez, I hope this is something. I hope they get what we're trying to do." For years, I thought he was talking about his editors.

Here's the frustrating thing. I think Marty was successful in convincing the people he wanted to reach that it was a goof. Unfortunately, it didn't work as well with some of those readers who knew him just for the column. You know the people. They take everything seriously, and everything else personally. So, let me say this now for him: kidding! He was kidding! He was just trying for laughs. Just playing with words. That was the only agenda. Do you really think he meant it when he said if the government builds a fence along the Mexican border, they should put a warning track in front of it? Some people did. Allegedly intelligent people with big syndicated radio shows. Oh, what's the use? It's over. He hopes it was something. He hopes you got what we were trying to do.

(BAGGAGE HANDLING, cont'd, P. B-2)

BAGGAGE HANDLING (cont'd from P. B-1)

Okay, at the beginning, I made a reference to how Marty hasn't been well. And if, in the last year, the last ten months, you feel the column has gone a bit off course, or worse, been unfunny, let me apologize on his behalf and try to shed some light. For the last ten months, Marty has been in almost constant pain. There is nothing wrong with him physically, but from his right hip down his right leg he has had to endure bouts of spasms, stiffness, and immobility. He has had to lie on his back on a special pad to write the column. But he is starting to get better. Thanks to a wonderful book, *The Power of "Ow!"* by Dr. Samuel Abrun, my husband is getting in touch with some deep unconscious feelings from the past that are causing his pain. If it sounds like a lot of psychological nonsense, it isn't. It is just, to use an expression, his baggage. The book has had a tremendous impact on Marty, and he often tells me, "People should be reading Samuel Abrun, not me. He's the real deal. He's the self-help guru. He's what people thought I was." I figured I'd pass that along before the end of the column.

Whew, this is long. I hope if the editors cut, they cut from the top when I was rambling. I'm rambling now. This is where being funny would help. Okay, then. Marty loved the column, and he loved all of you. Even the ones who didn't get it. Especially the ones who didn't get it.

For the last time . . . Happy Baggage!

As you can see, they didn't cut anything. They "jumped" the column rather than lop off a few 'graphs to make it fit on the front of the section—a first—and Phil spent a good hour reveling in watching himself turn the page of his own newspaper. An hour which was pain-free.

He then turned to the last page of the B section, the obituaries, to look at what was always the best writing in the paper.

Typical Tuesday in Deathland. An ACTOR KNOWN FOR TV ROLES he vaguely remembered. A FINANCIER, 99, POPULARIZED OFF-SHORE ACCOUNTS he was delighted to not have heard of. The WIFE OF INNOVATIVE LONG ISLAND DRY CLEANER, 84 whose daughter had once worked at the desk next to him at the AP.

And further down, crouched in the left column corner, trying not to get Phil's attention:

LENNY MILLMAN, 61
Activist, Smoker
Lenny Millman, the colorful, self-

appointed "Small Tobacco Lobby-
ist," who defied city laws to exercise
his "First Amendment right to poor
health," died April 12 following com-
plications from minor back surgery.

Mr. Millman, a former night-club
owner, private investigator, and news
researcher for 1010 WINS, became a
minor New York City celebrity after
tough antismoking legislation was
first passed in 1995.

Showing up in his trademark year-
round outfit—leather vest, leather sandals, and leather satchel—at various
well-known Manhattan landmarks,
(including St. Patrick's Cathedral) he
would light a cigarette and see how
many he could smoke before security
personnel or the police would show
up and escort him off the premises.
His biggest splash, literally, came last
July 4, when he somehow boarded a
Macy's fireworks barge and got off four
or five puffs before diving into the
East River.

Born and raised in and around Boston, Mr. Millman was married three
times and had at least four children.

12

Phil, my boy, you have got to make a choice."

"I know, Dr. Abrun," said Phil. "Start seeing one of your therapists, or continue to see mine and have pain."

"No, fuck that," Abrun said. (*Hey, he swears!*) "Here's your choice: Continue seeing my daughter Janet, or get better."

"You're not serious."

"Oh, but I am," Abrun quietly chuckled, which, like that handwriting analyst in Central Park, he did when he was saying something particularly painful. "Look, no father is more proud of his daughter than me. I know how phenomenal a woman she is. And I know you're bright enough to see that."

Phil's squirm came over the phone cordlessly. "Dr. Abrun, I'm not comfortable with this conversation."

"You think I am *(quiet chuckle)*? Do you have any idea what she'd do if she found out we were having this conversation? Doesn't matter that it was my idea *(chuckle)*. She'd beat the shit out of us both."

This time the chuckle came from Phil. "No reservoir of rage there," he said, completely forgetting to whom he was talking.

Abrun cleared his throat and went on. "She does not buy my . . . stuff. Not anymore. That's her right as a physician, and as a *(quiet chuckle)* former patient. But I am not in the convincing business."

"I know you aren't, but with all due respect, I do not agree that she doesn't buy your program. She thinks it's, uh, incomplete."

"Hey, the Venus de Milo is incomplete! My ass is incomplete! There is no room for incomplete. Where there is doubt there is pain!"

"Dr. Abrun, I know that—"

"No, you don't! Look, we're wasting time with you. I've got people who want to get better. Who *(chuckle)* buy this. Stuff." And the author of *The Power of "Ow!"* hung up the phone with the full force of that power.

Phil stared at the receiver, hoping for something more civil than a dial tone. He had to settle for a cold coda.

"Did I call it?" said Janet, standing across the room. "Did I friggin' call it?"

13

Apricot and paint. That's what Janet's lips and cheek tasted like.

"I had to put some cream on," she said as she gathered her things to leave. "I'm a little red around here."

"Is it my beard?" Phil asked.

"The beard doesn't help, but my face tends to, uh, do things occasionally when things happen."

"Things, and things?" Phil said. "You are a diagnostic dynamo."

"Hey, don't think you're the only one with psychogenic super powers." She smoothed her navy blazer and gave him another latex-colada kiss, and they made plans to meet for dinner whenever one of them had the balls to call next.

Phil splashed some water on his face and looked in the bathroom mirror at the rogue droplets that clung to his beard. He smiled onto himself for the first time since God knows when. "You look like a guy," he said to the mirror, "whose story is just over halfway done."

He opened the medicine cabinet and stared at all the things he had not taken since February. Oh sure, there was the occasional three Arthritis-Strength Tylenol, toothless tablets he would pop when he felt nostalgic for swallowing pills. But the heavy-duty stuff—the pre-Abrun, "this might help" *PDR* miniannex of the narcotic and near-narcotic prescribed by Dr. Glindelvoss, the orthopedic surgeon and disk freak, who hadn't shown in the hospital and hadn't bothered to call since Phil had left St. Clare's—that was still in attendance.

Percoset, Vicodin, OxyContin, Tylenol with Codeine. It was all there. Never worked. Never worked the way Phil had wanted it to. Shit, the third of a joint he'd had at Janet's apartment the other night had worked better. No, the best any of these pills could offer was erecting a see-through curtain in front of the pain. That, and nausea. And confusion, because the limp never went away. And he knew the pain was still there, hiding. So really, what was the point? Why take something when eventually you'd have to get over whatever you were taking and deal with whatever it was you took it for? Better to endure a real manifestation than launch another capsule manned with another neurological sous-chef.

All of that was why even though Samuel Abrun himself said it was okay to take painkillers (not anti-inflammatories because there was no inflammation, but painkillers because there *was* pain, and the narcotics might calm it down enough to improve one's retention while reading *The Power of "Ow!"*)—Phil made the decision his second day home from the hospital to . . . what was that Buddhist line of shit? Oh yeah, to make pain his teacher.

Some teacher. A teacher that never showed up in the same place at the same time. And yet there were instances, more than a few over the last ten-plus months, where he may have been rendered pain-free just by ignoring it. That night three weeks ago when he had walked all the way back from Café du Kips Bay after dinner with Janet.

So what kind of a pupil was he? What was this, when you get out of a chair, take three steps, think "Hey, feels pretty good . . ." and *just that thought* makes your whole left side seize like a mall-cop-busted shoplifter? Phil had asked himself that question hundreds of times. Which was the problem. He was expecting an answer from himself, from the same brain that had given him the pain, hired his teacher. But who was left to ask? Why wasn't there something Phil could take that could tell his brain and his teacher to shut the fuck up?

And now, all the childproof, amber plastic silos just sat there in the medicine cabinet. Just sat there. Say, you know who used to love all this stuff? Fellow by the name of Jim McManus. Especially the Vicodin. Before he let himself be diagnosed with APS, he'd gone a little nuts with the prescription painkillers in the late 1980s. A little nuts. Chevy Chase/Brett Favre/Matthew Perry nuts. Jimmy came out of rehab, clean, and even more of a rabid righty. Wouldn't that be something if that turned out to be one of the side effects of Vicodin? *May curtail fascism.* Somebody call the FDA.

Phil skipped into the bedroom *(Hey, I just skipped into the bedroom . . . ow!)*, grabbed his phone and started to dial. He pressed the Disconnect button and walked haltingly back into the bathroom to close the medicine cabinet.

One more look. He closed the cabinet door and couldn't miss the look on his face. It was a different look than the one that had just told the mirror he might be halfway through his story. He threw the door back open, wrestled the Vicodin open, and threw back two pills before dropping his head under the faucet. He wiped his beard on his sleeve and grabbed the phone and rejabbed the numbers in. This time, all of them.

Busy.

Redial. . . . busy.

Redial. . . . busy.

Redial. . . . busy.

Phil walked over to the wall unit and turned on the radio. Preset to 940-AM.

"Dorothy, I know where you're going with this, but let me run down, excuse me, I mean let me run through, run through, the political career of John Kerry and demonstrate why we have absolutely nothing to be worried about. . . ."

Redial . . . busy. Jim McManus had already hung up on her. Phil would have to wait until the next one, or just before. With the seven-minute delay, there was a brief window where a space arose in the queue of callers. That's when you hit Redial. He'd learned this in the mid-seventies, the hard way, on a rotary phone, dialing a late-Sunday-night show out of Boston called *The Sports Huddle* to try and make the three hosts laugh with a joke about Roger Staubach finding Jesus, but overthrowing him. Two hosts, Eddie Andelman and Mark Witkin, were Jews and gave him curtailed snorts. The third, a real Beantown Irishman named Jim McCarthy, said, "You're naught from around he-yah, ah yah?" and hung up.

Hmm. Another radio guy named Jim who didn't want to hear from him.

"*But, Jim, don't you agree that some of the oversights he unveiled during the 9/11 hearings were reprehensible? Didn't they bother you, as a defender of the Bush—*"

"*Excuse me, are we still talking about Richard Clarke? It's a month later and we still have to listen to him whine about how the government failed all of us? First of all, Richard Clarke does not speak for me. If he wants to say the government failed him, that's his right. But don't speak for me. Go be a Monday-morning quarterback in the privacy of your own toilet. Did the Bush Administration make the same mistakes that the Clinton Administration had with virtually the same intelligence? Yeah. You've heard me say that before. Me, Mr. Arch-Conservative Righty Spawn of Satan. I've said it. I've taken some heat for it. I've had my loyalty questioned, which, when you think about it, is ironic and flattering. But I move on. And we have to move on. What's your name . . . Drew?*"

"*Yes.*"

"*Drew, have you written a book?*"

"*No.*"

"*Are you on a book tour?*"

"*No.*"

"*I think you are. I think you're on Richard Clarke's book tour. I think you called to make the points he is making to try and sell his book.*"

"*No, Jim, I just wanted to—*"

"I know what you wanted to do, but why are you doing it, unless you're working for Richard Clarke's publisher, trying to sell his book?"

"I'm not doing that."

"Of course, you're not. Not directly. But there is no Richard Clarke without the Richard Clarke book tour. That is why I will never have anyone on this show within six months after they've written a book. I want the person, not the book tour. I want the issue, not the commercial. I want to be a destination for serious discussion, not a stop on some marketing . . ."

Ringing. Phil had hit Redial at *"Of course, you're not."* He knew Caller Drew had been long dispatched. He knew his brother's riff about never having anybody on his show who had written a book. (Or, as Phil would mumble at the radio, read one.) He knew it was a riff that would go uninterrupted, complete with those frequent three-beat talk radio pauses. The kind . . . that let you know . . . that what is being said . . . here . . . now . . . demands your full attention . . . your full attention . . . So . . . stop reading the paper . . . stop folding the laundry . . . stop playing with your children . . . or your cock . . . and take a lesson.

Click. "Jim McManus Show," said a voice.

"Am I on?"

"Hah!" said the voice. Definitely his producer. "First-time caller?"

"Yeah," Phil said, "but longtime listener."

"Name?"

"Phil."

"Where you calling from?"

"Uh, The Creek."

"Does the creek have a name?"

"Nah. We just call it The Creek."

"What do you want to talk to Jim about?"

"Uh, Marty Fleck?"

"Marty Fleck getting canned?"

"Uh, yeah."

"Great!" said the voice. "But it's going to be a while. Probably in the last hour. You'll have to stay on the line. Can you hang on?"

"Sure," Phil said. "Where am I going?"

Once on hold, you got to listen to the Jim McManus Show in real time. Which meant six minutes, fifty-three seconds earlier than the radio public (Seven minutes, minus the standard FCC seven-second delay to bleep inappropriate language, like "shit," "fuck," and "Noam Chomsky.") He lay down on The Pad, speakerphone by his ear, and let the Vicodin tell his brain. . . . He closed his eyes and saw the four of them, the four sophomores, walking him toward Shit Creek. Oh right, Phil thought. *This* is why I don't take Vicodin.

Eyes open.

"Who told you I don't like Ralph Nader? I love Ralph Nader. And you should, too. I should send Ralph Nader ten percent of my paycheck. Ralph Nader not only put George Bush in power, he put me in power. Hah-hah!"

Eyes closed. He might as well tell himself the story. He'd been putting it off for at least ten months, and at most thirty-one years. Might as well tell himself the story. On hold and in the hold of Hydrocodone. Where was he going?

"Didn't you call last week about the antiquated computers at the CIA and FBI? Please. Who are you working for? Mercy, do you think they'll track down Bin Laden by sending him an e-mail for Cialis?"

Here I am, Phil began in the silent voice that had narrated his life as if a documentary crew had been following him since he began walking. Here I am, about to be taken to Shit Creek. It is an early June night, and the last exam of my freshman year at Cabot Hill Academy is tomorrow. I am in the basement of my best friend's dorm, Tim Lyons, and he's killing me in Ping Pong. My big brother, Jimmy, is home. He graduated two days ago. I go home tomorrow.

Here come the four sophomores, down into the basement. Three of them, I expect. Chaw Keefer, Dyke Sheehan, and Bobby Burkalter. The fourth is Reggie Naulls, one of six black students at Cabot Hill. Football player. Six-foot-two, one-seventy. Fastest guy in the school. He's come along in case I try to run.

Mr. Camp, Chaw Keefer says to me, it's time.

"*So, instead of being relieved Saddam Hussein had no yellowcake uranium, we're supposed to be outraged. . . .*"

Mr. Camp, it's time.

One of the others asks if they should take Tim Lyons. Nah, says Chaw. He's just a dipshit. He's not Camp. If we came for the dipshits, we'd have to get everybody.

Here I am, being walked up the stairs and out onto Heritage Road. There's another hour or so of light, so a lot of people are still outside. Students and faculty. I would recognize them but my head is down.

Make it look like we're all friends, says Chaw Keefer. I am nodding and start talking to Reggie Naulls about a touchdown he scored against Cheshire. He smiles and I ask him if it was a set play. Shut up, says Chaw. I thought you told me to make it look—I feel the back of my neck get wet. I hear the others laugh. I know what it is. Tobacco juice. Right. That's why he's called Chaw.

Chaw Keefer. I knew him first as Kenneth Keefer. Kenneth Keefer, Spanish I. Let me think about that . . . Here I am, sitting in Spanish I. I am in the front row of the class for the first two months of school. I am five-foot-one, ninety-eight pounds. Which is also my grade for Spanish I—98.

Just before Thanksgiving, Mr. Sandoval begins class by saying, We're changing the seats here. I need the people who are in danger of failing up front. Mr. Keefer, I need you to switch seats with Mr. Camp.

Here I am, walking to the back row. The others snicker. Kenneth Keefer has his back to me. He finishes writing something, then leaves it folded on his old seat. Here I am, sitting down, opening the paper. *Hola, Jew.* That's where it started.

Here I am, almost at the end of Heritage Road, just where the dirt path to the lower level athletic fields starts. I don't know when I started hating you, Camp, he says. "*Hola,* Jew?" I say. Bobby Burkalter laughs. He was in that class. Bobby had to switch seats with Fritz Greacen. Nah, Chaw Keefer says. Way before that.

"*Where is your proof that the 'disappearing middle class' is disappearing? The Jim McManus Show would love to hear . . .*"

Let me think about that . . . Here I am, in the Locker Room B showers after freshman soccer practice. Way before Thanksgiving. There are about twenty of us in there. Chaw Keefer, Dyke Sheehan, and two other guys, Holcomb and Decartier, walk in from JV2 football practice. There's plenty of showers free, but they start dancing around my friend Ivan Upton, singing the Mexican Hat Dance. I know why. Ivan is smaller than me. No hair on his balls. Mexican hairless. Get it? Here I am, throwing my towel at Ivan. Ivan, let's go. Dyke Sheehan shoves me. What's your hurry? Gotta go. Better go ask your big brother where Shit Creek is. Right, Chaw? Yeah, go ask him.

I don't have to ask Jimmy. He had told me before I came to Cabot Hill. Shit Creek is the cesspool that forms on the lower level during the spring, after the river thaws. Let me think about that. . . . If anyone says anything about Shit Creek to you, Philly, it's just talk. I'll take care of you. Forget it. I'll take care of you. Like you took care of me. I'll take care of you.

"Sure, I wonder how many more listeners I'd have if I added 'God rest his soul' every time I said, 'Ronald Reagan' . . ."

Here I am, at the far end of the varsity soccer field on the lower level. Chaw Keefer asks me, Why don't you run? I say, I just ate. Bobby Burkalter laughs. We are approaching Shit Creek. It is fifty yards behind the JV2 baseball diamond. Even though I played JV2 baseball, I am seeing it for the first time. The trees become deformed and crooked and the grass is high and scary. Way way to the right is the Wachumtuck River, but Shit Creek has nothing to do with that. I say, hey, how about throwing me in the river? Nah, says Dyke Sheehan. Jews float. Isn't a Jew float with root beer? Shut the fuck up, Campstein. Reggie Naulls laughs. Bobby Burkalter laughs.

I am not scared. I am not scared. You don't have your big brother to protect you now, Chaw whispers. I am not scared. I am not scared. I am . . . lonely.

Man, is it dark here. Nowhere else on the lower level yet. Here I am, taking my shoes off. I am grateful until I realize my feet will feel all this. Well, at least I won't ruin my shoes—Nice throw, Reggie! I watch my loafers sink into Shit Creek. It takes a while. Like movie quicksand, or some vat Batman was trapped in at the end of an episode. Except much darker. Shit Creek. Shit Pudding. Jew float.

I walk to the edge. My foot sinks a little into the side. Can I take off my jacket? Bobby, Dyke, get a leg. Chaw, can I take off my jacket? Oh, let me do that. Thanks—Nice throw, Dyke! There's clapping. My madras jacket, my new one. Just lying there on top of Shit Creek.

Here I go. I run. I run into Shit Creek. Hey! Yuck . . . Hey! You dumb fucking Jew!

"Three weeks ago, I used those words? 'The black people'? Those exact words? Me? Jim McManus. Three weeks ago? Jay, pull those tapes for me . . ."

My feet sink into the bottom. Even with my socks on, it makes me queasy. Yuck. Yucky. I'll tell Mom my jacket was stolen.

There is just enough water to move around. Lots of bubbles. Detergent bubbles. Foam bubbles. Shit Creek bubbles. Come back here! Camp, you asshole! You dumb shit!

Here I am, putting my madras jacket on and swimming back to the bank. I am grabbing a weird tree and pulling myself up. Back on land. I am more muddy than wet. More shitty than muddy. Man, do I stink. I breathe through my mouth and move toward the four of them and they back away. Sorry, Chaw. You guys want to throw me in now? Reggie Naulls jumps way back. Nah, says Chaw. I see his hand grab the one spot on my jacket that has no Shit Creek on it. He shoves me hard. Here I am, losing my balance, bouncing off the bank and back into Shit Creek. I hear laughter. I'm back in. Don't cry. Don't cry. It's over. It's over. Don't cry. They're done.

Here I am, treading water, treading whatever, in Shit Creek, breathing through my mouth, watching Dyke Sheehan whisper to Chaw Keefer.

Dunk your head.

Why?

Your hair's still dry.

No.

You're not getting out until you go under.

Then I'm not getting out.

Reggie Naulls waves and taps Bobby Burkalter. They're walking away.

We're not leaving until you dunk your head.

Here are my feet, finding a rock. Well, I guess you're not leaving.

Just dunk your fucking head, Camp.

No. Don't cry. Don't cry. Wait. Turn around on the rock.

Oh, come on! Turn around! You asshole. Kike piece of shit.

Here are my teeth chattering. Here is my nose running. I can't wipe it. Afraid to. I close my eyes. I'll cry that way. Something hits my shoulder. It scares me, but doesn't hurt.

Did you hit him? I don't know. I can't see. Shit.

"The Liberals hate me because I'm onto them. The Far Right hates me because my Jesus does not believe in attending PAC lunches . . ."

Here I am, counting—877 . . . 878 . . . 879 . . . 880 . . . 881 . . . 882 . . . 883 . . . 884 . . . 885 . . . 886 . . . 887 . . . 888 . . . 889 . . . 890 . . . 891 . . . 892 . . . 893 . . . 894 . . . 895 . . . 896 . . . 897 . . . 898 . . . 899 . . . 900. I turn around. It is dark. Chaw Keefer and Dyke Sheehan are gone. They've been gone for about nine hundred seconds.

Here I am, wiping my hands on the grass by the JV2 baseball diamond. I take off my socks, ball them up, throw them back into Shit Creek. I wipe my hands again on the grass. They may be clean. It's dark. I touch my hair. Dry. *Dry.*

Run. Run. *Run.*

Here I am, in the Locker Room B showers. Showering in my clothes. Rubbing soap on my pants and shirt, rinsing it off, rubbing more soap on, rinsing. I throw my tie under some lockers. Here I am, wiping my face with paper towels. Trying to dry my clothes with paper towels. The regular towels are locked up. I can't change. I cleaned out my locker yesterday. I go home tomorrow.

"Indolent critics of No Child Left Behind . . ."

Here am I, running behind the houses on Heritage Road, trying to stay out of the streetlights so no one can see me. Everything is cold and dark, colder and darker than Shit Creek. And wetter. But faster. It is not far to Roland House, my dorm, but it is farther running through these yards. My teeth are chattering worse than before. I am colder. I am also nervous, because I know I have to go up the fire escape. If I run in the door and up the stairs, the guys will see me. They'll know. I don't want them to know. I go home tomorrow.

"*Unwashed Lotto ticket–buying bozos . . .* "

Man, the rungs on this ladder are cold. Oh, here I am, climbing up the fire escape in the back of Roland House. Everything is clinging to me. Everything hurts. Three floors I climb, then across the roof to Ralph Duncan's window. I'll go through his window. My room is next door. My room has no window in the roof. Ralph is always at the library. His dad is a diplomat and he lives in Brussels— Hey, Camp, did you get Creeked?

"*On whose watch . . .*"

Here I am, drying my hair, telling the other ten freshmen in Roland House about Shit Creek. Making jokes. I think I'll go in for a dip tomorrow morning before my geometry final. Wasn't it awful? The bathroom smells worse after you're in it, Osterville. Everyone laughs. Ivan Upton makes me tea on his hot plate the dorm master doesn't know about. I am putting on my sweatshirt. Still cold. I hold up my wet Shit Creek clothes. Who wants a whiff? There they go, back to their rooms to study for finals. I am putting my wet Shit Creek clothes in a Hefty bag and getting my suitcase out from under my bed. I go home tomorrow. Here I am, emptying my drawers when Fred Shulman walks back in. He is the smartest kid in Roland House. And the only other Jew.

They got me, too, Camp. When? In the fall. Second week. Remember when I went home? Yeah. I thought your aunt died. Yeah, aunt died. I almost didn't come back. I never told anybody. Uh, thanks. I kind of thought they wouldn't get to you. Yeah, well. Because of your name. Camp. It's hard to tell. Not for me. Yeah, well. And . . .

"*Let me finish? Can you . . .*"

And, you know, because of your older brother.

"*Absolute crap . . .* "

Here I am, sitting against the door of my room. It is dark. What time is it? Shit. Shit. I want to go to bed, but I'll lie on the floor.

"*Stand By for Truth, Manus . . .* "

Hey, where did this pad come from?

"*Rummmmsfelddddd . . .* "

"*Disenfran . . . eyes . . . vo . . .* "

"*Ten thirteen on a Wennzz . . .* "

"*Geneeeev . . .* "

"*Susceptibullll . . .* "

"*They call her Val-al-al-al-lurreee . . .* "

"*My old man . . . stem-celled his . . . arkinson . . . zees . . .* "

"*No Haiti then . . .* "

"*Les Assspinnn . . .* "

"*MollyMollyMollyMolly, am I shoutingggg . . .* "

"*Ambling into hist . . .* "

"*Forrrrmerrr apologissssss . . .* "

"*Would have . . .* "

"*ave you believe . . .* "

"*Would . . .* "

"*Lieve casualties . . .* "

"*Suuuuuunites . . .* "

"*Puhleeese . . .* "

"*Arty Fleck afterrr thuh . . .* "

"Phil?"

"—"

"Phil?"

"—"

"Phil!"

"Wha? Huh?"

"You dozed off, buddy. Don't tell Jim."

"*Jim . . . Jim?*" Ah—it was McManus's producer. "Nah, I won't," said Phil. "Sorry. Antihistamines."

"I'm sure. Can you get off speaker?"

"Yeah, sure."

"Now?"

"Oh . . ."

"Fine. Stay up, now. We're ready for you."

"Do I have time to go to the bathroom?"

"Jesus, no!"

"Okay, no problem."

Through the receiver, he heard the brief oncoming wave of anachronistic static and the pneumatic pop on the other side, as if he had been wirelessly summoned into the studio. Not as if. He had.

"Okay, we have Phil from The Creek on the line. Hello, Phil."

"Hello, uh, Jimmy? First-time caller, longtime listener."

"Good to hear from you. I mean it. Unfortunately, we're up against a hard break. I'm sorry."

"I'm sure."

"Can you call back another time?"

"Why, Jimmy? Are you unavailable?"

"Yeah. I'm really sorry."

"Yeah. Maybe another time. Like when you're in danger of losing your other testicle."

Phil delivered that line calmly enough to saunter by the seven-second delay. Jim McManus gave an unintentionally long pause, looked at his producer, who was laughing on the other side of the glass like it was "good radio." He realized they were still on the air.

"Calling from The Creek, huh? Say, where is that?"

"You know where it is, you abandoning, ungrateful cocksucking motherfucker."

And then they weren't.

14

Ladies and gentlemen, we have a new record.

In the last two hours, Phil had gone to the bathroom ten times. Peed ten times. And not the "Oh drat, I was being impatient and have to go back." Legitimate pisses. Pisses that would stand up in court, if only he could stand up in court without having to excuse himself every twelve minutes. Thank God he was alone. Thank God it was just him in the apartment. Who could live with this? Who could act as if this were normal? Other than Phil. Well, at least he had an answer if anyone asked if he was working. *You working? / Yeah, part-time job. / Yeah, what? / Redoing a bathroom.* Okay, so he left out "in." Redoing *in* a bathroom. But really, who was going to ask him if he was working? Really. Who was left? Who gave a shit? More to the point, who gave a piss?

Later, during his twelfth or thirteenth trip to the toilet, Phil had decided to dump out the last of the Vicodin, one at a time, into the bowl and work on his aim. It gave him something to look forward to, and it punished the pharmaceutical messenger. Because let's face it, he never would have had that truncated radio exchange with his brother if he hadn't been in the throes of *Delirium Limbaughs*. Which, of course, is nonsense. But who was around to call him on his shit? Who was left? Abrun, gone. Irish Shrink, gone. Jim McManus, disconnected. Marty Fleck, buried. Lenny Millman, decomposing.

Okay, Janet was left. But, with all due respect, are you serious? Janet? Just how long would she, might she, stay around to scale, then repel Mount Neurotica in the Psychogenic Alps? Please. *"Honey, how about a movie?"* / (tile-muffled voice from behind bathroom door) *"Only if it's playing in here, sweetheart—7:20, 7:32, 7:45, 7:56, 8:07 . . ."* How gifted was she? How desperate was she?

Phil held off flushing and answered the phone.

"Yeah?"

"Janet. What are you doing?"

"Pissing and limping."

"Well, zip up and go for a walk."

Phil hung up and looked for his jogging shoes. Okay, okay. She was pretty damn gifted.

He made it in sixteen minutes to the southernmost entrance of Central Park, where the hansom carriages line up for out-of-town pigeons. It used to take ten. By then he was warmed up enough to lift his gait to a kind of step-skid, the way a trainer makes his way across the ice when a hockey player is injured. The walkway to the Central Park Zoo was lightly trafficked. Early afternoon early April early in the week. The weather not quite good enough for office workers to come up with excuses why they stayed out that long for lunch. No charcoal sketchers. No *"Your name on a grain of rice!"* painters. No hot-dog vendor. No graphology expert. No hot-dog vendor who used to be a graphology expert.

The zoo was doing a little business. Twenty kids in identical purple sweatshirts were waiting for the sea lions to beck and call. They yelled, "Seal!! Seal!!!" Nothing. Phil stopped, which he regretted because it would involve starting again. The unique stiffness of the misbehaving first step. One sea lion was on its back on the lower rock, inert. *Put a speakerphone next to his ear,* Phil thought, *and that could be me two hours ago.*

He repowered up and skidded under the dancing animal clock and the short tunnel before the petting zoo and slowed to a clip-clop. Say, you know what's great for a headache? Ice cream. Ice cream on an empty stomach. Phil made it to Seventy-second Street and bought a chocolate éclair from a Good Humor cart on the corner of Fifth. He ate the thing in five bites, then spent another five minutes picking chocolate flakes out of his beard. Of course, his headache got much, much worse, but somewhere, that was the idea. Take his mind off his throbbing ass, and on down. And it worked. Phil was distracted enough to decide he'd walk another ten blocks up Fifth, a half-mile, then tackle the steps of the Met.

Bad idea.

Before everything was converted to meters, the world record for the half-mile was 1:44.6. Phil Camp's pace was off by about thirty-seven minutes. He slowed to the point where what he was doing looked closer to bad tai-chi than walking. A more self-possessed, quicker-thinking man might have put his head down and saved face by repeating, "Now where the hell is that contact lens of mine?"

Not today. Not since who knows? Phil moved against a head-wind of dogs, runners, school-paroled children, nannies, multiple strollers. And zero cabs. Why had he listened to Janet? What did she know? Where was the self-esteemable act here, that he might attain museum steps before nightfall?

At Eighty-first and Fifth, Phil reached the pre-Met sidewalk agora of artists and photographers. He'd do the steps, then sit in the restaurant, the good one, and eat and drink and, if all went well, blubber until somebody got him out of there. The left leg was now half-collapsing every time he put weight on it. He tried an Abrun mantra: *There is nothing physically wrong with me,* but it kept coming out *There is nothing phy—fuck you!!*

He decided to buy an umbrella, a full-length one with a wooden cane handle, and get himself a temporary left leg for ten dollars. It would help with the steps, too. Finally, a good idea. If only some-one was selling umbrellas. Great. The one friggin' stretch of side-walk in Man-friggin'-hattan without a guy selling umbrellas. No room. Too many derivative paintings and iterative photos.

Against his better judgment, Phil stopped. His eye caught a photograph he'd seen stacked on the street thousands of times. The threshold to Strawberry Fields, that portion of Central Park renamed in 1981 to commemorate John Lennon. A stone-tiled sunburst compass engraved with the word IMAGINE, Lennon's now-ironic ode to a nonviolent world and his unintended recessional. Only this time, when Phil looked at the framed reprint, he did not see IMAGINE.

He saw IM AGING.

He stuck his face close to the glass. IM AGING.

Only when his reflection came into focus did the letters behave. IMAGINE.

Phil looked around frantically for a witness. Instead, one block North across Fifth, he saw a man getting out of a cab.

And he ran.

He sprinted half a block, juke-stepped three tourists and a Doe Fund worker emptying a trash can, cut hard to his right on the light change, and scampered across Fifth by going into a gear unsum-moned since the spring of 2003. He arrived in plenty of time to see the doorman at 945 Fifth hold up one gloved hand to stop him, and with the other open the rear left door of the cab. Seconds or hours later, one of those indigenous Manhattan creatures, the Upper East Sideasaurus—half woman/half relic/all dough—emerged under the building's awning. She was gilded and beyond thin, ele-gaunt, and it was clear most of her body weight could be measured in Troy ounces. And old. At least a good quarter-century from the last time she had been described as a biddy. She crept to the cab in the time it would have taken the driver to hop out and do an oil change. But make no mistake, right now, racing dusk to the door, she was moving faster than Phil had between Seventy-second and Eighty-first. Would have kicked his already kicked ass. So, he had to laugh.

You'd laugh too if you'd run for the first time in a year, pain-free, after misreading a photo.

Phil laughed, and the pain came back. He thought he heard himself yelp, but it was the doorman at 945 Fifth, whistling down a cab for him. Nice guy. Phil gave him the ten bucks he would have spent on an umbrella and headed home. "I have a surprise for you," he said to his left side. "No," misinterpreted the cabdriver. "No can't make change."

"That's okay," Phil replied. "I can."

Fifteen minutes later, he was back in his bathroom, not peeing. That's right. Not peeing. *The Power of "Ow!"* lay open to Page 29, face down next to the sink. Phil was face up, looking at himself in the mirror of his medicine cabinet. Staring at a full, thick white beard . . . of lather. The Gillette Sensor had a clean blade. The hot water was running. Good word, running.

"So long, Grandpa."

That was how Phil Camp greeted himself, and said good-bye.

Whatever adverb denotes less speed than "deliberately," that was how Phil proceeded. It took almost twenty minutes. He wanted to give his body and his mind time to catch up to what was going on. He shaved the left side of his face first, and like something you'd hear advertised in a Vegas lounge, the ache adroitly jumped to his right knee. Jumped. He had it on the run. Which is where he was five minutes later, out the door of his building, running. Around the block, just once, then back through the lobby and up the fire stairs, twenty-three bounding flights, to his apartment. Inside the door, he bent over and put his hands on both knees, equally, then on his hips, huffing and wheezing like, well, like just another well-meaning but out of shape forty-six-year-old. Just another. He'd be sore tomorrow, he knew it. Eeee-fucking-hah.

He had almost caught his breath when Janet picked up the phone on the other end.

"Hello?"

"All right, all right," Phil gasped lightly, "I'll marry you."

15

Janet thought, he's kidding, right?

It was possible. Oh, it was more than possible. The exchange on the phone had been so brief (*"Hello?"* / *"All right, all right. / I'll marry you."* / *"Hah-hah! Let me get back to you . . ."* / *"Unbelievable. Janet, I just ran for the first time since—"* **(Intercom buzz.)** *"Dr. Fitzgerald, they're calling for you on four . . ."*), it may have been a goof. Phil sounded good. A little wheezy, but euphoric enough to make a joke? Why not? He was funny. Wasn't he? He was capable of this. Sure. Why not? Until recently, he had been paid to be funny. "Baggage Handling" by Marty Fleck. And Marty Fleck was funny, wasn't he? But Marty Fleck hadn't proposed. Marty Fleck couldn't. He was married to Stacey Fleck, remember? And neither of them were real. What if the whole thing was some kind of elaborate—

"Janet!" she yelled at herself. "Breathe! Try not to be as nuts as your patients."

But what if he hadn't been kidding? How had Janet ended up as the homewrecker who had come between Phil Camp and Samuel Abrun? How was *that* working out for her?

Not well.

Nobody appreciates it when their life's tenets are about to be disproved. Tenets like: *Men are intimidated by smart women.* A man thinks he wants the challenge. But how long can his ego coexist with a woman who would rather lead than be pursued? How long can the man accept that he will never be properly taken care of? (Nurturing? Enemy of intellect? Feh!) That he will never be the strong one? That he'll wake up one morning and see her in front of the mirror, trying on his dick and balls? So, they run. *Men run.*

This is what Janet knew: *Men are intimidated by smart women.* And: *Men run.* Knew it like someone with two decades of field research to back it up. Flirt with them, make out with 'em, blow 'em, blow 'em away enough with your brains to make them love you for your ultimate unattainability. But expect no more.

Okay, the ex-husband, Galen, the Queens guy with the fireman family. That was an exception. That was a moment of weakness that lasted three years. Janet looked around, her sightline obstructed by a suddenly crowded field of younger, cagier, prettier women even more adept at the behavioral science she thought she had created. So, she married the guy with the fireman family. That time, Janet let herself be led. And we all know how that turned out. He left anyway. *Men run.*

She had all the data. So then, explain this. How come the one guy, the one guy who couldn't run, when, thanks to her, he finally could run, ran *to* her? Tenets anyone?

Actually, she could explain it. Oldest reason in the world. He wanted to marry his nurse. Happens all the time. Bob Dole did it. Okay, bad example. Not that anybody was calling Janet a nurse, not that anybody would friggin' dare call Janet a nurse. Except Janet. Come on. The guy you're seeing calls you in pain, you tell him to zip up and go take a walk and two hours later you get a proposal? Forget looking at rings. First, go shopping for some thick-soled white shoes.

Besides, and more to the point, his Acute Psychogenic Syndrome would return. It always does. Maybe not in the same place or in the same way, but APS will eventually find another attractive spot on the body, a spot with plenty of exposure, and time share. This is the "symptom imperative" her father talked about, one of the points on which she not only agreed with him, but felt he didn't hammer enough. So, what happens then? They get back from the honeymoon, and suddenly, Phil can't move his neck or he can't stop hyperventilating, or his elbows are riddled with eczema. Or a million other things the mind can storyboard. What happens then? Oldest story in the world. Man who marries his nurse grows to resent her for not actually being his nurse. Man runs. *Men run.*

Except that this time, on the way to building yet another theorem that concluded yet again with *Ergo: Men run,* Janet made the mistake of imagining the honeymoon. Her honeymoon. And that made her happy. And she didn't need to take the time to think about whether she'd rather be right.

Happy. Janet could get use to the idea of being happy.

Again, she was interrupted by a buzz from the intercom. "*Dr. Fitzgerald, your—hey!*" She heard the hollow bounce of phone receiver hitting desk, then a thoroughly invalid touch-tone code, then a clumsy click she recognized as the Speaker button being activated. Throughout the struggle, she recognized the voice. A couple of muffled "Excuse me, honey's, followed by "I know all about these things! You think we don't have these things on Thirty-third Street? Janet! This is on, right? Janet!"

She picked up her phone. "Come on in, Dad."

Despite a couple shelves of evidence to the contrary, Janet was always happy to see her father. He was passionate, he was brilliant, he was relentlessly engaged, he twinkled even when he didn't want to, and most important, if it came to blows, she could take him. And he knew it. But despite that, he never stopped confronting her with his love, his interest, and his exasperation. Never stopped coming. How flattering. How maddening. If Janet let herself think of Samuel Abrun as a man, here was a man not intimidated by a smart woman. But she didn't, because that would have flattened her first tenet.

"Dad, what a pleasant surprise."

"How come you weren't at the group today?"

"I haven't been coming to the group for about a month now."

"And when were you going to get around to telling me that?"

"What?" she half-laughed. "Didn't you notice I wasn't there?"

"Of course I did. Do you think I'm an idiot?"

"Well, I didn't until this part of the conversation." Sam Abrun twinkled even though he didn't want to. "Dad," she continued softly, "you told me if I wasn't going to share, I couldn't be there. It wasn't fair to your patients."

"My *other* patients."

"Oh, for Christ sake, are we keeping my file active twenty-nine years later?"

"You're welcome." Samuel Abrun let his face show hurt, and may or may not have meant it. Didn't matter. It was not the first time for this face, and the only thing it always achieved was that Janet began to no longer be happy to see him.

"Dad, we're gonna have to do this later."

"What did I tell you?"

"You told me a lot of things. And continue to."

"But what was the first thing I told you?"

She felt her lips starting to shut their purse, which was her version of the lump in the throat. *Crying during an argument equals losing.* Another tenet. She tried diplomacy. "Maybe I misinterpreted when you told me I couldn't come to group if I didn't share. But that's something we'll talk about." Lips closed. "Later."

"The first thing . . ." His voice cracked, and his eyes leaped from twinkle to glisten. He pulled a handkerchief out of his white lab coat and blew and wiped whatever he had to. *Crying equals losing.*

She could be magnanimous here. "Dad, listen to me," Janet whispered. "I need you, I need us, to have this conversation later."

He could not. "The first goddamn thing I told you," Samuel

Abrun bellowed, "don't, for God sakes, *do not* get involved with your patients."

"I am so sorry. My mistake," she said. He brightened for as long as it took his daughter's eyes to match her Fuck It—More Black hair. "I thought you meant don't get involved with *my* patients. I didn't realize you meant it literally. Don't get involved with *your* patients."

"You know what I mean."

"Frankly, I don't. I know what you say, but I have no idea what you mean. What is this about? You've helped thousands of people. Thousands. You've changed their lives forever. And the ones you weren't able to help or change either weren't ready or didn't want it."

"What's your point, Janet?"

"My point is, with all these people, why, why is this guy, why is Phil Camp, so important to you?"

"You know," said Abrun, "I could ask you the same thing."

"But I'd have an answer."

"Which is what?"

"He's important to me because I may be in love with him."

Normally, a line like that would cause a conversation scuttle or organ music and a fade-out to a commercial break. Not today. Dr. Samuel Abrun, ground-imploding author of *The Power of "Ow!"*, lightly wagged his right index finger. "I think," he surmised, "he's important to you because you may hate me."

Janet laughed. "I am so glad we didn't wait to have this conversation later."

"Think about it."

"Do I have to? This is beyond demeaning."

"Think about it. You're *(Charlie Rose–type pause)* enraged that I give this time and attention and . . . stuff to so many strangers. Always have been. So, first, you become a psychiatrist and spend your professional life committed to trying to find fault with my theories, my proven theories. Then, when that doesn't succeed in emasculating me, you resort to seducing one of my patients, taking him away as you must feel I have been taken away from you. It's all unconscious, that's why I don't blame you."

Janet realized she had to unlatch her agape mouth first before she could resume talking. "Well," she hissed, "it's a giant relief that you don't blame me. So, let me ease your mind, Dad. I don't blame you for coming up with the kind of probing psychiatric insight into your own daughter that could only be achieved after reading half an article in *Cosmo* and sitting through a Dr. Phil lecture at the Learning Annex."

Abrun tried to stifle his laugh. He couldn't.

"You know why I became a psychiatrist?" Janet went on. "It was because I wanted to augment the work you did. You're the one who saw it as a threat."

"Well, I guess one woman's augmentation is another's nitpicking and deconstructing," he said. "And I am not threatened by you or anyone else in the medical establishment!"

"By all means, reduce my years of research to nitpicking."

"Nitpicking! That I place too much emphasis on rage, not enough on sadness and shame and guilt. Not enough about the 'Symptom Imperative.' I know, I know. I've heard it. But the point is *(finger wag) you* place too little emphasis on rage. That's your protection."

"What do I need to protect?"

"Your rage against me, of course!"

"Dad, you're out of your element here."

He started chuckling. Bad sign. "Sweetheart, I invented that element."

"Whoa."

"You're afraid if you ever felt that rage, if you ever let it come to the surface, you might—"

"Dad, I'm begging you."

"—kill me."

Abrun added a nod to his chuckle as Janet walked around him and opened the door to her office.

"Dad, you have to go now. Before I kill you."

"You're not listening."

"So, kill me."

Abrun started to walk out, turned back and reached up to touch his daughter's cheek. "Professional favor, Dr. Abrun-Fitzgerald?"

"What?"

He twinkled, but respectfully. "Can you at least stay away from Phil Camp until he's better? Until we're done?"

Janet gave her father a formidable hug. "Dad," she whispered in his ear, "I am not anyone else in the medical establishment. I am your daughter. I love you. And while we're setting the record straight, your patient seduced me. And I believe it was quite conscious. Quite conscious. So, your issue is with him. Take it up with him."

"I have," he choked out.

"I know. One other thing. That was some reaction by you just now when I said I might be in love. Let me tell you what that means. It means I'm happy. It would be great if you had acknowledged it, but I guess that was too much to ask. You were a little distracted. You think I'm going away. I'm not . . ."

She broke the hug, looked down and turned him quickly toward the door. She knew he was crying. She didn't want to see it. *Crying equals losing.*

16

She wore a bright red dress that was much too flashy for this time of night or year. Satiny, floor-length, cinched at her enviable waist. And on her shoulders, hints of straps that aspired to angel hair. It was clear she had taken a long time with her makeup. Enough so he'd notice. Who couldn't? She giggled all through dinner when she wasn't talking. It took her an hour and a half to finish her steak. She'd take a bite, then remember something that had happened in the last month that she had forgotten to tell him or had already told him and just had to tell him again. And plans? Man, she had a lot of plans. Who could have this many plans? Three times, she pretended to read the wine list, then held up her hand to signal the waiter. Three times, Phil laughed, then shook his head and waved the guy off. Instead, he let her order the pear tart flambé for dessert, with just enough burnt-off brandy to fall safely in between celebration and misdemeanor.

"You know, I was worried we wouldn't see each other anymore," she said, accusing him with a forkful of pear. "But I knew the best thing to do was give you time."

"When did you get so smart?"

"I've been smart since I was twelve. You just didn't notice it until recently. Typical man."

"Can you ever forgive me, Elly?"

Elly Vogelbaum nudged him neighborly. "Bring me back here every year until I go to college," she said, "and all is forgotten."

"Done."

She nudged him again. "And buy a calendar that works."

"Oh right," Phil winced. He bowed his head, then moved the candle from the center of the table to just north of the pear tart. "Happy incredibly belated sixteenth birthday, Elly."

Shortly after his endorphin-sponsored proposal to Janet Abrun-Fitzgerald, Phil Camp had scrambled across the hall, pounded on the Vogelbaums' door, and invited Elly into the hall to kick a soccer ball with him. Until the onset of all this psychosomania, kicking a soccer ball in the hall had been the overwhelming extent of their relationship. *Thwop . . . thwop . . . "Good one . . ." "Watch this . . ." Thwop . . .* Monday to Friday, 4 to 5 P.M., or 7 to 8 P.M., or until someone on the twenty-fourth floor opened a door and asked how much longer. This time, they kicked for ten minutes and he felt the wind of the last ten months and two hours. Phil put his hands on his knees and trapped Elly's last solid cross with his flexed foot. His left flexed foot.

"I think I owe you a nice dinner," he had said.

"At least."

"You free tonight?"

"Nice dinner?"

"Oh, I don't know," he said. "Depends if you think the Four Seasons is nice."

Elly squealed and raced back into the apartment. Moments later, she came back into the hall, a cell phone six inches from her glum ear. She handed it to Phil and mouthed, "Guess who . . ."

God must have picked this day to bestow upon Phil insight, his legs back and the brief ability to say exactly the right thing to any subset of single woman. Janet, Elly, Wendy Vogelbaum.

"Wendy? It's your favorite putz from across the hall. No, the other hall . . . Wendy, tell me exactly what you need me to do for you to make this happen. Exactly what you need . . . You . . . Okay. No problem. Anything else you need from me, you need to let me know." He put his hand over the phone and mouthed "tomorrow?" and Elly jumped six times. So, yes.

Wendy Vogelbaum, single working victim, would never admit Phil was doing her a favor, but taking her daughter to dinner freed her apartment to host the monthly meeting of the women's goals group she belonged to. The idea of the group, called "Ch-ch-ch-ch-Changes," was for the six women in various Draconian stages of marriage and nonmarriage to meet once a month and discuss specific goals for their lives—career, intellectual, spiritual, philan-thropic, financial, recreational—in a supportive setting, but whose only real goal was to make it through two hours without redrawing plans for the vaporization of all men over twenty-five. Without Elly and her unbittered ears, "Ch-ch-ch-ch-Changes" would be able to discourse, and drink, freely. So, tomorrow. Have her back by nine. School night. House rules.

Phil came a-calling at five forty-five (Wendy did not get home until after six), bearing miniature roses and a box of ginger Altoids from the deli around the corner. Elly had little time for the roses and was more impressed with the Altoids. "Ginger! My mom loves these. How did you know?" "Lucky guess," he had said. Which was much more tactful than *"How did I know? You mean, other than every time I knock on your door, I hear a tin clicking and your mom snarling at me, smelling like a Zinfandel snap?"*

Phil had thrown on a tie at the last minute because he wanted to look more like a chaperone and less like a scoutmaster. He wore the one suit that still forgave him enough to fit after a year of only pool-running for exercise. It worked. He felt almost forgiven.

He suggested that Elly put the roses in water before they leave, but the fifteen-, no, sixteen-year-old was a lap ahead of him. Flash-ing her carefully-mascaraed and shadowed eyes, she said, "Let's put these in the fridge and say they're for Mom. That way, she won't be pissed off at me for wearing her earrings, or this dress."

Her syntax indicated that the dress may have also belonged to Wendy, but in what decade?

"You like this?" she hoped. "I was a bridesmaid for my cousin, Merri, last December. I knew I could wear it again."

"And you got to," said Phil.

"Like it?" Again.

"Elly, how did you know that red is my absolute favorite color?"

"I knew," she said. "The red pens you always use."

I do always use red pens! Sixteen-year-old girl, and Phil Camp was completely overmatched. And that hadn't changed even now, as he was sticking his American Express card in the leatherette check caddy. "We still have an hour before you have to be back," Phil said. "Wanna walk to the front of the park?"

"Nah, here's what we'll do," she said. "I mean, here's what I'd like to do, and I know you'll want to help me out."

"Elly . . ."

"And when I tell you, I know you'll get it." You see? Overmatched.

"Do I have a choice?" said Phil, and then, not waiting, "Of course, I don't."

She tossed her napkin on the table. "Great. It's very simple. I want us to take a cab up to Seventy-seventh and Park. Jake Linder lives there. He is kind of my boyfriend. He just had knee surgery and is resting at home. Serious. He tore his ACLU."

To his credit, Phil gave a concerned grimace, and did not say, *Tore his ACLU? Whew, that's tough. I believe the recovery period is usually a year, then three years of appeals . . .*

"ACL, huh? Whew, that's tough."

"Yeah. I texted him and said I would stop by and see him, but I didn't tell about the dress." Elly wiped her hands with the napkin. "Phil, I want him to see me in this dress. You can understand that, can't you?"

"You know what? I can!"

"That's all," she said. "We walk in, which is much less weird than me walking in alone in this dress. We say hi. We chat. We're back by nine, and I should be fighting with my mom by nine-thirty."

"Sounds like a plan." The waiter slid the check caddy onto the corner of the table. Phil signed, then stood up and acted as if he were walking away. He looked back at Elly. "Can you take care of the tip? Sixty should do it." She dropped her jaw in real fright, saw him smile and point, then did the bored eye roll/half-laugh. It had taken just over two hours for Elly to let herself be just over sixteen.

"You're gonna like Jake," she said, as he stuffed some bills inside the check caddy. "He's an athlete. You know, like you used to be."

"Ow."

"And he's cool."

"Like I used to be?"

"Oh no," as she led Phil outside, "you're still cool. Cooler since you shaved that creepy beard."

I did shave that creepy beard! Overmatched, but slightly strutting. Oh, screw that false modesty. Not "slightly" at all. The strut was still there, with equal weight on both legs. And the agony of the last ten-plus months now coursed somewhere through the Manhattan sewage system, riding a makeshift raft of Phil's beard clippings.

They walked to Lexington and Elly ducked into the Staples there and bought a five-pack of blank CD-ROMs to make the stop at Jake Linder's look like an errand. It was just after eight when they were motioned onto the white-glove-operated elevator at 853 Park. Next stop, nineteenth and twentieth floors. The Linder residence.

Bruce Linder was the founder and CEEverything of Linderlines, the second-largest fleet of buses and ambulances in the five boroughs. That evening, he was six miles upriver in his Yankee Stadium box seats, ten rows behind Giuliani, watching a crucial late-April tilt between the Yankees and Athletics. Jaycee Linder, CEO of Bruce Linder, was at the 92nd Street Y, watching Mitch Albom interview Michael Chabon, or the other way around. (Or maybe it was Peter Kaplan interviewing a panel of authors, all named Jonathan. Or David Remnick interviewing David Foster Wallace. Or Dee Wallace-Stone. Or Robert Stone. Something like that.) The two oldest children, Nick and Noreen, were away at Berkeley and Bampf, respectively. The maid was off. The cook never answered the door.

"Little help, Orestes?" the voice came over the call box. "I'm in the playroom."

The white-gloved elevator guy locked his cab and guided Phil and Elly through a massive hall and what anyone could have mistaken for the playroom into what should have been the playroom, and was.

Jake Linder muted the Yankee game and spun his wheelchair around in time to see an eager flood of red, like a rolling loose bolt of Valentine's Day textile, devouring the floor. Elly stopped to do a giggling curtsy.

"Wow," Jake said.

"I was hoping you'd say that."

He looked past her, just for a second. "Mr. Camp?"

"Phil. Hi, Jake." The kid was handsome, wiry, and polite. What girl wouldn't be in a rush to see him?

"You got to take her out looking like this? That's not fair."

"No, it's not," said Phil. "That's why I'm going to go into that other room and stare at your books and let you two visit."

"I told you he was cool," said Elly.

The library was on the other side of the hall. Normally, this was an ideal pastime for Phil. Looking at titles and scolding himself for all he hadn't read, of how unquenched the allegedly thirsty could be, before seizing upon some familiar volume—a Roth, a Dinesen, a Jong—and pronouncing himself "not so bad." And once judged "not so bad," then he could get down to the real business, judging those whose library it was, deciding how many books the owners had actually read. How many *ex libris* were *libres recta*. They never fared well. You can go sit through Michael Chabon or anyone named Jonathan all you want. It don't count as a read. Which makes your library just bound wallpaper. Decor masquerading as literature. *White Fang* Shui.

Tonight, though, it was just a halfhearted scan of cloth and leather and embossed gold-spine type. Nothing in the way of gratuitous self-negation followed by even more gratuitous disdain bubbled to the surface. How could it? Phil Camp was standing, his clean-shaven face with nothing to reflect in, his pain scattered, his weight-bearing (it bears repeating) equally distributed on both feet. Equally. You could look it up.

And if that wasn't enough of a distraction, he kept looking back in the direction of the playroom with one drumming thought: *What parents leave their son alone just out of the hospital?*

"You can come back now, Phil!" Elly yelled. They had been alone maybe ten minutes. Her heels impatiently clicked on the floor toward him. "He wants to meet you."

"You're done already?"

"Yeah. We'll see each other tomorrow at school," her voice lowered and she grabbed his elbow. "I got the 'You really look hot' twice from him. I'm done." She took him elbow-first back to the playroom. The game was unmuted. As they crossed the hall, a new thought replaced *What parents leave their son alone just out of the hospital?* The thought was, *What father leaves a daughter like this?*

Jake Linder lounged in a Fieldston Lacrosse T-shirt three sizes too big. Despite the wheelchair, there was not an ounce of self-pity on him. "I'm sorry you didn't get to meet my dad. He's a big fan of Marty Fleck. I mean, you."

Phil fake-furrowed his eyebrows at Elly.

"Jake!"

"Was I not supposed to say that?"

"No, that's fine. It's good not to have secrets." Phil saw the angle of elevation on Jake's leg and asked a question whose answer he already knew. "How bad is the knee?"

"Whole deal. Tore the ACL. Friggin' jackpot."

"What's that, eight months?"

"Yeah." Jake was surprised. "I thought it was a year. How'd you know eight months?"

"In another lifetime, I was a sportswriter. Don't worry. Rehab will keep you busy. The time will fly once you're out of the chair. You'll be back playing lacrosse next season."

Jake began to darken for the first time. "Oh no. I'm fucking done with lacrosse."

"I'm sorry," said Phil. "I just assumed because of the T-shirt . . ."

The kid tried to smile, but he wasn't old enough or hypocritical enough to hide how he felt. "The T-shirt is to remind me."

"Jake is a great soccer player, and an awesome wrestler," said Elly. "Awesome. You should sue that asshole."

"Ells . . ."

"So," Phil said, "the thing you're really pissed off about is missing next wrestling season."

"Yeah," Jake whispered as he turned toward the TV. "Jesus, Giambi looks terrible."

"Tough going off the 'roids," Phil said. "If he gets any thinner, he's going to have to change his name to Jason Giambi-Hilton."

The kid laughed. Hard. Which made Elly laugh. Which made her say, "Even I got that." Which made everybody laugh longer.

"Jake, tell him what happened. You should sue—"

"You have time for the story, Phil?"

"Sure." They'd be back at the apartment late, after nine, and between that and Elly's outfit, they'd both take a beating from Wendy Vogelbaum. But what was he going to say to this kid? *"Nah. Save it. You'd probably rather be stuck here alone waiting for your parents to give a shit."* "Sure," he said. "Where are we going?" Elly lowered herself cross-legged next to the wheelchair, to sit under her red tarpaulin of a dress. Phil let himself be swallowed by a leather couch. The TV was turned off.

"Last fall, I made the varsity soccer team at Fieldston, but I was mostly a practice player. That was fine with me. We ran a lot. The coach is like a Marine. He thinks he's a Marine. Coach Dunholm."

"Coach Assholm," Elly said.

"Is that yours?" said Phil. She blushed into her dress. Jake continued.

"Coach Dunholm is also the lacrosse coach and the assistant athletic director. He's been there forever. He's got a brush cut and calls all the players 'Miss' and 'she' and 'girls.' Stuff like that."

"A real modern thinker."

"Yeah," Jake smirked. "It never bothered me because I was just using soccer to run and play a real team sport. Good guys. But for me, wrestling is the bomb. I mean, you're on a team, but you know, it's not, you know . . . Okay, so this past winter, I wrestled at 127. And I'm kind of kicking ass. I lost one match all year, to this guy from Horace Mann, Gisser, but I know I'll see him in the regionals at the end of the season.

"Every week, Coach Dunholm shows up to our practices and asks me about coming out for lacrosse. I tell him I'm not interested, but he won't take no. He goes, 'All your soccer pals will be there—Miss Wynn, Miss McLoughlin, Miss Shapiro, Miss Singer—and I need another girl I can develop.' I don't even know how to do the basic shit with the stick. I keep saying no, but he stays on me.

"Okay, so our dual meet season is over and I go to the regionals. It's all private schools. Up at Albany Academy. I make it to the finals against Gisser, but I have to default because I twisted my knee in the semis. Stupid. I was way ahead of this kid from Fairfield Prep and I tried for a fireman's carry and didn't plant right. I twisted my knee. It hurt like a bitch and the trainer up there told me not to chance it and get an MRI when I got back to the city.

"I couldn't schedule the MRI for a week and my knee began to feel better after doing the ice, heat, and rest for a few days. Four days. On the fifth day, I decided to get on the bike and see how that would feel. I was just starting to test it when Coach Dunholm walked into the cardio room. He asked me why I wasn't dressed for lacrosse practice. I told him about my knee and the MRI in two days. He took me into the trainer's room, put me up on the table, and moved my leg in a few directions, to test the range of motion. Then he rocked it back and forth and tapped on a bone just under the kneecap. 'Does that hurt?' he said. 'Yeah,' I said. 'It sure does.' 'Well, that's your problem,' he says. 'It's your Osmond's Ladder.'"

"Osgood Schlatter?" said Phil.

"That's it. 'You have Osgood Schlatter knee. That's why this bone protrudes like this,' he says. And there's the bone, sticking out after he rocked my leg. And he goes on. 'This is very common with sixteen-year-olds. It's a growth thing, like teenage tendonitis.' Said I had 'activated it' when I twisted my knee. Then he says the team is running light drills outside in a half hour. I told him I'd rather wait until after the MRI, but he did the 'Miss Linder' thing."

"So, you went to practice," Phil said as Jake nodded. "And it wasn't light drills. They were hitting. *Oy*."

"No! No hitting. I didn't know what I was doing. The first time I started cradling, and I dropped my stick. It must have bounced up, and somehow, my legs got tangled up in it. And then I heard a pop.

"They took me to the emergency room. The orthopedist there told me I had a third-degree sprain of the ACL, a complete tear, and a first-degree sprain of the meniscus, which is a slight tear. Slight. The meniscus injury was from the original twist, and that's usually nothing. The worst is you have to take it easy for a month. But I didn't and I went out and had this, uh, lacrosse accident, it's now a year. A fucking year." He scrunched his nose, as if that would turn off what was welling up in his eyes. "I won't be able to wrestle again until senior year. All because I let myself get bullied and misdiagnosed by that asshole."

You want to be a hero. You want to say something so uplifting that it turns an AME pastor's head and can galvanize spirits and joints alike. But Phil Camp's emotional circuitry rerouted a torrent of cold sweat at the utterance of the word "misdiagnosed." Fixed fast in the gravity of someone else's real affliction, Phil suffered his most recent psychosetback—a throbbing bolt of sympathetic spasm to his left knee, the emphatic realization that he had no words to offer and that he would not make it all better for Jake just by listening. It was too familiar, as his puddling shirt confirmed. He had nothing to say. So, he said what people, nonheroes, say.

"Did he say anything?"

"Who?"

"Dunholm."

Jake sniffed. "He said something like, 'Now you can get your MRI.' That's all I remember. I was in a lot of pain."

"You should sue him," said Elly.

"We should go," Phil roused himself from the couch. His knee was now fine. Of course, it was. *Say something!* He walked over to the wheelchair and shook Jake's hand. "I'm glad you told me this story. A similar thing happened to my brother, which I'll tell you about another time. It's not important right now. Let yourself get better. Attack your rehab. Nothing defines an athlete like the way he handles rehabbing an injury. And you are an athlete."

Jake smiled and Phil's sweat stopped flopping. "You're a wrestler," he went on, "be a wrestler. Your next season will be senior year, but that season begins with recovering from this, which will start soon enough, and you'll hate rehab worse than two hours of shooting takedowns in an unventilated room or starving yourself to make weight. Until then, help out and be active with the team."

"That's what I was thinking about."

"I knew it. Great." Phil put his hand out to help Elly and her dress struggle to their feet, an irony which was not lost on him. "And as for Dunholm," Phil paused and decided he might as well try. He tapped Jake's bad leg. "This is a gift. I know it doesn't seem like it, but it is. You never have to play for this guy again, you never have to pay attention to this guy again." He inhaled sharply to prevent his voice from gulping. "And . . . if you heal right, completely, and you will, you'll never let yourself be talked into anything this important again."

Phil looked at his watch—nine-eighteen. "We're screwed, Elly Vogelbaum."

"Is that what happened to your brother?" asked Jake.

"Huh?"

"Your brother. What you said. He healed like that?"

"Yeah. Yeah."

"Wow. You'll tell me the story?"

"Sure," said Phil. And then, to himself, *Sure. When I let myself remember it.* He felt a buzz just above his hip. Like someone had flicked a switch in his gluteus. Shit. Strut begone.

"What does that mean, Phil?" asked Elly.

"What?"

"'When I let myself remember it,'" she and Jake said in unison.

Phil had not said it to himself. Engine room, release the flop sweat.

He smiled weakly. "Forget that. That's just something old people say. I'm aging. No, next time, I'll tell you about it. Until then, let people take care of you." Phil nodded blatantly in the direction of the red dress.

"Thanks, Mr. Camp. Phil. Thanks a lot."

"You going to be okay until your folks get home?"

The kid snorted. "Sure. *Mah nishtanah?*"

Phil and Elly took a second for their nonobservant heads to translate. *Mah nishtanah. "Why is this night different?"* The first line of the Four Questions from the traditional Passover Seder. *Pesach.* Which may have been last week. No, the week before.

Elly waited until they were out on Seventy-seventh Street to pull Phil's arm down and kiss him on the cheek. "Who's better than you?" she said.

"Well, for starters, that kid," he said.

The doorman opened the cab door and Elly climbed in first and furled in her dress like she was coiling a main sheet. Phil took a while before alighting ass-first on the backseat. A while.

"Jesus, Phil," said Elly. "Did your leg fall asleep?"

"Something like that."

"And what's with the sweating?"

He began what he thought was a lie—"Just thinking about running into your mother"—but when the droplets tripled he realized it would pass for the truth. "Aren't you?"

"Nah. We still have twenty blocks and twenty-four floors."

For the first time all night, Elly would be wrong. They turned the corner on Fifty-fourth and she saw the righteous silhouette under the awning, smoke billowing from its head. Luckily, it was real smoke. Sneaking a cigarette with the doorman. Uh-oh. Potential lung disease. The ultimate guilt gambit. *You have disappointed me into cancer. Happy now?* Except her mother didn't look disappointed. And the guy she was smoking with didn't look like the doorman.

"Shit," said Phil, "fucking waiting for me."

"Get over yourself, Phil," Elly said. "She's waiting for me."

Phil rechecked as the taxi pulled up to the awning. "Oh, your mother. I didn't see her. I was talking about the guy smoking. My brother."

The doorman, the actual doorman, opened the cab door on Phil's side. Elly popped out on the left into the still street. Wendy Vogelbaum and Jim McManus broke briefly from their chance nicotine dalliance to look at someone else. At the same time, unrehearsed, they puffed out, "Where the fuck have you been?" Then, again lockstep by syllable, they looked back at each other and said, "You know him/her? How?"

17

Janet had left a couple of unreturned messages on Phil's answering machine. The first one, *"Phil, it's Janet. There's a complete nut job out there doing an uncanny impression of you. Somehow, he got my number and proposed to me yesterday. . . ."* was barely out of her mouth when she recognized it for the *Sex and the City* spec script dialogue it was. She disclaimed the line with the blunt postscript, *"As you can tell, I'm not ready to talk yet."* The second message, recorded around nine, was purposefully lame. No judgment. Those were her words. *"Phil, Janet. This is purposefully lame. You sound like you're ready to talk. I can tell by the quality of your screening. Maybe I'll stop by after work. Wait. (sniff, sniff) I think I smell gas. I'll be right over."*

She took the subway two stops to Fifty-first Street and walked the last three blocks as if she was trying to convince herself that she wasn't in a hurry. She turned the corner, and saw Phil under the awning, bobbing to avoid the animated gestures and raised voices of three people Janet didn't recognize. It looked like the period just before licenses and insurance company numbers get exchanged. It did not look social. Not at all. If it had, Janet would have ducked back onto Lexington and hailed a cab home, jabbing her cell phone until she was able leave a message whose catchy opening ten bars would be *"So, who's the little twat in the red dress?"*

"Phil!" she yelled. All four of them stopped and looked. "Well, this is awkward."

"You have no idea," said Phil. "Everyone, this is Janet Abrun-Fitzgerald. This is my neighbor, Wendy Vogelbaum, her beautiful daughter, Elly, and my brother, Jim McManus."

"Jim McManus, the radio guy?"

"Yeah," gleamed Jim. "Same guy. Abrun like Samuel Abrun?"

Janet fanned herself. "He's mah daddy. . . ."

"Honey, we're a little busy here," barked Wendy.

"It's Janet."

"Oh. Well then, good-bye, Janet. Let's go, Elly." You'd think on that bark, Wendy Vogelbaum would have wheeled and headed in, but she didn't. Instead, she took a step toward Jim while Elly tugged Janet's cardigan and smilingly whispered, "I know who you are."

"That makes one of us," Janet said.

Wendy stubbed her cigarette against the stanchion of a parking ordinance sign. "I have to go be a mother," she told Jim. "But if you finish your business with Phil and then want to finish that pack, knock on my door on your way out."

Phil stood there and watched, grateful that he was, for the moment, the attention of no one. That ended when he felt Elly's arms around his waist and looked up to see Wendy tent-poling her eyebrows in the direction of his brother. The loose translation of which was *Put in a good word for me to your brother and you get to keep your nuts.*

"Happy birthday, Elly. I had a ball," said Phil.

"Thanks, Phil. You're the bomb," she said. "And good night, you guys. It was nice kind of meeting everybody." As they passed the doorman, Elly, skipping backward, blurted, "See, Mom, I knew I could wear this dress again."

"Elevator," Wendy singsonged through clenched teeth. "Wait till we're on the elevator. . . ."

"Jimmy, can you give me a second with Janet?"

"Sure. Regards to your father."

"Regards to Ann Coulter," Janet said.

"Seriously?" said Jim.

"No."

"Because she's a friend."

Janet began refanning herself. "Well then, in that case . . . no."

Phil took Janet back to Lexington, where they just beat the light in an ungainly crosswalk to the southeast corner.

"I see we've returned to the Ratso Rizzo gallop."

"Yeah," said Phil. "Well, it was a nice thirty hours."

"You know how common it is for APS to come and go."

"I know."

"It can do that because there's no structural damage. The brain decides."

"I know, Janet."

"But do you know why I'm telling you this now?"

"To cheer me up?"

"Hell, no!" she smiled. "I'm saying this because I want to know if the marriage proposal is still good, even though you're back to limping."

"The offer is still out there, but do you want damaged goods?"

"I don't, but I don't know anyone's goods that aren't damaged. You should know that, Mr. Put-a-Handle-on-That-Baggage-and-Don't-Leave-It Curbside."

"What?"

"I'm babbling," Janet said. "What's your brother doing here?"

"Fuck if I know."

"He's cute."

"You're babbling again," said Phil.

She hip-checked him. "Maybe if you're jealous, you'll propose."

Phil caught the playful force of the hip-check on his right side, then did a half-fake, half-real stagger to regain his balance. Nothing he hadn't done privately dozens of times in the last year, just maneuvering around his isolation. This time, he was not alone. He looked up to see the concern on Janet's face. She was always pretty. That dark, bold confidence like a rich sauce forever on the stove. But this, this look of concern, was new. It did not flash. It hung, vulnerable and luminous.

"I'm okay," he said. "Are you?"

"Sure." She straightened up. The rich sauce back atop the burner.

Phil kissed her forehead. "I am jealous. But I've already proposed. And I meant it."

"You want my answer?" Janet asked.

"You want to give me your answer standing on Fifty-fourth and Lex with my brother over there waiting to tell me God knows what?"

"Uh, no?"

"I'll see you tomorrow."

"That's what the guy says in the movie before he goes upstairs to bed and gets whacked."

Phil put his hands on her shoulders as she hugged her cardigan. "Great. Now you've ruined the movie." They kissed long enough for Jim not to miss it.

"Thanks for breaking up the scene in front of my building," he said.

Janet hailed a cab. "My pleasure. Wendy seems fun. I haven't had another woman glare at me like that since I won the *Monday Night Football* pool at the Blarney Stone five years ago."

Jim McManus was in an animated discussion about immigration with Ramon the doorman, so he had missed the kiss.

"How long you been going out?"

"Couple months."

"Marriage?"

Phil waited for the elevator to close. "Maybe."

"Abrun's daughter . . ."

"Yeah."

"You know, this ain't gonna cure you, Philly."

"Yeah, I know."

"Well, then," Jim intoned like station identification, "it must be love."

They got off the elevator just in time to see Wendy Vogelbaum, who had clearly been waiting offstage for this cue, walk in front of them on her way back from the garbage chute room, wearing a long T-shirt and bare feet beneath a pair of prizewinning calfs. She feigned embarrassment at being "caught" in such an outfit, then pointed to Jim and pantomimed knocking on her door and smoking. Jim pointed to his brother, now fumbling with the lock, did a watch take, and shrugged. Wendy reached into the neck of her T-shirt, pretended to pull out a good-sized revolver and fired three fake rounds into the general vicinity of Phil's ass. The recoil was slight.

Jim weakly stifled a laugh.

"Wendy," said Phil, his back to her still as he held open the door, "he'll try not to keep me too long."

Phil headed directly for the master bathroom while his half brother retoured his flat, yelling questions that were half-judgment.

"Have you painted since the last time I was here?"

"Has Abrun's daughter seen this place?"

"Is that a wrestling mat?"

"You're aware they make TVs that are much bigger and flatter now, aren't you?"

"Nice oven. When was the last time you used it?"

Phil emerged, rubbing his hands. "I may use it to rest my head in the second after you leave."

"Calm down."

"You want anything to drink?"

"What do you have?"

"Water. Diet Coke. Pineapple juice," Phil said. "I could make you a Vicodin colada."

"You prick."

"I'm trying to experience my repressed anger."

"Uh, that ain't repressed, Philly."

"You got some balls coming here."

Jim McManus exhaled and lowered himself into one of the expensive suede chairs that would have been great for the company his brother no longer had. "Actually, that's why I'm here," he said. "I'm here to talk testicles."

"What?"

"Like maybe when you're in danger of losing your other testicle."

"And again I say, 'What?!?'" said Phil.

"One of the last things you said to me when you called into my show the other day. I asked if you could call back another time and you said something like, 'Sure, another time. Like maybe when you're in danger of losing your other testicle.'"

Phil stood at his desk, his back to the confrontation, pretending to check his e-mail. "I don't recall saying anything like that." He tapped his keyboard unconvincingly. "Doesn't mean I didn't. Of course, I was pretty looped on Vicodin at the time. You remember Vicodin, don't you, Jimmy? For a while, it was one of the four major food groups for you."

"I hadn't thought about it until about twenty seconds ago, when you hit me with the 'Vicodin colada' line, or do you not recall saying that?"

More tapping. "Okay, so I don't recall and you hadn't thought. Great. So, where are we now?"

"Philly, could you turn around, look at me, and sit down?"

Tap tap tap. "Why?"

"Because I'm asking."

Phil turned around, desperate to sit. He was exhausted, vanquished by the unlimited refill of emotions that had written this evening. Elly, the kid Jake, Janet. An evening that was not over. The emancipation of his leg had been brief, thrilling. Freedom from pain. But now, he was back to the day before yesterday—a torso uneasily astride a fixed simmer of discomfort—changed, but back nonetheless. He had no desire anymore to stand. Stand up. Stand by. Stand against. And so, he let his brother see him do what Phil called "the move." He sat on the edge of the couch, then, one hand on the arm, the other on a strong, boxy coffee table, swung himself down to the floor, and rolled one full revolution. Onto The Pad.

Jim waited for him to sit up before he said, "Now that. That move looks familiar. Except your dismount is more fluid."

"I've been doing it longer," Phil said.

"It is a son of a bitch."

"Was that true what you wrote?"

"Where?"

"On the back of Abrun's book."

"That I had to do my show lying on my back? Yeah. Not the entire show. But I could not sit for four hours straight. And I couldn't stand up for more than ten minutes. That left the floor." He eyed The Pad. "But if I'd sprung for the NCAA-approved wrestling mat, hell, I might have done the whole show on the floor. Even though it would have looked rude to the guests."

"And God forbid you be rude to your guests."

"Hey, Philly, I swear. When you made that crack about testicles, my producer and I thought it was a joke. After we went to break, we laughed and I told him it was you, and Matt, my producer, said, 'That was your brother? He really knows how to tease the end of a call.' But I didn't put it together until today."

"What?"

"What," Jim sniffed.

"What? Say it."

"Is that what all this is?"

"All what is?" Phil asked.

"You don't think I appreciate you taking care of me thirty-three fucking years ago when that asshole doctor misdiagnosed me and I got sick and almost lost one of my nads?"

Phil bent both his knees so Jim's view would be obscured from seeing how calm he was on The Pad. "No, Jimmy. I know you appreciated it. You told me so many times. You told me you'd take care of me."

Jim stood up and looked down at his brother, still in his coat and tie from dinner, lying on The Pad with a three-day-old glass of Gatorade next to his head. Too old, like this conversation. Jim swung his left leg over Phil's knees and straddled his brother's chest. He lit a cigarette, took a long drag and before he could exhale, Phil had started coughing. It looked like they were mid-scene in some avant-garde production of *The Odd Couple*.

"So, that's it?" Jim said. "You're in pain, and you want me to take care of you now? Is that it? That's what the visit to the studio and being on hold for hours and all the rest of it is about?"

"No."

"Because if you ever stopped banging his daughter for five seconds to pay attention to what Dr. Abrun writes or says or—what do you mean no?"

Phil waved the smoke away as if the script said *Felix waves smoke away with brief bizarre breaststroke motion*. "I mean no, I don't expect you to take care of me," he said. "How fucking insane do you think I am?"

"Well," said Jim, "if the wrestling mat fits . . ."

That crack suddenly reminded Phil of the wrestling mat Jake Linder would not be on till senior year. He ignored his immobility and complete lack of leverage and tried to kick his knees out to the side and knock Jim over, then spring to his feet and beat the living shit out of him. That was the plan. But the best he could do was mildly jostle his brother, who had four inches and fifty pounds on him. Jim kept his feet, then picked up one, the left, and planted his shoe on Phil's sternum. Nothing painful. Nothing hard. Eighty percent toe, twenty percent heel. Just enough force. The force of a point well taken.

Another drag off the cigarette. Now, they had moved to an avant-garde version of *Sleuth*. "Okay then," Jim said, "what then?"

Phil closed his eyes.

"That won't work, bro. Look, I could kill you right now, and don't think I haven't thought about it. But that is the point. *You* have to think about it. I feel like my family left me three times. My parents, our parents, my wife and kids. Maybe four times . . . *Grandpa*. And it's not just sad. And it's not just about missing them. Sometimes, I've wanted all of them, all of you, back just long enough to hug

them and kiss them and throw them off a building. Both those feelings are in me. *Odi et amo*, pal. I hate and I love. Figure it out. I had
to, or I'd be on that mat lying next to you."

Jim removed his foot and tossed his cigarette into the too-old
liquid next to Phil's head. He straightened his sweater and superfluously smoothed his hair. "Look, if you don't mind, I'm going
to take a run at that overdue snatch across the hall." He started for
the door and turned around. "Hey, you know what? Fuck you. I
don't care if you mind. Maybe I'll finish with her, then go fuck Janet
Abrun-Fitzgibbons, or whatever her name is. Why not? It's good
luck before the wedding, right, Philly? I learned that from you."

Phil opened his eyes and sat up. He hugged his knees, the nearest
reef for him to grab. He could not stand. Who had that kind of time?
He could not speak. He was thirteen and two and forty-five and nineteen and eighty-years-old. And fifteen. And there was his brother.
Larger than life. Well, larger than *his* life. Standing. Leaving. Again.

"I love you, Philly, but I can't help you, you fiancée-fucking piece
of shit. I cannot take care of you now. I cannot protect you—"

"*I don't need you to protect me now!!!*" Phil screamed. "*I needed you
at Shit Creek!*"

"What?"

"Phil from The Creek." He threw himself back on The Pad and
closed his eyes. "Phil from The Creek."

Jim McManus nodded to himself. *Ah. Phil from The Creek.* . . .
Finally, things had been explained to his satisfaction. He looked at
his younger brother, lying on the floor, eyes glued fast by the past,
and as is the gift of any provocative broadcaster, said the next thing
he could think of, and the least thoughtful thing he could say.

"I'm gonna go. You look like you want to be alone."

Phil waited until he heard his apartment door click shut, then
waited however long it took to hear the click from the door across
the hall at the Vogelbaums, before he began to call out, "*Phil from
The Creek . . . Phil from The Creek . . . Phil from The Creek . . .*" It was
a rhythm at first fixed and comforting, but rose to a cadence that
could madly dash to its only destination: momentous sobs.

18

Okay, fellas, one more question and then we gotta catch a flight."

"Have you given up on Pete Falcone?"

"Who asked that?"

"I did."

Joe Torre gave his pissed-off good sport look from behind three bouquets of microphones and lenses. "Jesus," the Yankees manager said, "you look like Phil Camp. But much, much older. Who you writing for?"

"The Watchtower."

With that laugh from Torre, and the sycophantic undertow of chuckles it brought, the postgame press conference broke up and the young harried beat guys from the papers, radio, websites, and cable outlets who had been elbowing Phil for the last forty minutes on their way to Mike Mussina's locker, A-Rod's stool, or Bernie Williams's guitar case now filed past him with nods that only served to bounce the bile in their eyes.

"Pete Falcone?" one writer had the courage to confirm with Phil, "bad Mets pitcher in the late seventies?"

"Yeah. When Torre was managing over there."

"You know," the writer huffed, "we could all say shit like that."

Nine hours after his brother left, Phil had awakened on The Pad, drenched in sweat, and marveled at how good a night's sleep one could get weeping himself into a stupor. And no trips to the bathroom! Zero. Well, sure. Between perspiration, tears, and drool, what fluid was left in him?

While on the john, for the first time in however long (who could keep track anymore?), Phil had called the roll:

No job.

No shrink.

No Samuel Abrun.

No answers.

Midway through, just as the attendees were announcing themselves (*Pain in ass? Here. Pain in neck? Here. Pain in left leg? Here. Pain in knee? Not here. Wait. Here. Lower back? Here. Groin? Here . . .*), Phil's machine had beeped.

"*Mr. Camp, Mr. Walker. They found out I was a day of service short of a pension upgrade and put the ball in my locker at the Big Yard this afternoon. If you feel like spotting tendencies and picking up padding next to Munson, call me.*"

Translation: The AP had no one to cover the rescheduled game at Yankee Stadium that Tuesday afternoon, so Phil's former colleague at the news wire, Glenn Walker, had volunteered. This was how Glenn Walker asked for help. Through oblique sports analogies that only other sportswriters might get. Shit, forget help and forget other sportswriters. This was the way he spoke about anything to anyone. Walker, now an agate editor at the AP, hadn't filed a game story since the breakup of the Soviet Union. He wanted company, and all Phil had to do was gather some postgame quotes. The reference to "Munson" was Thurman Munson's memorialized locker in the Yankee clubhouse. Was Phil interested?

No shrink, no Abrun, no answers, but a job.

In ten years, since his last time there on business, the Yankee clubhouse had reconfigured itself from locker room to a combination Ambassadors' Club lounge and Virgin Records outlet. Rap, salsa, country, and rock collided midair over deliveries of chicken Caesar, wings and biscuits, and arroz con pollo. There was no longer a tray of cold cuts in the middle of the floor for a working stiff off the street to backhand. The money the players made had never rankled Phil. And the only company other than the Yankees involved with bigger contracts these days was Halliburton. But Christ Jesus, $200 million in payroll and you can't spring for some community salami to pick at? Infuriating. Seriously, what's next for these pampered pricks? Turn the Child Lost and Found into a "champagne room" with gratis lap dances?

"Camp, get over here!" Torre screamed and waved.

"Excuse me," said Phil to two sneering radio guys fraying their rotator cuffs trying to stretch their mini-cassette recorders close enough to catch the broken English whispers of Mariano Rivera. He made his way to Torre's office door. *I'm walking well,* he thought.

"Nice hobble," said Torre. "What the fuck are you doing here? Pete Falcone. I almost shit."

"I'm doing a favor for my buddy Walker. Running quotes."

"Walker? AP?"

"Yeah."

"Or AARP?" he winked.

"Joe, would you like me to bring everyone back so they can hear that?"

"Nah." He squeezed Phil's shoulder. Phil figured he'd take a shot. It had been ten years since his last question.

"Jeter came out in the seventh. Half day off?"

"He's had a little back tweak. Went to get some treatment before going to sit on a plane for six hours. It's nothing."

"He's hitting .181."

Joe Torre laughed to clear his throat. "It's May 3, and he's Derek Jeter." Another shoulder squeeze. "Phil. Go home. Take a nap."

Phil dawdled in the clubhouse, watching gym-fit college kids pack and toss duffles into the middle of the floor. He chatted with Kendall, the one security guard he recognized from his last trip here in 1994. Before he left, he walked over to the coveted corner coop of three lockers. Derek Jeter had emerged from the trainer's room after the press had left, and was now getting dressed methodically, as if he had to stop and shoot a layout on his way to Kennedy.

"How's the back?" Phil asked.

"Who are you?"

"Phil Camp. Friend of Joe's."

Jeter looked around to make sure the room was media-free. "Back's fine. Little spasm. I get 'em once in a while in the cold. It's an old injury. Got treatment."

"Yeah, Joe told me." Phil exhaled. "I heard the word 'back' and I had to come over. Look, I'm not a doctor, but I know about this type of thing. I've had it myself. There's nothing wrong with you. It has nothing to do with the cold."

It was May 3, and Derek Jeter looked at Phil with the kind of bemused incredulity he gave a marriage proposal squealed from a box-seated fifteen-year-old. Somehow, Phil translated this look as, *"Please. By all means, continue."*

"Back spasms," Phil went on, "are not caused by any changes in the body's structure or in response to a previous injury. Or by the weather. Back spasms are caused when the brain wants to distract you from what is unconsciously enraging you. There's a book that can explain it better than me. *The Power of 'Ow!'"*

Phil then lowered his voice in an attempt at discretion, but the timbre raced an octave too far, past discretion into creepiness. "Go ahead and laugh." Jeter wasn't laughing. His head was down and he was working some links through a stubborn French cuff. That's where his focus was. That's where it had to be at this moment. All of which was lost on Phil, who leaned in closer. "It's clear there's a lot bothering you. You're furious A-Rod is here. You're furious you have to be supportive of him when you have no support. They've all left. O'Neill, Brosius, Pettite, Don Zimmer. No support. That's what the back represents. Support. Meanwhile, you have to stand up for this $125 million half-a-fag?"

Derek Jeter stood up. "Need a hand, K," he said, then gave a small up-flick of his head as he edged toward the bathroom, which Phil had no choice but to misinterpret as *"You have a point. Thanks for your courage in bringing this to my attention. I'm definitely going to think about this,"* instead of what it was, a signal to Kendall the security guard to gently walk Torre's old friend outside.

"Good to see you, Kendall. I gotta get up to Walker in the box," said Phil, before his voice suddenly became quite strained, the result of a large hand pinching the back of his neck. "Kendall—wha?"

"Mets send you?"

"What?" Phil squeaked. "I'm running quotes for Walker."

They were out in the underpass now. Kendall heard footsteps and took his hand off Phil. "I let you stay here after the other guys left because I know you and we cool, and you go fuck with Jeter like some card-show motherfucker?"

"Fuck with him? I was just talking to him about his back."

"Well, he didn't want to hear it."

"Of course he didn't. They never do." Phil rubbed his neck and raised his voice. "Winfield, Mattingly, Kevin Brown. All the needless surgery."

The clubhouse door opened and Kendall spun and stood in front of Phil as Jeter glided out with Jorge Posada and Alex Rodriguez. A-Rod. Jeter saw Phil and again flicked his head. "Thanks, sir," he said.

"Anytime."

Kendall waited until they were out of sight before turning back to Phil.

"Get out."

"What?" said Phil. "You're telling me that wasn't nice?"

"He's nice to everybody! He calls me 'sir'! That boy is pissed."

"Oh, for Christ sake, Kendall, what do you know? See you in ten years."

Phil started walking toward the elevator that would take him to the press room. Four strides in, he felt a sharp pain in his ass. Different. And on the right side. It quickened his step and throbbed hard long after he had pressed the call button and regained his limp. He never bothered to stop and look back. He knew what had happened. Kendall had kicked him.

Walker was in the press cafeteria, eating its idea of a turkey sandwich. He was the only member of the print media in the room. He had already shipped his story, and he was clearly basking in his status as the First One Done. Glenn Walker was almost fifteen years removed from the ballpark fray, with barely enough hair for a DNA sample and a belly that demanded to be housed only in sweatpants. He and his wife should have been living in Westchester by now, but he had taken investment advice from a retired umpire and they were still in the West Side walkup. He needed his gall bladder removed and a thing on the inside of his thigh looked at. He had missed Giambi's home run in the fourth, Matsui's diving catch in the sixth, and a pickoff by the Kansas City reliever in the eighth because he was off peeing. But he had beaten the beat guys, all the regular Yankee writers, young and unyoung, who tilted against the windmills of deadlines and replates every day. So what if it was an afternoon game and many of them had to file two stories before hustling to the airport to catch a decidedly noncharter, undoubtedly nondirect flight to Oakland. He had beaten them. Beaten them bad. Beaten them like Secretariat beat Sham at the Belmont, or some other murkier, smirkier Glenn Walker sports analogy.

"You done?" asked Phil.

"Oh yeah," Walker beamed. "For ten minutes."

"You sent it without quotes?"

"Nah. I Durochered the new kid at *Newsday* to give me what he had. Told him if he didn't he wouldn't get to play in the New York–Boston media game at Fenway."

"He's not going to play anyway, is he, Glenn?"

Walker wiped his mouth, then kept his hand to the side. It was the first signal that he was beginning a conversation whose references would need to be footnoted. "Herb Washington," he muttered. Phil thought for a second and remembered. He remembered Herb Washington,[1] and he remembered this was how Glenn Walker communicated.

"So," asked Phil, haplessly fanning through a reporter's notebook, "do you want what I have from Torre?"

Walker stood up and put on the world's oldest living windbreaker. "No, I'm good. I talked to him."

"When?"

"Five minutes ago. He called up here."

"Did he give you the line about Mussina being like a self-cleaning oven?"

"No, we never got to that. We talked about you."

Phil brightened. The effects of Kendall's kick were now a murmured twinge. "Really? Hah! That's great. What did he say?"

"He said if you talk to his players again, he'll have his people in Jersey fix your other leg."

"Was he laughing?"

"He was laughing like Rick Pitino when you ask him about Ping-Pong balls."[2] In other words, no, Torre wasn't laughing. Not at all.

"Did I get you in trouble?"

"Nah. I should thank you," Walker said.

"Why?"

"You stopped before Jeter goes Clubber Lang on you.[3] If that happens, then I'm filing three stories a day for a month. And then there's Tommy Mattola at the arraignment.[4] And then Victor Kiam tells a joke."[5] In other words, thanks for not getting popped and making yourself an item that won't go away.

"Uh, good," said Phil.

"But your career running quotes is over." No analogy given.

"I understand."

Six hours later, as Phil was multitasking (watching *SportsCenter,* making out with Janet, and waiting for the Irish Shrink to return his call), the phone rang. Phil uncharacteristically pounced, not waiting for the machine.

"Hello, Dr. O'Reagan."

"No," said the voice. "Phil, this is Rick Cerrone." Rick Cerrone was PR director for a little outfit called the New York Yankees. Not good. Pete Falcone not good.

"Uh, yeah."

"I got your number from Glenn Walker. Sorry to be calling so late, but we just got into Oakland."

"Uh-huh."

"Jeter wanted me to get in touch with you. I hope I'm delivering this message right. . . ."

Phil's brain gave the order to his leg. *Prepare to buckle.*

"Uh-huh?"

Rick Cerrone continued. "The name of the book? He forgot to write down the name of the book you recommended?"

ENDNOTES

1. Herb Washington was a world-record sprinter who appeared in 104 games for the Oakland As in the early seventies strictly as a pinch runner. Never had an at-bat in the big leagues. Just ran. Claimed he owned a fielder's glove, but no one remembers ever seeing him wear it. That would require remembering who the hell Herb Washington was. Take the people who remember Pete Falcone and divide by a hundred thousand.

2. *Rick Pitino . . . Ping-Pong balls.* A reference to the 1997 NBA Draft lottery, when Pitino, the new coach of the Boston Celtics, had the overwhelming statistical odds to win the lotto-style drawing for the Number 1 and 3 picks and draft Tim Duncan and it really doesn't matter who else. When the pneumatic tube had finished hocking up the balls in order of selection, the Celtics finished with picks Number 3 and 6.

3. Clubber Lang was the volatile fighter played by Mr. T in *Rocky III.*

4. Former Sony president Tommy Mattola was the ex-husband of singer Mariah Carey, Jeter's first high-profile girlfriend.

5. Victor Kiam was the president of Remington and one-time owner of the New England Patriots, who was sued by a female reporter, Lisa Olson, for sexual harassment in 1990 when she claimed three players in various stages of undress accosted her in the locker room. Four months later, just when the story had finally died down, Kiam was videotaped at a banquet telling this joke: "You know what the Iraqis and Lisa Olsen have in common? They've both seen Patriot missiles up close . . ."

19

The Irish Shrink wiped his eyes and blew his nose. He stood up to put his handkerchief back in his pocket and, instead of sitting back in his leather club chair, walked across the room and sat on the couch next to Phil.

"So that," he said, "is Shit Creek?"

"Yeah."

He bowed his kindly white head and leaned in. "Phil, when I say I haven't heard something or don't know what you're referring to, I mean it. I'm not fucking with you. This isn't *Punk'd*." He straightened up, buoyed by his reference, a pop culture analogy less than five years old. "That is the way I am with all of you. I'm flaky, I know, but I'm not delusional. I know all my patients have the same goal: to be former patients."

Paddy O'Reagan patted Phil on the good knee, stood up, and walked back to his club chair. A club of one. "Okay," he said, "we're caught up. Do you want to continue?" And with that, he propped up the side of his face with his open palm and went back to being the Irish Shrink.

Phil looked at the clock that sat atop the rolltop desk. It was always seven minutes fast. He smiled and dropped his head. Two after.

"We don't have time to discuss what I needed to talk about," he said. He wasn't wrong. Between Janet, Abrun, Abrun and Janet, Jim McManus, and Phil from The Creek, he had five minutes left to talk testicles.

"The session begins now. If you want to make it official, you can get up and come in again, but we have another fifty minutes. Our time is not up." And that's why he was the Irish Shrink.

"If I had to get up, walk out, and come back in again, we'd only have ten minutes," said Phil.

The Irish Shrink snorted, then gave a sharp, decidedly non-Freudian intake of air. The only appropriate response.

Paddy O'Reagan had telephoned that morning to say he had a four o'clock open that afternoon. Phil began to apologize for his actions at the end of his last visit, his push-punctuated notice of termination, but the Irish Shrink had said, "Let's save all that for when we see each other. But I will say this: My wife loved that you knocked me down."

"I like this guy," Janet had said over a pre-session pep talk/lunch at Café du Kips Bay when Phil recounted the conversation.

"I like his wife," said Phil.

"Get your own wife, pal."

"Okay. How's August?"

Janet was jabbing the last of her salad. "August? Three-months-from-now August?" She ate the salad to muffle what would have been yelling. "I know you have some things to talk about at four o'clock today with the Celtic therapist or Riverpants or whatever you call him."

"The Irish Shrink," Phil corrected.

"Thank you. But this, *How's August?* has to be Topic One."

"Why?"

Janet had stopped jabbing. "Look, as a forty-seven-year-old single gal with no cats, I am thrilled you want to get married so quickly. As your girlfriend, I am honored and paralyzed by the fact you needed all of half a dozen dates before trying to set a date. As the daughter of Dr. Samuel Abrun, I am giddy but suspicious. As a therapist myself, I'd like to leave my work at the office."

"Said the woman who sleeps under a comforter made of sixty percent down, forty percent *Physicians' Desk Reference*."

Janet laughed the laugh Phil had been dying for the whole meal. "You should write."

"Yeah, I should."

"My point is—"

Phil had interrupted. "I know what it is. You, and everyone who knows about us, all five people, think I think you'll cure me of this nonsense because of who you are. And that's the reason I want to get married. Something like that."

"Exactly like that."

"You know what? At first, I thought that. But it made too much sense. In the same way looking for one explanation for all this makes too much sense. One explanation, like I'm a grandfather. I got thrown into a cesspool. I want to kill my father. I want to kill my brother. Through a third party, I want to contract my mother to kill my father. And I must have decided there must be one solution. But it couldn't be further from reality. The truth is, I'm like this because of a bunch of shit. All buried under shit. Buried alive. And the truth is that it will go away only as the result of a combination of things. Whatever they are. Whatever that is. Whatever 'is' is . . ."

"Uh-huh."

"And speaking of a combination of things," Phil went on, "of all the things I love about you, one of them, and we don't have the rankings yet, is that if I have to continue to hang onto this garbage, this fucking pain, for a while, and I mean *a while*, you, above everyone, will understand that one person cannot cure. Which makes you the only person who, if I limp down the aisle, won't ask why."

Janet Abrun-Fitzgerald took a responsible sip of red wine. A gallon or so less than she would have wanted to take. Her drenched eyes had given her away.

"What about Labor Day?" she asked.

"Four-months-away Labor Day?"

"Yeah."

"My favorite holiday."

"Great," she whispered.

Phil looked around the table and quickly grabbed a discarded napkin ring, which he pushed toward Janet. He wiped his mouth and kissed her.

"Okay, now I have to tell you about the episode with me and Jimmy a million years ago that I'm bringing in this afternoon. . . ."

Janet kissed him completely unprofessionally. "That," she said as she pushed back from his mouth, "is the Irish Shrink's case."

"Okay, then," said the Irish Shrink at 4:57 P.M. (5:04 P.M. on the desk clock), "what are you here for?"

It was the one question Phil couldn't begin to answer. Oh, he could answer it. He just couldn't begin. He wanted to lie on the floor, take a couple of Vicodin, and have it slur out of him with zero monitoring, like some hypnotist's stooge.

"Got any Vicodin on you?"

"Sorry."

"Then I guess this version will have to do." Phil cupped one of his hands. "Do you know what a twisted testicle is?"

"No."

"It's fairly common among boys after puberty. One of your nuts gets twisted or stuck in the wrong part of the scrotum. You need a twenty-minute outpatient procedure to relieve it and you're fine in a week."

"Never heard of this, Phil."

"Well, you're fucking excused, Doc," Phil groused in a raised voice he was not originally in on. "Sorry."

"Go on."

"My brother Jimmy, when he was still my brother Jimmy, was a tremendous athlete. Great football player. Smart. Like Tom Brady. He started at quarterback for the varsity as a sophomore for the last half of the season. And Cabot Hill was a school that had PGs."

"PGs?"

"Postgraduates. Guys who had finished high school and were great athletes, but didn't have the grades to get into the Ivy League or the Little Three."

"Little Three?"

"Williams, Wesleyan, Amherst. So, they came to Cabot Hill and prepped for an extra year. Sophomores rarely made the varsity, let alone started, let alone started at quarterback. I was three years behind Jimmy, but I knew I was going to Cabot Hill after eighth grade. That was always a lock. The summer before eighth grade, when I was thirteen, the same summer we began caddying and the name change and all that shit, around the last week in July, Jimmy started getting sick. He kept telling me one of his balls hurt him from the golf bags banging against it. And he could swear one of them was larger than the other. He showed me. Yeah, I guess so. Then he got a fever and my mom took him to the doctor. Dr. Oates. What a fucking prick."

"And that was when he was diagnosed with the twisted testicle?"

"*No!*" Phil screamed. The Irish Shrink's face was thrown off his palm. "Dr. O'Reagan, you need to let me get through this."

"Okay."

"I think you know how tough that was for me to say."

The Irish Shrink nodded.

Phil turned his head to the side and felt his neck crack. "Dr. Oates, that prick, said Jimmy had epididymitis. A week at home on antibiotics and he'd be fine.

"Fine. . . . A week later he was in bed, hundred-and-three fever, and his ball was the size of a tomato. Only redder. He couldn't get out of bed. And things did not change for almost a month. Under a million blankets. I stayed home and took care of him. All day I would stay in the guest room, putting ice bags on his giant ball, making sandwiches, changing sheets after he'd sweat through them, putting the blankets on, taking them off, changing channels, reading the sports section out loud, cleaning up after him, getting the piss jar."

"The piss jar?"

"It was one of those large-mouth glass jars with 'Ball' embossed in script, but we didn't call it the 'Ball jar' because that made him laugh, and it hurt when he laughed. I don't know how many times a day I had to help him with the piss jar. And this is years before Mel Brooks and *History of the World* and the piss boy. He'd go in the piss jar, and after he'd finish, I'd hold it up and say something like, 'First Prize,' or 'Who wants soup?' or 'You want this or orange juice?' or 'I'm going to pour this in a Mott's bottle and give it to Dad' and he'd laugh and cry and beg me not to make him laugh. But then later, he'd start giggling and say 'How 'bout some soup?' That's when he was awake and not hallucinating."

The Irish Shrink offered his free hand, the international sign for "Go on . . ."

"He had this fever for days and he was on a strong antibiotic, so he would fall asleep and then he'd start screaming. Scare the shit out of me. He'd bolt upright, his eyes would be open, and he'd say shit like, 'Philly, Thomas Jefferson is in bed with me and he won't leave!' And I would say—and I don't know where I came up with this and I don't think I could come up with this now—'Jimmy, I think he just left. I'll lock the door. Why don't you go back to sleep?' And he fell right back to sleep. Which is more than I can say for me. But I got used to it.

"Another time, he fell asleep around ten at night and I stayed up to watch *30/30 Theater*, which ended at eleven. I was about to turn out the light, when Jimmy woke up, jumped out of bed, and started walking toward the bureau. This was about ten days in, when the thing was as large as it would get and he was barely able to get out of bed in the morning when I had to change his sheets. His testicle was so big he could hardly walk bowlegged. So, I was stunned when he got out of bed. He's pulling clothes out of the bureau.

The problem was we were in the guest room, so the drawers of the bureau were filled with sheets and cloth napkins and that kind of spare shit. He's pulling the stuff out. I say, 'Jimmy, what are you doing?' He says, 'Getting ready to go caddying. I hope we don't get Dad.' I thought he was kidding, but then I saw the look on his face. Serious. So, I say, 'Don't you remember? There's an outing in the morning. They're using all carts. We're going out in the afternoon. With the women. Go back to sleep.' And he turned around and waddled back the few feet. That was the farthest he walked in three weeks. He had no recollection of it the next day. He thought it was funny. He cared more about what was on *30/30 Theater*. He was more upset that he'd missed it."

"I'm going to have to interrupt now."

"Okay."

"Two questions. What was *30/30 Theater?*"

"It was just what they called back-to-back episodes of *Sea Hunt* and *Highway Patrol*. We loved it. It ran during the summer on UHF and must have cost them like a nickel. They also ran *Ensign O'Toole* at three in the morning and we would watch that if Jimmy woke up and was thirsty or needed his ice changed."

"I don't remember *Ensign O'Toole*."

"You shouldn't. It ran a year in the early sixties. Dean Jones and Jack Albertson and every episode was called 'Operation Something.' 'Operation Whodunit.' 'Operation Geisha.' That kind of shit. So, Jimmy and I would call lunch 'Operation Tuna Fish' or changing his sheets 'Operation P.U.'"

"How do you remember all this? The TV shows, I mean."

Phil looked quizzically. "Because TV marked my day. Our day. Every day. That's how we got through."

"It's remarkable."

"Not really. Because of Jimmy's condition, we couldn't do anything. We couldn't play games. I would read to him in the morning from the *Globe* sports section. Then we'd kind of wander around with game shows, you know, *Price is Right*, *Joker's Wild*, that kind of stuff. *The Galloping Gourmet* came on at noon, and we loved that because we would be getting hungry and one time a pot blew up in Graham Kerr's face and he yelled 'Dag blast it!!!' and then there was a tape splice and he's in a completely different shirt and tie. We watched the show hoping that would happen again. He'd also always pick the fattest woman in the audience to taste what he made at the end of the show, so that was pretty much a fixed fight. Then, I'd make Jimmy some lunch, which for a while was either consommé or chicken soup without the noodles, while he dozed off, but I'd be back up by one for *All My Children*. That was the highlight of the day."

"A soap opera?"

"Yeah. We got into it big time. Jimmy made me promise to always wake him for *All My Children*."

"Why?"

"We had started watching it during spring vacation as a goof when we both had the flu. We picked it right up. The great thing about soap operas back then was that there were no repeats. It is a dependable constant in people's lives. No wonder they are so popular. I kept watching *All My Children* all through college and well into my time here in New York. I told the AP I could only work at night during the week, because by then I was going twelve-thirty to four Monday to Friday afternoon. I would do that four-bagger on ABC. *Ryan's Hope* to *All My Children* to *One Life to Live* to *General Hospital*. When I started going on the road with the Mets, half the guys on the team watched the soaps."

The Irish Shrink, unbeknown to Phil a longtime Met-hater, wanted to say "That seems about right," but opted for "So, you said *All My Children* was the highlight of the day. . . ."

"Right. Half of it was set at a hospital, and one of the characters was this guy Chuck, who Jimmy could imitate." His chuckle quickly dissolved into softly choked sniffles. "Jimmy would always say what a terrible doctor he was, how he knew nothing about medicine. Yet . . . yet . . . yet at the end, he said Dr. Chuck would have done a better job with him than the fucker Oates. That was at the end, when we found out that he'd been misdiagnosed."

Phil gave a rumbling inhale of snot through his nose, the signal that he was returning to material more easily discussed. "At two was this terrible game show, *The Wizard of Odds*. It was hosted by Alex Trebeck, ten years before he got *Jeopardy*. After the lame theme song, which I can still sing, Alex Trebeck would run out, and the audience would jump up and give him a standing ovation. For no reason. Drove us nuts. After a week, I started screaming, 'Sit down!' and Jimmy laughed, even though it hurt. He loved that. He started doing it with me. We would do it louder and earlier every time. That's all. We never watched the show. We just watched it to see him come out so we could yell. Then, I would switch to the two o'clock movie and hope it was a war movie. If it wasn't, we'd watch *The Big Valley*. No. I'm sorry. It was *Dennis the Menace*, then *The Big Valley*, then *Andy of Mayberry*, which we would whistle the opening theme to, then *The Beverly Hillbillies*, then *Love, American Style*, *Gomer Pyle*, *McHale's Navy*, then it was time to make dinner and he'd fall asleep and I'd wake him up for the Red Sox at seven-thirty. That went until around ten or so, then *30/30 Theater*, which was on the same channel. For the life of me, I can't remember what we watched or what was on during the weekend, except that the Red Sox played in the afternoon."

"What else do you remember?"

"Not a lot."

"Not a lot?" said the Irish Shrink.

"Just changing his ice over and over again. And the sheets. And the piss jar. And he took erythromycin four times a day. For a couple of weeks. So I was responsible for that. Then his fever broke and he slowly got better. Slowly. He could start to eat real food. Tuna fish. And go to the bathroom. I would help him once he got there, but it worked better if he waddled over. Like the night he did the thing about caddying. So, it was like that until he was well enough to see Dr. Oates and we got the news. A month? Five weeks?"

The Irish Shrink leaned in as far as his kindly white head would take him and still be seated. "Phil, I need to reiterate what I said earlier today. That I am not a wise guy. I do not manipulate. I do not ask questions I know the answer to. So, I have to ask, where were your parents in all of this?"

Suddenly, Phil's tone turned to one more suited for deposition-answering. "They were around. My father was looking for work and playing a lot of golf. And my mother was playing a lot of golf. That's what they did during the summer. They were around. They just weren't involved. My dad would come in at night if we were watching the Red Sox and my mom was watching something else downstairs. He would sit on my bed in the guest room for maybe an hour and he would make fun of the Red Sox manager, Eddie Kasko. Every time Kasko came out to make a pitching change or they'd show him in the dugout, he'd say, 'This guy has no idea what he's doing.' That's if he was in a good mood. If he was in a bad mood, which was, I don't know, two-thirds of the time, he would sit on the bed and complain about how he couldn't see anything. The beds in the guest room were at a right angle, an 'L,' and the TV was small, so I put it on the table directly in front of Jimmy and I would sit across the head of my bed and watch that way. When he was asleep, I would move it toward me. But most of the time, this was the setup, and my dad would start in. 'How can you watch like this, Phil? Jimmy has the better view.' Like I said, he'd last about an hour, then say, 'You have no idea what you're doing' and say good night.

"That was the only time I remember seeing him, unless I was up early and made him breakfast. He would have cereal, unless I came down. Then I'd make him eggs and toast. He would keep saying, 'Do you know what you're doing?' and I would say yes. Never said thank you. One time, I complained to Mom, and she said, 'Well, I'm thanking you.'"

"And where was Mom?"

"Mom would get up and be downstairs around nine, when my dad had left for the club or to go look at some real estate thing. She would call me if she needed help putting her golf clubs in the trunk of the Buick. She always thanked me, especially then, because I hadn't bothered Dad about hiring anyone to take care of Jimmy. I guess it was a tough time for my dad. I say that because I would say to her, 'Mom, I'm glad to do it, but it was supposed to be a week and Jimmy's not getting any better.' And she'd say, 'Your father is going through a tough time.' So, that's how I figured that out."

"Did she check in on Jim?"

"Oh, sure. Couple times a day. She wouldn't stay long. She'd bring some juice and say, 'You probably want to sleep,' then leave. And he would have just woken up!" Phil giggled like a thirteen-year-old. His cheeks went McIntosh red and his upper body shook as if he was improperly wired. He held a finger up and vainly tried to throttle it all down. "Hang on . . . Hang on . . . When Jimmy started to get better, I would do Mom. Every time, I mean every time, I brought him some food, whatever time of day, I would lay it down and whisper, 'You probably want to sleep' and really exaggerate tiptoeing out and closing the door. He loved that. The only thing he liked better was when she would actually do that and leave and we would go nuts. Go crazy."

"Did she ever talk to you about your brother?"

"Of course! As I was loading her clubs into the trunk, she would thank me that they hadn't had to hire anyone to take care of Jimmy. That kind of outlay would have really upset my dad."

"Who kept in touch with the doctor?"

"She would call him once a week, I think, and tell him Jimmy *seemed* to be doing better. How would she know?"

"Did the doctor ever come to your house to look in on your brother?"

Phil's eyes went black as Janet's hair. "Dr. Oates? Now, why would he have done that? Why would he have come to the house of a kid he had obviously fucked up with his diagnosis? Why would he have gone to those lengths? Drive fifteen fucking minutes to possibly give better care to a patient than was currently being provided by a fucking thirteen-year-old. You're a doctor, you tell me."

"Phil—"

"Don't bother. I'll tell you. He knew he fucked up. He would have called attention to the situation if he had showed up. So, he enlisted my mother. Put my mother to work for him, which I have to give him credit for. She was usually busy putting people to work for her. He did that over-the-phone concern thing. Acted like he was doing all he could for Jimmy by listening to her. Totally softened her up. But all he was doing was saving his own ass. Malpractice insurance insurance."

Paddy O'Reagan laughed at the wordplay for a second. A second too long. "How can you be so sure?"

"Because of everything that happened at the end! Christ fucking Jesus, are you going to defend this guy who almost permanently disabled my brother?"

Now it was the Irish Shrink's turn to get angry. "Absolutely not! Oh, for Christ sake, Phil, I asked you a question. How can you be so sure? You want to turn me into Dr. Oates, fine. You want to *do this for real?* Let me know, and we'll go at it. But I think you'd rather answer my question."

Phil wiped his eyes and maybe his nose on his sleeve. "I'm sure, I'm sure because of the way it all came down at the end. After Jimmy's infection went away, it took another week or so for his sack to shrink down to its normal size, and then some. He went to see Dr. Oates in the morning. She took him. I was not allowed to go. I remember it was a Monday because, well, the course at the club was closed on Mondays so they could repair the greens and fairways. The range wasn't closed, and I had the feeling she thought she would get this out of the way and still have the afternoon to go hit some balls." Phil snickered. "Yeah. She had balls to hit." He was not joined by the Irish Shrink, who now knew better.

"So, they get back just after one, and I'm sitting downstairs, watching *All My Children* on the big TV. Jim comes in, sits next to me. I can tell he wanted to watch, so I wait for the commercial. 'How'd it go?' I say. 'One wing to fly,' he says in a fake deep voice. What? That's what this prick Oates had told him. 'Well, my boy, you've got one wing to fly.' Then, he starts laughing. It doesn't hurt him to laugh now. His ball had become the size of a baked bean. And here I am, laughing and crying. Now, *All My Children* comes back on. They're in the hospital. Dr. Joe Martin was talking to Kitty.

'I wish Dr. Joe had been my doctor,' Jimmy says. 'What about Dr. Chuck?' I say, figuring he'll start laughing or do his impression. 'I'll take anyone but that fucking prick Oates. He misdiagnosed me. It wasn't epididymitis. I should have gone to the hospital right away. It's a twenty-minute operation, Philly. Twisted testicle. Twenty-minute operation!' What? 'You're better in a week!' What? 'Now, because of this prick, I get an infection and wind up in bed for five fucking weeks. And I can't play football this year.'"

Phil reached over to the end table and grabbed the box of Kleenex for the first time in the six years he'd been seeing the Irish Shrink. He let himself wail a good six seconds, one for each year of therapy, then whispered, "Don't cry, Jimmy. Don't cry. Sit down, Jimmy. What do you need?" Phil threw the Kleenex box against the rolltop desk, a move that startled the Irish Shrink, who was awaiting softer sobs. "Jimmy stood up, picked up a glass paperweight, and heaved it at the TV. The screen shattered. He jumped up and ran up the stairs while I ran to get the broom. I figured he wanted to be alone. I'm sweeping up the glass when I hear yelling. Mom and Jimmy. My mom is saying, *'Don't be silly. How would it look if we sued a doctor?'* I run to get the vacuum. I don't want to hear this. They're screaming. *'You're ungrateful. You're just being selfish.'* I am plugging in the vacuum. Just before I turn it on, I hear, *'Taken care of me? The only one who has taken care of me is Philly.'* There was noise from the vacuum, but I could still hear them. Crying. Screaming. *'Fuck the both of you. You're both fucking cowards.'*

'Don't you dare talk to me that way. I'm your mother.'

'Well, you suck. Go to the club and take a fucking lesson.'

"I want to run. My brain is screaming 'Run. Run. *Run!*' Why don't I run? I'll tell you why. I am not done vacuuming."

The Irish Shrink nodded. "I believe you, Phil. I believe that's why you didn't run. You took your job seriously."

"Sure, I took the job seriously. But I also liked it. *Go to the club and take a fucking lesson.* That's what he said. What a beautiful line. She didn't have a clue. My mom. Not a fucking clue. She thought I was taking care of Jimmy for her! Or for my dad. Please. I did it for three reasons. Because no one else was going to do it, and because I knew I'd be good at it."

"And the other reason?"

"Because I'm selfish."

"How do you get selfish?"

Phil half-smiled. "The Irish Shrink asks a question he does not know the answer to."

"Hey, that's why I'm the Irish Shrink."

"I am selfish because by taking care of Jimmy I do not have to caddy, which I hate and am not good at. I do not have to spend time with my parents, and yet I get their approval because I am a hero. Instant self-esteem. I save them money and they are free to go about their business, whatever that is. Oh yeah, golf. I watch TV all day, make a meal or two. A dream summer for a thirteen-year-old. It's all good for me."

The Irish Shrink grabbed his pinkie as if there were a fourth point Phil had omitted. "And you get to be with your older brother, who at sixteen would normally be out running after girls."

"That's right! I idolized him. Like I said, it was all good for me. Jim was the one who suffered. There was always some doubt after that as to whether Jimmy would be able to have kids. But he was sixteen and that was far away. But not that far away for me. I think, I think that's when I made the decision not to have kids. Must have been. I feel a little guilty about how much praise I got for taking care of Jimmy. From my mom. But especially from him."

"I'm sure he would have done the same for you."

Phil was under the impression that he had been looking at the Irish Shrink throughout this exchange. And that would have been true, if Paddy O'Reagan had been lying on the floor, with his kindly white head looking up in the space between Phil's Stan Smith Adidas. Such a move is a common victimless act of self-protection, as if the exposure of revelation—in this case Phil copping to his perception of selfishness and guilt—had its own face-yanking gravity.

But as is the case with thinking you're looking at the other person, you're the last to know and the first to correct it. That's why it is victimless. Phil looked up.

"I said," the Irish Shrink said, "I'm sure he would have done the same for you."

Phil's head started to drop again. Started. Maybe two inches. Just far enough for him to turn fifteen. And eighteen.

"Jimmy, where's Shit Creek?"

"Shit Creek is the cesspool that forms on the lower level during the spring, after the river thaws. Why?"

"Nothin'."

"You let me know, Philly."

"Yeah."

"Forget it, Philly. They won't come near you. They know me. It's just talk. I'll take care of you."

"Yeah."

"Listen to me. I'll take care of you. I still owe you for two summers ago."

"Don't say that, Jimmy . . ."

The head went all the way down. The Irish Shrink let Phil have his silence or his screams. There was some time. Not enough, but there was some.

"So that," he said, "was Shit Creek."

Phil nodded. "Never forgave him. Thought I had. I mistook not thinking about it, refusing to look at it, as forgiveness. But I must have thought about it. I know that's why I fucked Mickey. His fiancée. No resistance there. Why take care of him anymore? The next day, I find out they're off getting married and he's not my real brother. His father's not even Jewish! It was as if the assholes who creeked me knew before I did. Years before I did."

"You mentioned about Jim not having children."

Phil pointed. "I know where you're going, but I guess he checked out okay. And he did have three kids."

"Well, two."

"Again, I know where you're going. That's why the Grandpa thing fucked me up. What happened? Was it Mickey joking, now that the two of them were no longer together? And if she was joking, why did she tell Jim?"

"Maybe"—the Irish Shrink was talking a lot, even for him—"maybe, on some level, you thought you were taking care of your brother by giving him a child."

Phil laughed, and startled himself. "You are giving me way too much credit. I was horny. I was drunk. I never got laid. He always got laid. I was angry. I saw his fiancée's tits. She grabbed my dick. There is no unconscious shit here. Selfish."

"How do you get selfish?"

"Do you remember me telling you about the handwriting analyst I saw in the park years ago?"

"Vaguely." The Irish Shrink stood up to rummage through the rolltop desk for that session's notes.

"Dr. O'Reagan, sit down. We're almost out of time," said Phil, playing therapist out of necessity. The Irish Shrink sat down. "The handwriting guy said a lot of things. Mostly about me being stingy."

The Irish Shrink gave a ravenous nod. "Now I remember."

"At the end of the, uh, session, he tells me I had four children. I was, I don't know, twenty-four? I burst out laughing. I said, 'Pal, I'm not married, I've never been married, and I don't want kids.' But then the old guy said, and I hadn't thought about this until now, 'Zey vere eatn.' I said, 'What?' And he said"—Phil was now into a fully formed vague but true Eastern European accent—"'Zey vere eatn. Yu no? Zeh wummon take summthun und zey dizzahpeer.'"

"Phil, I'll be honest. I've never heard that expression."

"Neither have I. Before or since."

"They were eaten . . ." the Irish Shrink mumbled.

Now Phil tapped Paddy O'Reagan on the knee. "You know what?" he said. "Now I'm not sure if he said, "'They were eaten' or 'three were eaten.'"

"Well, then. You know what you have to do."

"No, I don't know." Phil's groin issued a stinging rebuttal. He flinched. "Shit, you mean go see his daughter? Jamie? Come on.

Give me a fucking break. For real? I mean, an old man in the park with a folding chair is hardly a DNA lab."

The Irish Shrink twinkled. "Where there is doubt, there is pain."

"I've heard that. Who said it, Keats?"

"Fellow by the name of Dr. Samuel Abrun."

"Give me a fucking break."

"I'd like to, Phil. I'd really like to. But, you know . . ." And the Irish Shrink tilted his head in the direction of the rolltop desk, then flexed his eyebrows toward the clock.

20

Only the elite clueless would have thought people had gathered so early in the parking lot of the Best Western Kfar Maccabiah, three miles outside of Tel Aviv, for a sporting event or concert. Alcohol consumption was minimal, face-painting nonexistent. And the reading matter was universal. In various stages of tatter, every person had their nose in or ear to *The Power of "Ow!"*

That was your ticket of admission. If you had bought Samuel Abrun's book, just show it at the door and take your seat and receive the free two-hour lecture that had never been given within five blocks of the West Side of Manhattan, let alone fifteen miles from the West Bank. You bought the book, you bought the man. You had not camped out in a parking lot to be convinced by a radical theorist. You were already converted.

Of the tens of thousands who had been transformed by the work of Samuel Abrun, no group was more disproportionately represented than Orthodox Jews. And not just because they could potentially avoid expensive surgery and a lifetime of pain for $14.95.

Okay, maybe that. No, Samuel Abrun, first-generation Italian-American, spoke directly to their Old World–cobbled view of hospitals. Medicine was a noble profession, healing the most honorable pursuit, but the hospital? That was the place you went in and never came out. And now here comes Abrun, this modern-day Dante, giving them specific directions on how to bypass Limbo. And his guide was not Virgil, but Freud. Freud! Mr. Unconscious Hisself. Mr. "It's a Bird, It's a Plane, It's Superego!" Freud: The Misunderstood Jew Jews Love to Misunderstand. All this for $14.95. There is no hero like a bargain hero.

Abrun had been convinced to make the trip by his wife, who had wanted to go to Israel ever since their daughter Janet had gone for two weeks eight years ago and stayed six, and by his accountant, who told him if he gave one talk he could write the whole thing off. The lecture was set up by two of his patients, Sheldon Wilowitz and Josh Aidekman, who jumped at the opportunity to present their back savior in the Homeland like a debutante. "You know, Dr. Abrun," said Josh, a Long Island real estate developer, "just say the word and we could all make some long coin on this venture."

"I'm sure we could," Abrun had said, "but that would make me another scumbag profiteer of the medical establishment."

"Yes." Josh coughed. "Of course."

"Just make sure they've read the book."

"Of course."

"And if they have questions, they should submit them in writing to someone during the lecture."

"Why in writing?"

"Why?" Abrun snapped. "Because with this large a group, one stupid question from a raised hand and I might get cranky. I'll be on vacation. My wife and I will be at the Hotel Daniel and Spa. We'll be paying five hundred dollars a night. I don't want to get cranky."

At least five hundred people wound up being turned away at

the doors of the Best Western Kfar Maccabiah. So, you want to talk cranky? Here's the general assembly. Eight hundred and fifty shoving lottery winners gangwayed in at 10:05 A.M. and were joyously in their seats a full hour and forty minutes before the lecture was scheduled to start. There was one bit of excitement at a quarter to twelve, when four seminar poachers pried open a fire door backstage, walked out from behind the curtain, and set up four lawn chairs in front of the front row. They were received with slightly more rancor than Hamas and quickly dispatched by eight large self-deputized Chassids.

Noon came and went and two maintenance workers walked onstage and removed the podium, setting up a standard microphone and stand in its place. Josh Aidekman emerged and announced that Dr. Abrun had been delayed and should be there within the hour. The grandiose groans lasted as long as it took the self-deputized Chassids to stand up and fold their arms. And then, eight hundred and fifty Jews did what they often do when they unexpectedly have to pass the time in an enclosed space with no natural light. They started singing.

At 1:22 P.M., Sheldon Wilowitz appeared behind the mic. And with the happy voice of a tower-cleared L-1011 pilot, declared, "Ladies and gentlemen, thank you for your patience. And now, to my knowledge making his first appearance outside the United States, the author of *The Power of "Ow!" How the Mind Gives the Body Pain*, Dr. Sa—"

An ovation shook the hall with a whistling, whooping force that tried to turn time back to when the audience had first been touched by *The Power of "Ow!"* or, at the very least, back to 12:01 P.M., the scheduled utterance of Abrun's first words. The din jarred everyone's eyes to stage left. Nobody saw Sheldon finish his introduction and adjust the microphone stand all the way down.

Out came Samuel Abrun. Cheers turned to laughter to exaggerated movie set murmurs then brave applause. And then all three at once. And that's because when out came Samuel Abrun, he made his entrance in a wheelchair, a *wheel*-fucking-*chair*, pushed by a woman too uncomfortable-looking to be anything but his wife.

"Thanks, Martha. Please give a hand to my bride of forty-eight years, Martha." The audience did as it was told. Martha nervously smiled and walked off.

"I'm sure you want an explanation for the wheelchair," Abrun continued. "I wish I could tell you that I was trying to open with a joke and I thought it would get a nice laugh, but the truth is I tried to lift my wife's and my luggage at the airport rather than wait for some help. I did it twice. Once because I'm a fool, and the second time because I'm a damn fool." He waited for his laugh, and got it.

"I guess I must have pulled something." The movie set murmuring was revived.

"Of course, if I had acted like a seventy-three-year-old man rather than thinking I was a thirty-seven-year-old man, I wouldn't have been wheeled out here. But as a wise fool once said, aging is enraging . . ."

Cheers, whooping from the crowd, as if it recognized the first few bars of one of his hit records. Maybe it was a concert.

"If this is a pulled muscle, it will heal in two days. If it's APS, I'll be on my feet by the end of this lecture. But this"—he banged the side of the wheelchair with his wedding band—"doesn't change anything except your vantage point. Actually, I'm only about six inches taller without the chair." Giggles.

"So, are we okay?"

Applause. *My friends, I'll say it clear . . .*

"Okay, Slide Number One . . ." The cover of the book everyone clutched came onto the large screen. "You are here because you have read this book and accepted the diagnosis that Acute Psychogenic Syndrome, APS, and nothing else, is the source of the pain in your back, neck, leg, hip, arm, or shoulder . . ."

I'll state my case, of which I'm certain . . .

Dr. Samuel Abrun had another two hours of talking to do before he could begin his written-off vacation. As always, he hoped to reach those who were suffering needlessly, to snake the plumbing of their unconscious with his words. But this time, he had two additional wishes: that the Vicodin he had swallowed in the car on the way over from the Hotel Daniel would kick in by Slide Number Five, and that none of the 850 in the audience would spot the two ice bags wedged between his and his wheelchair's lower backs.

21

Sandy Collewell's left hand simultaneously met Janet's right hand on the neck of the chardonnay bottle.

"Let me," Sandy offered.

"That's okay," Janet replied. "I've been doing my own pouring since I was six."

Sandy withdrew and instead tilted the basket of focaccia across the table. "No wonder we haven't been able to organize this dinner for two months, Phil. Your time has obviously been accounted for."

"Actually, other than a couple of breakdowns, the calendar has been wide open," Phil said. "I thought it took this long to organize the dinner because the only way you could get it expensed was to wait for the one weekend of the year when Rutledge files a restaurant review."

Don Rutledge stopped buttering. "I gotta file? Shit."

"Relax, Mr. Beard," said Sandy. "You already reviewed this place two years ago. The piece never ran."

Rutledge pushed back his ampleness to look at the cover of the menu. "Montebello. I thought the name sounded familiar. Did I like it?"

"Very much."

"Who was my dinner date?"

The other member of the Collewell party of five, Stan Feigensen, sheepishly raised his hand.

Rutledge laughed. "I guess that would make you Mr. Beard, Stan."

The Marty Fleck Pre-Memorial Day Memorial Dinner, six weeks in the conniving so that Excelsior Publications would pick up the tab, had its first raucous group guffaw only ten minutes into the fray here at Montebello, the venerable Northern Italian ristorante two blocks from Phil's apartment. The actual delay in scheduling had been caused by finding a Friday night the city room could afford to miss both Rutledge and Feigensen, the two most competent news-papermen left at Excelsior and, not coincidentally, Phil's only two male friends there. Rutledge, a long-ago colleague of Phil's from the *News*, had brokered the original talks that brought Marty Fleck to Excelsior. Now sixty-two (114 in newsroom years), Rutledge, who was manual-typewriter reliable with his litigation-eligible remarks, believed the dinner was to celebrate the fact he had gone ninety days without saying the word "fag." The docile Feigensen, two years older, eighty pounds lighter, and fifty decibels lower than Rutledge, had been virtually the only editor of "Baggage Handling," and in its seven-and-a-half-year syndicated run had changed maybe two dozen of Phil's or Marty's words. That made him a good friend.

A different seven-and-a-half-year syndicated run had recently ended for Sandy Collewell as well. In the last few weeks, she had answered her last *"Dear Jew . . ."* letter to Marty Fleck and denied a last media request for the hermit columnist. She had returned to doing actual corporate-type PR work for Excelsior, which meant kissing the ass of less-troubled corporations that still bought print ad space and wining/dining away their unsub-tle threats to take their business to that Internet-web thing the

young people were all yammering about. She deeply resented
this resumption of her job specs, but not nearly as much as she
bristled at Phil's request that morning that she add one more to
tonight's reservation. Phil thought Janet deserved a fraught-free
night out, and a glance at his pre-hobble life, when his repressed
nature was merely quirky.

"It's just going to be a bunch of newspaper talk and inside shit,"
Sandy had said.

"Certainly not from me," said Phil.

"Corporate will be all over my ass about five for dinner."

"I see. . . . So, why don't I pay for Janet and me?"

"Phil, that defeats the whole purpose."

"No it doesn't. It defines the whole purpose! Marty Fleck has
to pay for his own last meal." Phil had clapped his hands over the
speakerphone. "I love it. And as someone in PR, you should love
it, too."

So, Collewell party of five, Collewell party of five, *buona sera* . . .

"I thought I was going to hear newspaper stories," said Janet.

Sandy held up the focaccia in front of Janet's face. "Why don't
we wait until we hear the specials, hon?"

Phil elbowed Rutledge. "Tell the Fallon story."

"I need another drink for the Fallon story."

"You have one right there," Stan Feigensen said.

"It's a long story."

"The Fallon burning-building story?"

"No," Rutledge said. "The one Phil likes."

"The Fallon Dave Zyglewicz story," Phil said.

Stan mumbled, "That is a long story"; then yelled for the first
time ever—"Waiter!"

"John Fallon, the pressman?" said Sandy. "What a character."

"No," Phil said as Janet beamed, "Burt Fallon, the old sportswriter at the *Gazette*."

"Worcester?"

"Schenectady," Rutledge, Stan, and Phil chorused. Janet drained
her chardonnay to avoid whooping.

"Would you like to hear some specials?" the waiter asked.

"Oh yes!" Sandy said.

"Give us five minutes," said Phil. "But in the meantime, we need another bottle of this and double Wild Turkey on the rocks?"

Rutledge pointed at Phil. "You remember how I take my coffee." He rattled the ice in his glass in lieu of clearing his throat. He began his remarks to the table, but was playing directly to Janet, indirectly to Sandy. "Burt Fallon was a classic, bitter old drunk of a sportswriter at the *Gazette*. By the time I came to Albany to work at the *Times-Union*, he had already lost his license six times. So, he couldn't leave the office to go out and cover anything, unless it was five minutes from a bus stop. He lived two blocks from the paper and the guys used to joke that he was saving vacation time up so he would have enough days to ride a bike to the airport. So, he couldn't go anywhere. He was a glorified clerk. He worked four to twelve in the office, taking local results over the phone and loading them in for the composing room with slugs like "Little League Shit.""

"Bowling assholes," Phil interrupted, which received a harmless glare from Rutledge.

"Rim jobs," stage-whispered Stan. The table looked at him. "That was the slug for girls high school basketball. Rim jobs."

The table exploded, led by Rutledge. "That's right!" he said. "Fallon was always pissed off, but one of those guys, as long as he wasn't pissed off at you, it was entertaining. I only met him a couple of times, and it was always, 'How's your pecker?'"

Janet was wiping her eyes for the third time, and was still a couple behind Phil.

"Cheer up," said Rutledge. "Anyway, this is nineteen seventy-three and me, Fallon, and Gus Dougal go to the Armory to see Dave Zyglewicz fight."

Sandy took a high percentage shot. "Gus Dougal, who used to work at the *Post*?"

"Same guy, except back then he was the night slot at the *Gazette*. Tremendous guy, Gus, rest his soul. Big guy. Big drinker himself. He used to call everyone 'Jackson.' Whether he knew your name or not. 'Have a little more chardonnay, Jackson?'" Janet and Sandy dutifully drank.

Phil leaned toward Janet. "Dave Zyglewicz was a local fighter from Albany, who once fought Joe Frazier at the Gar—"

Rutledge put a hand over Phil's mouth. "He lent his face to Frazier for a minute, thirty-six seconds at the Garden in nineteen sixty-nine. . . . Okay, now it's four years later, and Zyglewicz is trying to make a comeback, other than getting his condition upgraded from critical to guarded. He's fighting some lean, fast black kid at the Armory. Zyglewicz's old pal, Fallon, is ringside, filing a story. I'm sitting in the next row with Dougal, a big fight fan, and more important, Fallon's ride back to the paper.

"So, the fight starts. Now, a round is three minutes long, but if you discount the time Zyglewicz was either on his back, getting to his feet, or looking for one of his eyes, that leaves about twenty-two seconds of actual fighting. It was one of those mismatches where when the kid landed a right that sent Zyglewicz's mouthpiece flying out of the ring, everybody thought the same thing: 'Lucky mouthpiece.'

"By the second round, this kid had chased Zyglewicz down and reopened all of Frazier's cuts from four years before and a few new ones of his own. Well, Fallon couldn't take it. As Zyglewicz crumbles for the third or eighth time, Fallon, already with half a bag on, jumps out of his seat and starts to climb into the ring, screaming, 'Stop the fight! Stop the fight!' Halfway up the turnbuckle, he's grabbed around the waist by Dougal. I'm just sitting there watching this. And this is what I love. Dougal has Fallon around the waist and yells, 'Fallon, you asshole. What are you doing? If that spook kills him, you'll make Page One, Jackson!'"

"What happened?" somebody asked.

"What happened? They stopped the fight. Dave Zyglewicz lived, Fallon got canned after he set the men's room on fire rather than take a bus to the Little League World Series, and two years later, Dougal goes to the *New York Post* and starts writing headlines like FOUR DEAD IN MIDTOWN CHOP SPREE."

The waiter returned just as the table pounding ended.

"Are we ready?"

Janet blurted, "I'll take the Midtown Chop Spree."

"Love this broad!" Rutledge coughed. Even Sandy saluted.

"Is there a quieter section of the restaurant, like maybe something on the West Side?" a professional-type voice bellowed behind Phil's suddenly spasming back. Collewell party of five turned. "Oh, hello, Phil," the pro voice condescended.

"Hello, Jim."

"Phil, you remember Wendy from across the hall."

"Uh, yeah. Everyone. This is my neighbor Wendy Vogelbaum, and my brother, Jim."

"You never told me about this place, Phil. And only two blocks away from the building. Wendy and I have been here like six times."

Which would make you my fucking neighbor as well, thought Phil. But instead, in a blaze of boundary setting, he said, "Well, enjoy your meal."

"We always do. Hello, Abrun's daughter." Janet blushed and Jim's eyes batted down to the next broad, Sandy. "This looks like a celebration."

"Celebration/wake," cooed Sandy. "This is the Marty Fleck Memorial Dinner. I'm Sandy Collewell, Phil's old publicist at Excelsior. We were just remem—"

Jim McManus lit up like Karl Rove's Blackberry. "Phil! You didn't tell me!" Phil scowled hard enough for the table to see, but his brother was way ahead of him. "Or you *did* tell me and I forgot. Wow, am I embarrassed. Okay, everybody up. We're going into the back room and the Marty Fleck Memorial Dinner is now on me."

Jim waved at the continental-looking gentleman in the suit who owned or fronted Montebello and gave a demonstrative point to the back. That brought Sandy quickly to her expense account-purged feet. Off the hook for the meal and a shot to flirt with Phil's brother, whose date was at least a size and twenty spinning classes behind her. The waiter lifted Rutledge's double Wild Turkey and he rose with it. Stan Feigensen followed, his natural inclination. The four of them fell in orderly step behind Jim, Wendy, and the continental guy in the suit. It was a thoroughly bloodless commandeering.

Phil and Janet had been sitting against the wall in a banquet. Janet started to slide out. Phil touched her wrist.

"I don't want to do this."

"Phil, I don't think you have a choice."

"Oh, I have a fucking choice."

Janet saw he was serious. Fortunately, she was not yet drunk enough to be annoyed. "I know," she said, "but I know you well enough that it's going to bother you more not to do this."

The continental guy in the suit came back to the banquet. "We're ready for you in the back room, Mr. Fleck."

Janet snorted and Phil pushed the table away hard enough so the continental guy had to move uncontinentally fast to catch it before it toppled over.

"It'll be okay," she said.

Phil stared past her.

"Free meal. Is that anything?" More staring.

"Come on," she bade. "We'll drink his liquor."

The back room at Montebello looked like it hadn't been used for customers since Clemenza's going-away party. Four tables to the right, just off the kitchen, were filled with spare candles, sugar bowls, focaccia baskets, and busboys' well-thumbed glasses of water. By the time Phil had tentatively walked in after Janet, a large round table to the left was encircled with seven chairs and covered in white linen bleached, starched, and ironed to the point where it had gained the properties of a mineral.

(That Phil had walked in "tentatively" was not due to Acute Psychogenic Syndrome. It was the way he chose to walk in. How about that? He did get to make a choice after all.)

Rutledge, reunited with his Wild Turkey, waved his free hand. Everyone, including Janet, was seated, awaiting the guest of honor.

"Phil," Rutledge yelled, "you never told us your brother was Jim McManus."

"Another drink, Don?" yelled Jim from what had become the head of the round table. Everyone laughed. Maybe the guest of honor had been seated.

Jim was shoulder-nudged by Sandy, who was on his right. "He didn't even tell me—and I was his fucking publicist," she said. McManus playfully pulled her glass of wine away and gave it to Wendy, who was on his left. Both women threw their heads back and roared. Phil looked away, toward an at-ease busboy, as if to say, *"Like I need another reason to hate this guy."* The busboy nodded, or looked into the kitchen. But he knew.

"How could you have not told your publicist?" Rutledge demanded.

Phil sat down in between Janet and Stan. It seemed like a quiet spot. "Sandy was Marty Fleck's publicist. And if you remember, Marty did not have a brother. He had two younger sisters."

"Flo and Edie," Jim quickly piped up.

"Hah! That's right! Hah!" Stan Feigensen had reached his word limit for the evening. "Who remembers that? I edited the guy and I forget about the sisters." Now he was babbling.

"I'd love to know how you ever remembered that, Jim," Sandy said.

"I'd love to hear the specials," said Phil.

The waiter began to speak, but the continental guy in the suit stepped in front of him and stole his act. "Tonight, as an appetizer, we have a lovely—"

"We know it's lovely. We know they're all lovely. Ernesto, right?" The continental guy in the suit smoothed his lapel and bowed. Jim didn't wait. "Ernesto, can you have the chef do for seven what he did for Wendy and myself the last time we were here?"

"But of course, Mr. Jim."

"Just knock us out. Any allergies?" Again, he didn't wait. "Just knock us out. Don't be afraid. Tell him it's for my brother."

"Very good."

Ernesto (the guy's name, as it turned out) wheeled and headed back to the kitchen, which left the waiter alone for Wendy to bark, "Zinfandel, *prego!*"

"You see, this way," Jim continued, "we don't waste any time with that," in his whiniest drag voice, "'*What are you having? What are you thinking of having? What do you have it narrowed down to? What is anybody thinking of having? You know what I might try? What might anybody try?*'"

"Fine with me," Rutledge rattled his glass.

"Me, too," echoed Sandy.

"Great," Janet said. "Jim, Jim McManus, I knew I could count on you to liberate us from the burden of choice." Phil conked her knee with his, which she couldn't decide whether to interpret as "thanks," "don't bother," or "now you've done it." Maybe all three. Maybe another glass of chardonnay. . . .

Jim McManus was already laughing. "Janet, you didn't think I'd take over this table and let other people order, did you? What kind of self-respecting demagogue do you take me for?"

Janet wisely opted for "don't bother." "Oh, I'm just cranky because until you showed up, I was taking over the table."

Jim stood up and raised his glass of water. "What do you say we put the focus back where it belongs?" He pointed his water at Phil, the only other person at the table not drinking. "To Marty Fleck, who for nearly eight years did twice a week, every week, what the great columnists, if they're lucky, manage to pull off twice a year—entertain, educate, provoke."

"Here, here!"

"Marty Fleck, who once said organized crime was going to offer a choice of executions: Gangland-style, or the new, spicier Szechuan-style."

"Here, here!"

"Marty Fleck, who when he took on the tobacco companies for pandering to children, said Joe Camel should get a biopsy done on that hump."

"Here, here!"

"Marty Fleck, who brilliantly summarized the Clinton impeachment by writing, 'I'd like Ken Starr to investigate me, because there's a few years during the early eighties where I can't remember anything . . .'"

"Here, here!"

"Marty Fleck, who just last month, when he listed the reasons the Republicans wanted to hold their two thousand and four national convention here in New York City, summed it up in three words: 'Pro-life hookers.'"

"Marty Fleck!"

"Marty Fleck, who playfully, yet deftly called attention to the scandal in the Catholic Church with the example of the fictitious Father Rawlings, who took fifteen children to a Phillies-Mets game, and came back with twenty-three."

"Father Rawlings!" shrieked Janet, who had not missed a toast, and may have added a couple waiting for Jim to finish each citation.

And on they flowed. For the next ten minutes, and ending only with the arrival of the first two appetizers, Jim McManus, off the cuff and on the record, gave close to fifty word-perfect re-creations of culled lines from Phil's column. A Child's Garden of Marty Fleck. He could not have known about the dinner, but the toast he gave was as encyclopedic and reverential as if he'd been contacted by a speaker's bureau two months ago to prepare special material for a small but well-paying corporate gig.

Collewell party of five, now seven, gasped and roared and pounded the round table like they were making a giant pizza. Though the unisoned *here, here!s* subsided around Fleck quote Number Seventeen, it was only because McManus had puddled his audience into weepy subjectification, if there is such a word. And if there isn't, there should be.

Phil was hopelessly tombed in it all. Maybe, maybe he might have remembered half a dozen of his own lines. Mostly, he just sat, slack-jawed, while Janet occasionally slammed into him, nondrink-holding shoulder-first. And on his other side, Stan Feigensen would sporadically murmur, "Can you believe I let that go through?"

There was a slight surcease during the white bean and fennel soup and the beet/goat cheese salad, but that was understandable. The table needed to catch its breath and Jim McManus needed to refuel. The break should have lasted longer, but without a conversational monarchy, this was a group that could not peacefully coexist. With a mouthful of beet, Wendy made the mistake of saying, "Why, Phil, if I had known my neighbor was this talented, I would have been much nicer to you." And Sandy responded, PR-bereft, "Oh, Wendy dear, I'm sure Phil thought you were very nice. You know, for a dyke." Janet yelped, but the tension was not allowed to register. Don Rutledge gleefully unveiled a loud, uncanny catfight hiss, the kind that can only be summoned by the insensitive. Then Jim dropped his fork, looked at Wendy, and said, "Oh my God. I must be a lesbian!" And everyone laughed. And women's wineglasses were refilled. And all was well, because Jim McManus resumed talking.

"*Everyone has their baggage, but if you're gay, you will always have that one extra suitcase to carry. And society will make you carry it.* Do I have that right, Phil?"

"Jimmy, you must. You know my stuff better than me."

"Good," said Jim. "Because while it's unfair and wildly subjective to pick the best thing you ever wrote, I have to say that that one line was the most profound."

"I have to ask," Rutledge had to ask, "how can you, Jim McManus, right-wing nut bar, fucking whacko Bush apologist, and don't get me wrong, I'm a fan."

"I can tell," said Jim.

"I mean, I'm a listener. How can you spend seven years trashing a guy who turns out to be your brother, and yet be more entertained by his stuff than any of us, and remember it better than fucking he does?"

Jim McManus smiled a smile that radio forgot. "Fair question, Don. And I'm only going to explain this once, because much as I'd like it to be, this night is not about me." He looked at Phil and smirked. "My brother is thinking, 'Will I have a chance for rebuttal?'"

McManus had overreached, and he got his first awkward laugh

of the evening. The line was fine, but radio guy that he was, he just hadn't considered the possibility the table would look away from his voice and toward Phil, whose face was writing all the rejoinders he would never commit to paper. He could only utter one. Would it be the right one?

"Phil?" said Janet. The right person had asked. He grinned.

"Jim, as much as I'd like the chance to rebut, this night is not about me." Phil let that new mist of awkwardness linger before out-bombasting, outsincering, outsuckering his broadcaster brother. "It's about Marty Fleck!"

In the stare of that moment, there was a chance for this night to return, however briefly, to a celebration on Phil's terms. So, he pounced with raised glass. "To Marty Fleck!"

"Marty Fleck!" The other glasses were lifted and stayed up in time for the waiter to hand Jim his bottle of light beer. He held it high above his head.

"I remember when you could empty one of those down in four gulps," said Phil.

Jim put the bottle down, then moved it like a chess piece in front of Stan. "That was a long time ago."

"I think I'd like to see that," Wendy slurred.

"Me too," said Rutledge.

"Nah. Then I couldn't answer your question, Don."

Rutledge shrugged. "Who asked a fucking question? Throw it down!" That got a preappetizer laugh.

Jim took a sip of his water. "Let me get through this instead. You were asking about why I can say what I do about my brother. It's all Big-Time Wrestling. Talk radio is about holding your average eight-minute listener to the thirteenth minute and the next commercial spot. You need enemies and villains, sure. And there are plenty out there to rail against. Us against them. The sinners and the haircuts. That's easy. But what really works is when you find an original enemy, and you righteously pound that villain to the point where the eight-minute listener thinks, 'He's either kidding about this obsession, or he's nuts. I'm not sure. Let me hang in.' And then it's after the break, and he's still there, thinking, 'Maybe he'll say something else about this guy. Because if it's a joke, I want to be in on it.' And if you do it correctly, that original enemy becomes your personal property. Your personal villain. And all those other guys on the air, all the other sharks in the pool, stay away. That's when you become the mako that gets to stick more than his fin above the water every once in a while."

Stan and Rutledge cocked their heads.

"I know," Jim nodded to the editors, "too many hack metaphors. Clearly, I am not a writer. Which is my next point. For over seven years, I had the ideal personal villain. Marty Fleck was the perfect combination. A great writer, who twice a week gave me a fount of fresh material far from the mainstream. What does Sun Tzu say?"

"Lift with your legs, not your back?" said Wendy while looking in the wrong direction for the waiter.

Jim twirled his index finger and pointed to Wendy's Zinfindel-essness. "Close, babe. Sun Tzu said, 'Know your enemy.'"

"I thought that was Michael Corleone."

"Never-the-fucking-less . . ." Rutledge said, as Sandy pushed the chardonnay toward Wendy to tide her over.

"My point is," Jim resumed, "that's why I remember every line. Why shouldn't I? Marty Fleck was ultimately writing for me. Twice a week, I opened my newspaper and was handed a funny, provocative twenty-minute segment. So, I let myself be educated by my personal villain. Why would I disrespect someone who was instrumental in shaping my on-air identity? Not only that, someone smart enough to never fight back. So, Marty Fleck never disrespected me. Why would he bother? Why should he bother?"

"Big-Time Wrestling," Phil said.

"You stole my line."

"Some line," Stan mumbled.

"So, you were in on it, Phil?" Sandy asked.

"Of course he was!" snarled Wendy.

"No, he wasn't," Janet said. "Isn't that right, Jim?"

Jim McManus stuck two fingers in his water glass and flicked fake sweat in his face. "Hey, who invited the shrink?" He dabbed his cheeks with his napkin. "Of course he wasn't in on it. Look at him. Does that look like a guy who was in on it?"

Phil dunked most of his left hand into his water and gave his forehead a good splash. "Thanks, bro," he said with mock relief before backhanding his dripping palm to the side of his mouth. "You think they went for it?" he basso-profundoed.

Collewell party of seven had enough time to appreciate the take before the table was encircled by three waiters with six entrees and three vegetables. Phil was stunned by how hungry he was. *Jesus, the guy meant it,* Phil thought. His brother meant it. Son of a bitch. That's when he decided to devour the entire Marty Fleck Memorial Dinner. Feast on the edible, drink in the nonedible.

And so, son of a bitch, Phil let himself be nourished. Everyone ended up saying a few words. None fewer than Wendy, who choked out, "My daughter, Elly," started weeping, and then barked, "Fucking happy now, Phil?"

With just enough detail to season his self-service, Don Rutledge told the story of the night last month when the wrong Marty Fleck column, "The Non-Gentile Cycle," had been e-mailed. Stan Feigensen, clocking in at just under twenty-five seconds, mentioned a line from the second year of Phil's column, when Marty Fleck was imagining himself as Saddam Hussein's publicist: "*Tuesday at eleven, we have the human shield auditions. We need at least a hundred, but don't feel you have to cast the whole thing in one day. If you put that kind of pressure on yourself, you're going to be stuck with people you're not happy with. . . .* ' I was thrilled to be stuck with Marty Fleck," said Stan.

"Jesus, Stan," Rutledge said, "You made me sound like an asshole."

"Too late," chimed Janet, and on that giant laugh, added, "That's my speech. G'night!"

Sandy Collewell was the only person other than Jim who gave her remarks standing up. During her tenure answering Marty Fleck's mail at Excelsior, as if waiting for this night, she had compiled a list of readers' salutations to their favorite columnist. In the interest of time and subjectivity, Sandy read only the top thirty.

Dear Marty Fleck
Dear Farty Meck
Dear Marty Dreck
Dear Mr. Idiot
Dear Nurse Idiot
Attention A-Hole of the Highest Order
Dear Rabbi Fraud
Dear Hackenstein
Dear Asswipenstein
Dear Jamba Jew
Dear Ronco Incredible Space Waster
Dear Funny as Face Cancer
Dear Fleck of Shit in My Morning Coffee
Dear Jew York Review of Kooks
Dear Six Fags over George Michael
Dear George Michael's Liberal Cliché Machine
Dear Mr. Fleck, aka Guy Who Can Blow Me
Dear George Won't
Dear Luckiest Man in the Fucking Universe (and I'm including
    Kelsey Grammar)
Dear Hebe Ho
Dear Metropolitan Diarrhea
Dear Cretins Clearwater Revival
Dear Weasel Tits
Dear Hack Club for Men
Dear Lame Edna
Dear Prick Handling
Dear Faggage Handling
Dear Gaggage Inducing
Dear Barfage Handling
Dear Hemingwaywaythefuckoff

Jim bounced up after Sandy took her sixth bow. He had been the
best kind of emcee; he had seen Sandy take papers out of her bag,
peeked over her plum-suited shoulder, and once he noticed it was

a list rather than a eulogy, he knew she had to be summoned last.

Throughout the meal, his instincts were as measured as the cream-to-brandy ratio in the sauce that covered one of the chicken dishes. While the others chewed, Jim offered more Marty Fleck bon mots, mostly from his celeb journo profiles of dead people. *(Albert Einstein was halfway through his smoked trout when he realized he'd shown up for our second interview without pants. . . . Lady Jane, Britain's nine-day queen, has some advice for Lindsay Lohan: Slow down! . . . Vasco da Gama has been trying to get the attention of a waitress for ten minutes. He needs some cinnamon. "Normally, I would walk into the kitchen and try to find it," he says, "but I'm tired . . .")* And when Jim knew it was fool-hardy to follow Sandy's list with anything funny, he served schmaltz and lauded Phil for his series of columns after September 11, called "Now, It's Everybody's Baggage."

"You notice I laid off you those two weeks," Jim said.

Phil smiled. "I did notice, but I figured you were just waiting to hear if Bush was going to include Marty Fleck in the Axis of Evil."

"Flexis of Evil," mumbled Stan.

"Dear Flexis of Evil . . ." yelled Rutledge.

You know it's a satisfying night out when both the men and women at the table head to the bathroom in shifts, and without coke. As if there are scheduled intermissions. While waiting for coffee and the kind of Italian pastries that can never survive the trip uptown, Sandy, Wendy, and Janet, sudden pals of the grape, camped in the ladies' room long enough to miss the men's room relay of Phil and Stan handing off to Jim and Rutledge.

Jim was already standing when he returned to the table, so Phil hadn't seen how labored Jim's last rise to his feet had been. But he couldn't miss his brother's uneven step to the bathroom. It was familiar. Where had Phil seen that walk before?

Where . . . He could place it. Of course! That walk. Deliberate and flinching. More balk than walk. A few seconds ago. Coming *from* the bathroom. Him. It was the only time in the last two hours that anything had hurt. And the only time this evening he and his brother had been apart.

The girls emerged, all talking and laughing and staggering at once, all trying to get the attention of themselves. They sat next to each other in unassigned chairs and continued making plans that ideally didn't involve daylight or sparkling water. All of them may have said something to Phil. But Phil was occupied with business over his left shoulder. His eyes were fixed on the end of the short hall just before the back room. Montebello's Restroom Row. Waiting for Jim to return. Waiting for his walk back in.

No limp. Other than dessert, it would be the only disappointment of the evening. There was a brief side trip to hand Ernesto his retro green American Express card and wave him off, but no limp. Maybe Jim's foot had fallen asleep. Maybe he was tired. Maybe he had been working on an impression of Phil for his big finale. But no limp now. Jim McManus and his tight-end built, Reaganomics-honed swagger strode into the back room to the only unfilled chair at the table. Next to Phil. Just before he sat down, Jim pulled out his wallet and carefully folded the small piece of paper he'd been staring at when he came out of the bathroom. He placed the wallet on the table, and squeezed Phil's shoulder as he lowered his head down to ear level.

"Nine years without pain," Jim whispered, "and all of a sudden, on the way to the john, my ass starts killing me."

"You okay?"

"Yeah. Just lasted a few seconds. And then I took my medicine."

"What?"

Jim opened his wallet, and dropped the folded piece of paper in front of Phil.

"You got a toast for coffee, McManus?" Rutledge growled. "Jim fucking McManus. I still can't believe you two are brothers."

Jim lifted the nearest cup. "Well, as that visionary cutting-edge genius, Dr. Samuel Abrun said, 'Think the unthinkable.'"

"Great," said Janet. "I can go back to hating you."

On the laugh, Jim took a sip of coffee. Not Montebello's best. He sat down, and pushed the folded piece of paper closer to Phil.

22

Phil waited until Janet was asleep to grab a copy of *Where Can I Stow My Baggage?* from underneath his desk. There were a few paperbacks lying in a dust-primered stack, next to the red, hard foam "Trakshun" neck cradle that looked like either the funniest pair of size 18C tits or a mold of Jennifer Lopez's ass at six months. So, that's where it had been hiding.

He lay down on The Pad and rested his head on the cradle. He started to look for the page where he might find the quote on Jim's folded piece of paper. He really didn't know where to begin. It had been so long since he had looked in his own book. At least eight years. Frankly, he had been surprised that the line seemed familiar at all.

"Why should I know this?" he had asked his brother at Montebello after he unfolded the piece of paper and read.

Sometimes, the only way you can love someone is from far away.

"Why should I know this?"

Jim had begun to laugh and coughed to a stop. "You're serious, aren't you? You should know it because you wrote it."

"Which column?"

"No. It's in your book."

"What page?"

Jim had scooped up the piece of paper and waved across the table to Wendy. "Uh-uh," he said. "This time, you gotta do a little work." He looked back across the table, where Wendy, sot-based, was trying to free herself from being lashed by her purse. "And now, if you'll excuse me, Wendy and I are going to take a two-block cab ride."

The "Trakshun" neck cradle did not help the page-leafing process. So, Phil sat up and flipped quickly, stopping to reminisce on a couple of Jeff Hong's cartoons. Eight years since he had looked in *Where Can I Stow My Baggage?* At least. And he was still embarrassed by this accidental acclaim that had befallen Marty Fleck. Nine years from the initial nova of publication, and Phil still wanted to scream, *"But it was a goof! I just wrote the thing to settle my divorce!"* Even now, that feeling was so fresh it snapped. And the only way the retroactive discomfort might have been greater was if it had been his name on the book instead of Marty Fleck's. But perhaps not. Maybe if it had been his name on the book, Phil Camp would have been forced to get over himself sooner. Or been forced to limp sooner. Or get over his limp sooner. Or . . . Jesus, you want to try and unravel all this? There aren't enough fifty-minute hours in the day.

Instead of perpetuating this fluke of book publishing, the genre which he alternately called Glib Lit or Shelf Help, Phil had decided to take on a column. Another goof? Maybe at first, to protect himself, but the unwritten goal was always to see if he could come up with something that people would read twice a week for a nugget that demanded a little less than complete emotional transformation. A contribution a bit more earnest and nudging than *Where Can I Stow My Baggage?*, the misappropriated musings of an unquestioned, answerless man. And with that, he had set out to make Marty Fleck worthy of the fuss and himself worthy of Marty Fleck. And, stop the vanity presses, it worked. Phil was free to be proud of Marty Fleck's column, to love what he did almost as much as he cherished his anonymous notoriety. He was well-off, well-read, and alone. Who wouldn't be grateful?

Who wouldn't be grateful? Oh, I don't know. How about the guy with the limp who hadn't looked at his work in eight years? It had taken almost a decade, but Phil and his restless brain had found a way to replace the involuntary wince of embedded embarrassment with the compulsory wince of physical distress. Referred pain. *"Well, who referred you, Mr. Camp? Marty Fleck? Oh yes, we know Mr. Fleck. . . ."*

Phil rotated his head clockwise three times and opened to the table of contents.

1. What's My Baggage?
2. How Much Baggage Do I Need?
3. How Much Baggage Will I Claim?
4. Does My Baggage Have the Proper Identification?
5. What Baggage Will I Carry On?
6. Can I Make My Baggage Fit Over My Head or Under My Seat?
7. No? Then What Can I Do Without?
8. Lost Luggage
9. Matching Luggage
10. Anything Else to Declare?

"Who came up with this shit?" he groaned. Then his ass groaned. Phil figured it was talking to him. He listened, and turned to chapter 6.

CHAPTER 6

Can I Make My Baggage Fit Over My Head or Under My Seat?

FAMILY:

I know what you're thinking. I don't, but I need a grabber to open this chapter. So, I thought I would act as if I am clairvoyant. You're thinking, "Marty, it's enough with the family stuff. We get it. How many times do we have to admit that the hand we were dealt in the delivery room was twos and threes and five suits?"

The Mob has the right idea. You angry with someone? Get someone else to kill him. That way, the relationship is over and you didn't really have to get angry. Okay, there's the issue of where to dump the body, but that's just annoying, not infuriating. And it's no longer your baggage, it's now your garbage.

Very few of us are lucky enough to be Made Men or Women, so we are stuck with the people we need to get out of our lives, but can't.

I have been trying to speak for everyone so far, and maybe I still am. But here, on Page 62, I, Marty Fleck, will share with you my two biggest fears.

Nobody is listening to me
Nobody is taking care of me

The fact that you're still reading on Page 62 means you're listening. The fact that you bought this book means you are taking care of me. So, there go my fears, right? More room in the baggage, right? Wrong. Because it's never enough. I can tell you're not listening right now. You want more material about the Mob. You want me to take care of you. And it won't be enough. That does it! You're too needy. I can't talk to you anymore, ———! (Please fill appropriate family member(s) here. Additional space is available in the back.)

Sorry I lost it there. That was not meant for you. And that might be the point.

Sometimes, the only way you can love someone is from far away.

Phil stopped after he read the next line *(Author's Note to Self: Find out if one can be sued for plagiarizing a fortune cookie. . . .)* and tried to remember if indeed he had pocketed that blade of wisdom after some 1 A.M. duck chow fun at Mon Bo. It certainly didn't sound like him. Or Marty Fleck. Not then. Not now. It was much too self-aware. And it takes a relentlessly self-conscious man to recognize that which is too self-aware.

How had this line found its way in there? How could he have possibly come up with a note so unapologetically kind in the middle of this 182-page sonata bravado? From how far away had that notion come? But there it was. There it had landed. For all the mantra-lapping world to see. Phil stared at the line and unbeknown to the rest of Phil, his head started to nod. Son of a bitch.

There was still coffee in the pot from that morning. Good. Old, cold coffee. The fetid fuel of Phil's pen. A few vile swallows propelled him, and for the next twenty minutes, Phil walked around his living room, the paperback of *Where Can I Stow My Baggage?* rolled up tight in his left hand like a program. As he patrolled his home, he alternately whacked himself in the forehead and hip. The left hip. You know what? It felt good. Nothing hurt.

Let's not go nuts here. *Sometimes the only way you can love someone is from far away* is no *Ich bin ein Berliner*. It's not even *Everybody's got a hungry heart*. But there it was. Page 62. Good enough for radio gasbag Jim McManus to write down and fold and carry neareth his ass. But while we're on the subject of nuts, every once in a while the blind squirrel does find the acorn. So, is that what this axiom was, the blind squirrel's acorn, or was there more? Was there more to the book Phil had dismissed? Was there more to Phil?

Phil sat at his desk with the cold coffee and his book, as if that had been the idea all along. He unrolled the paperback and started before Page 1, with the dedication ("To My Wife, if I still had one . . .") and began reading. The goal was to make it to Page 62 and see how he had wound up in his brother's wallet. He made it to forty-something and had to stop. Had he really written *All you have to do is work with people in your office. You don't have to not hate them.* Had he?

Or, *Why be uncomfortable and enclosed when you can get off the elevator at the third floor and walk down the rest of the way? Most times, the company is better.*

Or, *When you cheat, you're only cheating yourself. But if you admit to yourself that you're only cheating yourself, you can probably get away with it.*

Or, *I never met your dad, but I'd believe you if you told me he's an idiot. What choice do I have? He's your dad.*

Some of these lines he recognized and some, like the one reminded by his brother, he was forced to take at his own word. The transition from Phil Camp to Marty Fleck had been neither seamless nor particularly well lit. But for the first time, Phil was able to take credit for all of it. He laughed and nodded and then nodded off. The beep from his computer's e-mail alert roused him. He usually never heard it because his head was accustomed to lying thirty feet away. On The Pad.

There was one new message, from jmcmpg62@aol.com. The subject line read: "Got your address from Sandy Collewell . . . so blame her."

OKAY, BRO, THIS IS IT. SAM ABRUN'S BOOK DID HELP ME WITH MY APS. FOR A WHILE. BUT AFTER A YEAR IT CAME BACK, WORSE THAN EVER. WHENEVER I WOULD TALK TO HIM, HE WOULD SAY I HAD MORE WORK TO DO, OR TRY TO PUSH A VICODIN SCRIP ON ME OR SOME OTHER CONDESCENDING CRUD THAT WOULD DRIVE ME BATSHIT. YOU KNOW HOW THE GUY CAN BE. GOD FORBID YOU DON'T OBEY HIM. THEN ONE DAY, I WAS AT THE BARNES AND NOBLE IN LINCOLN CENTER. THERE WAS YOUR BOOK, RIGHT BY THE CHECKOUT LINE. I PICKED IT UP AND BOTH MY LEGS WENT OUT FROM UNDER ME. I KNEW ENOUGH FROM ABRUN TO THINK, "UH, THIS MIGHT BE SOMETHING."

I READ THE *BAGGAGE* BOOK IN TWO HOURS, BUT BY THE TIME I GOT TO "SOMETIMES, THE ONLY WAY YOU CAN LOVE SOMEONE IS FROM FAR AWAY" I WAS VIRTUALLY OUT OF PAIN. THAT WAS THE LINE WHERE I

NOTICED. ALL THAT I HAD READ BEFORE GOT ME THERE. A COUPLE OTHER PASSAGES AFTER THAT JUMPED UP AND BIT ME, ESPECIALLY THE "SECRETS/LIES" SECTION OF CHAPTER 8 (LOST LUGGAGE), AND THE "APOLOGIES DUE" IN CHAPTER 9 ("MATCHING LUGGAGE"), BUT I'M SURE EVERYONE HAS THEIR FAVORITE HYMNS.

SO GREAT, HUH? I'M CURED. THE PROBLEM WAS I WAS OUT OF PAIN, BUT NOW THE RAGE WAS RIGHT AT THE SURFACE. I MEAN, COME ON. FORGET THAT YOU GOT THE REAL DAD, HOWEVER EQUALLY SHITTY HE WAS TO BOTH OF US. I'M FURIOUS AT YOU FOR SLEEPING WITH MICKEY A MILLION YEARS AGO, I'M EVISCERATED BECAUSE MY FIRST CHILD MIGHT BE YOUR DAUGHTER, I'M ENVIOUS BECAUSE OF YOUR SUCCESS AND I'M INDEBTED TO YOU FOR WRITING THE SILLY LINE THAT CHASED IT ALL OUT OF ME. HOW COULD I POSSIBLY GIVE YOU CREDIT? SO, I GAVE ABRUN A BLURB FOR HIS PAPERBACK AND SQUARED OFF ON THE RADIO AGAINST MARTY FLECK. BIG-TIME WRESTLING. IT SEEMED LIKE THE WAY TO GO. AND IT WAS, UNTIL I SAW YOU LIMPING.

BY THE WAY, IF YOU HAVEN'T FOUND THE PAGE IN YOUR BOOK, MY E-MAIL ADDRESS GIVES IT AWAY. I READ THAT LINE AT LEAST ONCE EVERY DAY. THAT'S HOW IMPORTANT YOUR WORK IS TO ME. I TRIED TO LET YOU KNOW THAT TONIGHT. I HOPE YOU BOUGHT IT.

I'M WRITING THIS ON WENDY'S LAPTOP. SHE PASSED OUT A WHILE AGO. I LIKE HER. . . . DAMN YOU. I WILL TRY TO GIVE YOU A WIDE BERTH IN THE HALL. IF YOU NEED MORE ROOM, LET ME KNOW.
LOVE (FROM FAR AWAY?),
JIMMY

If Phil had been counting, he might have embarrassed himself at how many times he read the e-mail. Fortunately, he just continued to read. *Damn,* he kept thinking, *my brother can write.* That was the only thought safe enough to keep in his head. It was just after one in the morning and he was starving. Duck chow fun starving. Nah. Instead, he would grab the banana Janet was saving for her breakfast and try to make it up to her by kissing her neck when he climbed at a jostling minimum into bed.

He was two bites in when he heard a door close. Across the hall. He looked through the kitchen-door peephole, the clearest line of sight into the hallway, and saw his brother at the elevator. He watched Jim McManus stand there, only pushing the call button once. Once. Friggin' once. Who can be that patient when they're alone? He must get that from his real dad. Just before the cab arrived, Jim turned back toward the door of Wendy Vogelbaum's apartment and blew it a kiss. The elevator opened and Jim paused before stepping in. Why? Nobody was that patient.

Why indeed. As the elevator door low-rumbled back to close, Phil heard another sound out of the cab. A little deeper. A professional voice.

"Good night, Philly."

He thought about running after it, and he smiled. Phil smiled because he knew at that instant that he could.

He knew he could run.

23

If only that roar was the crowd of fifty thousand hearing the news over the public address system that Phil Camp was walking better, rather than the response to Gary Sheffield one-hopping the left-field wall for a sixth-inning RBI double. The blast put the Yankees ahead, 5–4, but Phil missed it. He was still under the stands, in the middle of his first men's room run. Bottom of the sixth, which made it over three hours since the last time he had peed. Over three hours. Somebody run that stat up to Bob Sheppard in the PA booth. *Your attention. Now going. Number One. Camp. Number One. . . .*

Phil emerged from the tunnel and reflexively looked at the right-center field Jumbotron for the replay that he knew would never be shown. Yankee Stadium never showed replays of any Yankee still living. So what? He could imagine what a Sheffield double looked like. But this? This even-plant saunter up the ramp? This was new. He still couldn't envision how it must appear for him to stride and not be noticed. But that? That was this. Phil Camp was walking

better. Had been for the last two months. Ever since the phone call
from the Irish Shrink. No, ever since the trip to Long Island. No,
the phone call.

He skidded nimbly down the short steps in the first-base field
boxes and got back to his seats just in time to see the concessions
waitress drop off the second ungodly load of food to Walker, Elly,
and Jake. With one hand, he gave the woman three twenties, and
with the other unwrapped and steadied a sausage and pepper hero
toward his mouth.

He saw their eyes on him. "Do I know how to throw a bachelor
party for myself, or what?"

"Down in front!" yelled a fat guy in a stress-tested Giambi jersey. Phil waved apologetically, scooted three seats in and plopped
himself next to Glenn Walker with no presetting of the left leg. And
no pain that couldn't be chased by a good play in the field. Or a
well-timed item from the concessions lady. Better. Not a hundred
percent. Not even eighty percent. But better. Better enough to be
hopeful. And hope is a thing with sausage and peppers.

"Are you going the distance on that po' boy, or are you just trying to get your work in?" said Walker. Phil tore the hero in half and
handed it to Walker, who put a giant pretzel around his wrist to free
up his grasp.

"Outstanding."

"Phil, aren't you worried you'll be sick for the wedding?" Elly
Vogelbaum said.

"I'm not worried," Phil smiled. "I'm confident I'll be sick for the
wedding."

Jake Linder, bequeathed the aisle seat by Phil because he was
still on crutches, laughed and clapped, which he had been doing all
night when he wasn't squeezing and kissing Elly. "When I get married, I'm having the exact same kind of bachelor party," he said.

"No you won't," Phil and Walker chorused.

"Yes he will," said Elly, squeezing and kissing Jake.

"So, it will be Jake, two old men, and the hot sixteen-year-old
daughter of his next-door neighbor?" asked Phil.

"Never mind."

Miguel Cairo flew out into the inkiness of a late August night to end the sixth. Jake and Elly split a sundae. Walker caught up in his scorecard with all the plays he'd failed to record while he'd been *in media prandio*. Phil watched the Yankee batboy clear away the accessories from the on-deck circle, which was only four rows away. Forty-seven years old, less than two days from his second marriage, sitting in the best seats he'd ever put his ass-hurtin' and not hurtin'-in. The seats were a wedding gift from a new friend. Fellow named Derek Jeter. Jeter, who had raised his average close to .290 since reading the first thirty pages of *The Power of "Ow!"* had come into the on-deck circle, four rows away, in the bottom of the first, and winked at Phil. The wink was intercepted by Elly, whose face went code red, and misinterpreted by Jake, who said, "Derek, can we focus?" and got a nod from the Yankee shortstop.

The wedding was scheduled for 4 P.M. Thursday. Well, that's the time Phil and Janet would meet at City Hall. It was the only break in Janet's schedule that week. Her redoubtable receptionist, Dana Truax, would serve as her maid of honor and ensure she kept her calendar open. The job of Phil's best man would be assumed by his former therapist, Paddy O'Reagan, hereafter to be known as the Irish Witness.

That's right. Former therapist. Going on two months now. Since the phone call. Which came after the trip to Long Island. And now it was August and Phil Camp was walking better. How much better? Better enough not to wait. So screw it, *You busy next week, Janet? / Next week . . . next week . . . All I got is Thursday at 4 P.M. / Perfect.*

City Hall had always been the only logical venue, given their relative past and parental present. Phil was still skittish over booking any house of worship, and after he told Janet the Trish bomb scare story, so was Janet. And any guest list was rendered irrelevant by the irreversible slide of Phil's Alzheimered parents (who were on different locked floors at a facility outside of Boston called Carlton-Willard) and the steadfast refusal of Samuel Abrun to attend any ceremony, even if the hiatal hernia that had bedridden him for much of the last two months eased up.

Dr. Abrun had been beset with half a dozen ailments since he and his wife had returned from Israel. (The lecture had gone over without incident, if you didn't count one of the Best Western Kfar Maccabiah maintenance workers thinking the puddle made by Abrun's dripping ice bags was the doctor having an accident on stage.) His lower back problems went away for a while, then came back, then went away, but left the door open long enough for heartburn, hypertension, psoriasis, gastritis, and the hiatal hernia to barge in with no intention of just staying the weekend. Abrun went into the office when he could, but he knew he was not the best advertisement to new patients if he couldn't bend over to examine them without groaning, scratching, or farting. Samuel Abrun was able to identify but not lick his own Acute Psychogenic Syndrome, to admit but not banish his self-inflicted wounds. He knew he had it, and he kept insisting the source of the APS was his fury over getting older. When his wife would rub hydrocortisone cream on his arm and suggest that all these problems might, just perhaps, be due to the fact that his daughter was marrying a former patient, he'd pop a Zantac and toast her with a glass of water. "Nice try, my bride," Abrun would say. "But this conversation is one genius short. Take it from the man who said 'aging is enraging.' That's all this is."

And just to prove what a good sport he was, he had thanked Janet the last time she stopped by the house in Larchmont and gave her a copy of *Where Can I Stow My Baggage?* He was surprised to learn that Phil and Marty Fleck were the same person, and wondered if he would have willingly treated someone who trafficked in such commercial crap. Sure he would have. Abrun treated everyone who bought him. Thus, or alas, he would not have been able to prevent his daughter and Phil from meeting. He was not God. Just someone who got mistaken for Him, and never bothered to correct the mistake.

Janet told her father that for all its generous servings of butteredup pop culture, Phil's book had some helpful self-confrontations. Sam Abrun, who could be as big a people pleaser as some of his patients, had even let Janet see him open the book and begin to read. He made it all the way to Page 30. Way before Page 62. Way before *Sometimes the only way you can love someone is from far away.*

But Janet was long gone by Page 30. She saw him start to read Phil's book and could only keep quiet for his first dozen sniffs and snorts.

"You know, Dad," she had begun.

He shushed her. "Please," he said, "I'm busy reading my *former* patient's book." Dr. Abrun repositioned himself in the bed and flipped to the back of *Where Can I Stow My Baggage?* "Is there an index? I'm looking for the first mention of 'disappointment.'"

Janet stood. "You just passed it."

She walked downstairs, gave her mother a hug, and said she'd send an invitation when she and Phil settled on a date. She hated lying to her mother, especially when her mother knew she was lying.

Janet made it two-plus blocks from her parents' house before throwing up behind a bush. She called Phil in New York, got the machine, and gulped softly, "I know it's tough for you to get around, but I need you to meet me at Grand Central. I'll be on the six o'clock." By then, he had picked up the phone, and she let him hear her cry.

They sat downstairs in the Food Court at Grand Central and talked long enough for four shifts of commuting herds to be loaded and primed and pumped into another time. In many ways, it was their first conversation. Well, the first one where Phil was not being helped or asked to explain what he meant. No, the only requirement here was for Phil to look at Janet and nod and keep his hands where they could hold and be held. And to listen. To listen in that manner in which men so often struggle.

No problem. He got to watch this woman he had until now known was nothing short of remarkable deliver on that promise to herself. She allowed each emotion—anger, sadness, guilt, shame, and their custom blends—to journey through her and linger where it needed. Janet had never wanted to be a cliché. The approval-starved daughter? She had been fed enough to live pretty well. The other cliché, therapist with screwed-up children, she had avoided. The third cliché, remarkable woman with the same needs as an un-remarkable woman, was now sprouting its bud in plain sight. His. And hers. Here in the Food Court at Grand Central, she allowed the right man a glimpse at the moment when the perpetual sentry in front of her vulnerability had left its post to go out for a smoke.

When it was over, she apologized for nothing, except for the two flights of steps Phil had to face to reach street level. At the top, she kissed his cheek and handed him a Larchmont timetable to throw away. That was the last time Janet had gone out to see her dad. Two months ago. Good Christ, a lot had happened two months ago.

Okay, the phone call. It had come from the Irish Shrink, maybe three hours after Phil had limped out of his office. It was their sec-ond session since he had returned from his trip to Long Island. Eight days before, Phil and Janet had taken the train out to Old Westbury to pay a visit to Jamie Popken. Jamie McManus Popken. His daugh-ter or his niece. And eleven-and-a-half-month-old Amy Popken, his granddaughter or his grand-niece. Or is it great-niece? Great.

Phil had thought about making the trip alone, but there wasn't exactly a ton of recent data that "alone" worked anymore. "Would you like me to go with you?" Janet had asked.

"Like?"

"Okay, do you *need* me to go with you?"

"Shit yeah," he said. "What if she's angry?"

"Like my father was angry when I took the train out to see him?"

"That was completely different."

"How?"

"That was Metro-North. This is the Long Island Railroad."

"You know," Janet said, "you're not as funny when you're full of fear."

"I know."

"I know you know. But what you may not know is that this," she pointed at his chest, "this full of fear thing, is attractive. To me."

"No it is not."

"Yeah, what do I know? Okay, I'll go anyway."

Phil got Jamie's phone number from his brother. It was the last time they had spoken. Two months ago. Not a conscious decision. Phil figured they were bound to run into each other in the hall, but he failed to allow for the possibility that Wendy Vogelbaum might decant enough Château de Courage to summon up the word "exclusive" and dispatch Jim into the hall for good. That also happened two months ago. He was grateful enough time had passed for Wendy to resist throwing some fraternal shame Phil's way when he asked if Elly and Jake could attend his four-person bachelor party at the Stadium. Not only had Wendy said yes, she thought it was a good idea. It might have had something to do with the fact that Wendy had stopped drinking. How long had it been? Oh yeah. Two months.

Jamie McManus Popken had picked up Phil and Janet at the LIRR station in Old Westbury. He saw her smile through the front windshield of the minivan. It was a nervous or brave smile, no teeth. When had she gotten so old? She had cut her hair, too short, and shaved her beard. No, wait. That was Phil looking at himself in the windshield. *Beep!* Jamie was two minivans down. She threw open her door and even though she bounced right out, he couldn't miss how long it took. Tall. Tall and lean. And though he wouldn't be absolutely sure until after they hugged, almost as tall as him. Five-foot-eight, easy. Forget the watery blue eyes, like his. Two brown-eyed parents. It happens. That's just a longshot that comes in. Stick with tall. Tall like Jim. Everything else on her—light hair, confident nose, feisty chin—was her mother, Mickey, just stretched out.

"Are you kidding?" whispered Janet.

"What?"

"That ain't yours. She's gorgeous."

"Are you going to be this big a help throughout?" Phil mumble-asked.

"I can't promise."

Jamie ambled easily over to them, breaking briefly to imitate Phil's limp. Yeah, she was definitely Mickey's kid. Isn't that enough? Cancel the lab work. Put the mouth swabs away. Mystery solved. She's her mother's daughter, but tall. Mickey's and Jim's kid. Why not?

After the hug (tall as him, easily), Phil began to introduce her. "Jamie McManus . . ."

"Popken," she corrected.

"This is my fiancée, Janet Abrun—"

"Fitzgerald," Janet piped up.

"Well, I hope we can fit all these names in the car," said Phil. His chuckle was not returned.

Phil coaxed his first laugh out of Jamie when it took three attempts to boost himself into the passenger side of the minivan ("Reason number eight-sixty-two why I don't live in the suburbs," he grunted). He handed her a gift-wrapped Elmoish thing that Janet had picked out for the baby.

Jamie held the package up to the rearview mirror. "Janet, I'm sure you picked this out, so thank you." She then let Phil fasten his seat belt before elbowing him and saying, "She's almost a year old. In three weeks. This is bad. Even for you, Uncle Phil."

Uncle Phil! The lab work had never been scheduled. Why not?

"I just wanted to wait until the kid and I could have a decent conversation."

"Not funny, Uncle Phil."

"If you want funny, I could try and climb into the car again."

Another unreturned chuckle. Now, Jamie turned to the backseat. "Janet, I'm thrilled you're here to see the baby, but I need—"

Janet flung the side door open. "Way ahead of you, Jamie. Take whatever time you need." And then, because she didn't have to be a therapist at that moment, she got to say, "Don't let Uncle Phil try to pull any of that charming shit."

Jamie stopped her brave smile and had turned toward him, her eyes at their watery blue capacity. "Look, I know you and I haven't exactly stayed in touch, and I know things have been even more fucked up since my folks' divorce, but I figured you might be interested in your first grand" —she gulped— "niece. Or great-niece. Whatever the hell it is."

Gulp indeed. Phil had grabbed her hand and apologized and run together some words to the effect of the never-ending distraction of physical pain and having had trouble getting around during the last year.

To no effect. "That's bullshit, Uncle Phil." She tossed the gift into the backseat.

"Yeah, you're right. Again, I apologize." Phil realized he hadn't brought anything for her. "Jamie, how about calling me Phil? Let's face it, I haven't been much of an uncle."

Another elbow from Jamie. "Well, here's your chance. Here's your chance to be a great-uncle." She beeped and waved at Janet to climb back in. "And try not to fuck it up with her."

They stayed just shy of two hours. By then, Phil was one of at least four people more than ready for a nap. Even the nanny, a quietly hustling Ecuadorian blur named Mariella, looked like she could go down for a while. Jamie and Amy put together a live highlight reel of all a one-year-old girl needs to do to win over a still-single guy. Which is pretty much just demonstrating toys, eating, and laughing. Janet had briefly tried to get the little girl's attention, but quickly realized her place was standing next to Mariella, eating and laughing, behind the action.

"Her personality has really started to develop," said Jamie. "She's got my temper and George, my husband's, concentration. And she loves the men. I guess that's me, too."

Phil would have to take Jamie's word for all that. Maybe he would be able to focus on Amy's developing personality and divvy up traits accordingly on his next visit. But on this day, Phil was thoroughly distracted by the surface area. By the physical plant of little Amy Popken. Squaring jaw to a welcoming smile to soft eyes underneath lids beginning to hood. Hooded eyelids. Item #1A in the genetic catalog of Jim McManus.

"Jesus, she looks like Jimmy."

"ARRRGG!" said Jamie. "When is somebody going to say she looks like me? I mean, I'm sitting right here."

"ARRRGGGG," Amy said. Got a big, big laugh, especially from her. So, she did it again. *ARRRGGG* . . . Repeating material and laughing at your own shit? Again, put the swabs away. For good. This was Jim's grandkid.

"I mean, people used to be polite," Jamie went on, "I might get a, 'Oh, I see a little something around the mouth that's you . . . ' but in the last few weeks, ever since she lost her baby fat, when they see her and my dad together, forget it. They double take like I'm the friggin' nanny." She looked behind her and saw Mariella had stopped folding laundry. "No offense, Mariella. *Perdóneme por favor.*"

"Jamie, I'd like to help you out," Janet said. "But I only met Phil's brother a couple of times and I look at her and, well, son of a bitch."

Phil fired a stare at Janet with the force to spin her around and send her back to look at the Popkens' living-room book collection. Jamie laughed, cupped Amy's ears, and mouthed "son of a bitch."

No wonder it had been so easy for Jim to give his brother the phone number in Old Westbury. No wonder he was able to love Marty Fleck as only a free man could. In the bat of a hooded lid, Jim McManus had been redrawn by the undeniable features of little Amy Popken. Her baby fat fell off, and irrevocably, he had become lighter. Lose a daughter, get back a brother. Gain a great-niece. Son of a bitch.

Janet pulled an interesting-looking paperback out of the shelf, and Amy, sensing a gambit from her dark-haired rival, scrambled up onto the couch and handed Phil one of her books, *Show Me the Way to Sesame Street.* And that's how he spent the last half hour in Old Westbury. Reading *Show Me the Way to Sesame Street.* Eight, nine times. Each time as interested as he knew she wanted him to be. Each time, more solicitous of her approval. The approval of Amy Popken.

The cab came to take them back to the station and Phil stood in the doorway for what would never be long enough, and got his leg squeezed by Amy. The left leg. And we'd all like to hear that his head twitched, his hip flexed, his tendons fired, and he waved the cabdriver off, and jogged three ten-minute miles in street clothes and Weejuns and made the 5:15 to Penn Station with nary a pant. But this is Phil Camp, remember? He bent over as far as he could, just north of her ears, and whispered, "Amy? Uncle Phil has to go home and take sixteen Tylenol. ARRRGGGGG!"

"ARRRGGGGG!" she said.

Jamie pried her daughter free and picked her up. "Good-bye, Phil," she said. "Great-Uncle Phil." Phil walked backward to the cab to amass all of the waving. Which worked out well, because walking backward, he looked closer to normal.

Janet stayed behind, to kiss Jamie, and thank her for being a better sport than Phil had any right to expect. "I know the problem he has with kids," Jamie said. "He had it with me for as long as I can remember. But today, this was great to see. I've been waiting for this most of my life, even when I stopped waiting for it."

A half-hug, and then Janet leaned over and kissed Amy on the forehead, which catapulted the little girl into a pep rally of kicking, screaming, and weeping.

"Somebody is very, very tired, "Jamie said.

"She sure is," said Janet, "but I'll nap on the train."

They shared a laugh and Jamie yelled for Mariella, who carted screaming Amy Popken back into the house. That left more than enough room for a full hug.

"Please," Jamie changed the syntax of a previous remark, "don't let him fuck this up."

"I'll try."

"He needs you."

"Yeah, well, maybe," Janet coughed, "but I know he's worth needing."

"Why's he limping so?"

Janet became much less of a doctor. "He doesn't know yet." She smiled and unnecessarily talked out of the side of her mouth. "I like to think it's so he can't run away."

A last laugh and hug and Janet bounded to the cab, where she found Phil pressed against the street-side door, his back turned three-quarters away from her.

"Hah! That was great!" She nudged Phil, who did not move.

"Until the end."

"What?"

"Until the end," he repeated, "when you made her cry."

Janet began to laugh, which she quickly realized was a mistake about the size of the *Mission Accomplished* banner. Not quickly enough. Phil turned around and she saw how angry he was.

"I'm sorry hearing that upset you," she said. "But you know she's a little girl and they get tired."

"Train station," Phil told the driver, who hadn't pulled away.

"And you know that's what's they do when they get tired. They cry."

"TRAIN STATION!"

The driver jumped. "Lady please needs to close door."

They rode the 2.8 miles in silence, gathering talking points for the train station parking lot open-air showdown.

"I fucking know babies cry when they're tired," Phil had begun, "but that doesn't happen the way it did, when it did, with me sitting in a fucking cab, if you don't hang around after the visit is *over*, with me sitting in a fucking cab, and try to make this about you."

"If I apologize for keeping you waiting, are we done?"

"No."

"I didn't think so, but I am apologizing anyway." Janet exhaled. "Okay, then. Why are you so furious at me? I ruined your exit, didn't I?"

Phil stared at her, as if it was too early in the argument for such insight.

"Okay," she said. "I apologize for that as well. And I mean it. But you got to let me know this was your plan at the end. I really, really thought I was helping. Yeah, okay, I was helping myself as well. You need to let me up on this. I have to be allowed to seek people's approval as well. Especially people who are important to you."

Phil's stare added some words. "How do you know who's important to me?"

"You're right, I don't."

"You're goddamn right you don't."

"Do you?"

Phil looked for the 5:15, or any set of railroad cars that could chug him from where he stood right then.

"You don't want to have this conversation," Janet continued. "And it ain't thrilling me. I'm going to say one last thing, not as a shrink, or Abrun's daughter, and not as your fiancée, which I may not be anymore after you hear this."

"I cannot fucking wait." Another longing gaze down the west-bound track. Where was that five-fucking-fif-fucking-teen?

Janet throttled the timbre of her voice back to an empathetic rumble. "You spent the better part of the day beyond relieved that that little girl is not your grandchild, and thus, Jamie is not your daughter. It was wonderful to see. I was hoping it might free you from everything that has locked you down, and frankly, leave some more room for me. But then you heard that little girl cry and it made you angry. Are you angry because she's crying and you can't do anything about it? Or are you angry because she's crying and you're not allowed to do anything about it, because it's not your grandchild? The answer, by the way, is not necessary to know. But the fact that all these conflicting feelings exist is. So, no, I don't know who's important to you. Have no idea. I think I am, because you thought enough to snap at me. I hope I am, because I'd like, love, to get through this shit, and readjust the scale so there's the possibility we can go back to taking care of each other. Big step coming here today. You got one answer. That's great. And unlike me with my dad, you probably want to come back."

Janet began to cry, remembered her credo, *crying equals losing,* and with a wrench-twist to her eyes, stopped.

"I'm sorry," said Phil. "I hope I'm still your fiancée."

Crying equals . . . fuck it! Here came the tears. And the 5:15. They were far into the parking lot and would have to hustle.

"By the way, asshole," she said after they plopped down into their seats. "Coming up the ramp just now, you were walking pretty fucking good."

That was the trip to Long Island. There is a happier ending. Phil got home, and only took four Tylenol.

Okay, the phone call.

Three hours after their second session since he returned from Old Westbury, the Irish Shrink called Phil and—what are the odds?—found him lying on The Pad thinking about either what he was going to do or what the fuck he was going to do.

They spoke for no more than two minutes. And it was gloriously one-sided. The Irish Shrink said, quite succinctly, "Phil, you've been limping for a year. We've covered all the major relationships in your life. You're getting married and seem very happy about that. You just saw a girl who you thought might be your daughter and a little girl who might be your granddaughter and you're pretty sure that is not the case. And you seem very happy about that. You've confronted deep rage about your brother and found out, quite by accident, how much he loves and respects you. And you seem very clear, even happy, about that. In other words, everything is better, except your leg. You are still limping, and not only that and maybe it's just me, the limp seems worse. Your pain seems worse. And you don't want to take narcotics, which I respect. But I've thought about this, and for me to continue to work with you when you are in this kind of constant physical pain and there doesn't seem to be an ongoing emotional crisis is, I think, cruel. As a patient, you are a delight. I look forward to seeing you. You are never late and you pay on time. But this is not about my needs. You need to get out of pain. I know pain is the touchstone of growth and all that shit, but this is too much of a distraction. So, I'm telling you, do whatever you have to do to get out of pain, and after that, if you want to resume the work here, I'm available. I know this sounds like the Irish Shrink being unconventional and kicking you out. But I am no longer the Irish Shrink. I am now Pat O'Reagan, your friend. So, as your friend, may I suggest trying acupuncture?"

Phil uttered the first of his only two lines in the conversation. "You know, I've actually been thinking about filling a bottle with M&Ms, writing 'Vicodin' on the side, and taking two every four hours to see what would happen."

Pat (*Pat?*) O'Reagan laughed. "That's an interesting controlled experiment. But seriously, if you're looking for something nonnarcotic, what about acupuncture?"

Then the second line, which he never finished. "Tried it a while ago. And Dr. Abrun says no acupuncture. He says you should not—"

"Hey, *fuck Abrun*! He ain't working. Ask his daughter how she likes seeing you wince around the house."

"Uh-huh."

"Phil, you need to get out of pain. I'm going to go now. Sometimes, we need to stop yakking. I'll be praying for you." *Click.*

Sometimes, we need to stop yakking. A bromide beneath Marty Fleck, but catchy nonetheless. And sticky. Phil got Janet to refer him to an acupuncturist and a physical therapist in the same office downtown. (Way downtown. Where his screams were out of earshot of her father.) He did that twice a week. Once a week, Monday or Thursday depending on the schedule, he took a town car to the Bronx and saw the Yankees's team chiropractor. That referral had been the first gift from Jeter.

The second were these seats.

"Get something, Derek," Phil yelled. Jeter, four rows away in the on deck circle, rapped his batting helmet twice with a closed fist. He was leading off in the bottom of the seventh. A hit here, and he'd be over .290 for the first time since last season.

And, like the maddeningly incremental climb of a batting average, so had Phil's progress edged up during the last eight weeks. There was still pain, but the humane kind. And if he had to yak, Janet had to at least pretend to listen. That was the law. The only thing that was still as grimace-worthy as before was getting up out of his chair.

"*And now, please rise . . .*"

Good Christ.

"*. . . and we ask you to join Dr. Ronan Tynan as we honor America.*"

Ronan Tynan, the Irish Tenor, stood just in front of home plate. Talk about maddeningly incremental. His version of "God Bless America," which the Yankees had first trotted out to after September 11, had metastasized from appropriately stirring to an extended jingo-jangle of mourning.

While the storm clouds gathered far across the sea
Let us swear allegiance to a land that's free,
Let us all be grateful for a land so fair,
As we raise our voices in a solemn prayer . . .
God ble—

In perfect pitch, Elly's cell phone chirped.

"Call back in five minutes," she whispered.

"He'll only be halfway through," muttered Walker.

"It was for you, Phil," Elly said. "Your brother."

Seven minutes later, with Jeter standing on first after getting hit by a fastball in his enviable tush, she handed Phil the phone. He had just taken a gulp of Diet Coke to wash down two M&Ms.

"Sorry, Philly. I got Elly's cell number from Wendy."

"That's okay. Good to hear from you."

"Maybe not. Dad died this afternoon."

"Yeah, well . . . Mom know?"

"Yeah. Yeah. Well, as much as she can know. I know the place, Carlton-Willard, left a message at your apartment, but I didn't want you coming home to it."

"Thanks for the call, Jimmy. I really appreciate it."

"You want to know when the funeral is?"

"Thursday at four?"

"Shit." Jim coughed. "How the fuck did you know?"

24

During Christmas or spring vacation the year they were both at Cabot Hill, Phil and Jim were up late one night watching *The Tonight Show*. In the middle of his segment with Johnny, Don Rickles looked down the couch at whoever the first guest had been, the only person in the building not laughing, and said, "You know, if you were Jewish and you sat like that for twenty-four hours, we'd have to bury you." Carson, Shegetz-in-Chief, almost upended himself in his chair, and the Brothers Camp knew how funny the line was without quite knowing why. The next morning, as their father catatonically awaited his breakfast, Jim reissued the remark with syntactic and denominational perfection. "Dad, if you sit like that for another twenty-three hours, we'll have to bury you."

This is the kind of memory that should not be rattling around as you walked toward the graveside ceremony that will be your father's funeral. But Phil figured if he kept his head down, the others might think he was overcome with grief rather than trying to avoid eye contact with his brother, who he knew was thinking the very same thing and probably taking the same measures. And neither of them could risk a snortling, chortling crack-up, which might force their mother to send them away from the table, again.

Might.

"There is a time and a place for laughter, and this is neither the time, nor the place," Shirley Camp used to say to her boys. In fact, it would have taken a hand recount to figure out which saw she unsheathed more while they were growing up: That one, or "I have a little shadow who goes in and out with me," her standard greeting for Jim and Phil whenever they sped into a room with no daylight between them.

Ah, it would have been wonderful to hear either of those sayings on this day, but Shirley was only as present as the vengeful god Dementia would allow. A light blue floral-print sundress hung loosely. She had lost a good bit of weight and kept patting the dress in her wheelchair as if to revive the recall of the last time she had worn it. She smiled and patted the dress and calmly went where she was pushed. Calm. You want to say happy. You could. She saw her sons and nodded, slowly closing her eyes. The original hooded lids. Calm. Quiet. Skin smooth. Fewer lines uttered than on her face. She might come up with "Hello," "Sure," or "That's nice," and might actually say it in spots where it made sense. Anything beyond that was rare.

They had both faded relatively young. Harry Camp had been diagnosed with Alzheimers ten years ago, at seventy-four, and less than a year later, just seventy, Shirley overnight went from caregiver to fellow afflictee, joining her husband like there was some neurological early opt-out package she couldn't pass up. It was 1995, four years from the first coinage of the phrase "compassionate conservative," so Jim could have given a shit about the old man. But when Phil told him about the mother they shared, he used his Gingrich Revolution–era influence to place them in Carlton-Willard, a multilevel assisted living facility in Bedford, Massachusetts, which normally had a seven-year waiting list.

"You know I'm only doing this, pulling these strings, because it's Mom," Jim had told Phil, repeatedly.

"Yes, I know, Jimmy."

"And I'm doing it purely out of obligation."

"I appreciate that."

"I'm not doing it because I'm a nice guy."

"Oh, I know," Phil would always say. And his words would always land irony-free.

Harry and Shirley shared an apartment for two years, as long as it took them to become strangers, then were adjourned to different rooms, then wings, then floors. Better that way. Better to bark fragments and nonsequiturs and indeterminate whimpers where they cannot land on a shared past.

So no, no one got to hear "There is a time and a place . . ." or "I have a little shadow . . ." Sorry. But Shirley Camp did manage two complete sentences that afternoon. Within minutes and yards of one other, Shirley served a bon mot to each of her sons that would etch more indelibly than any Kaddish couplet. When Jim took her hand as they were unloading the casket from the hearse and whispered, "He's okay, Mom. He's at peace," she said, "Sure. I gave him an Imodium." And moments later, when Phil walked Janet up to the wheelchair and introduced her as his fiancée, Shirley smiled, grabbed his wrist, and declared, "He's still got a lot of jizz in him." Regrettably, Jim overheard the remark and as Phil tried to catch his breath, sidled up to Janet, and soft-spoke, "Well, of course she's going to say that. She's his mother. Big surprise."

Jim, Jamie, and Amy had driven up in the minivan the night before. They picked up Phil and Janet at the Route 128 train station when the Acela hissed in Thursday afternoon at 1:30. In their second meeting, Amy and Janet got along as if they were old friends. From the backseat, Janet played peek-a-boo with the little girl long enough to gather a dozen gleeful squeals and even more eyeballed data to determine lineage.

"Jim, I'm telling you, she could be your daughter," Janet said, then catching herself, "Er, I'm telling you because I know your ego missed its noon feeding today."

Phil's neck stopped tightening and Jamie laughed. "She's got you down, Dad," she said.

Jim nodded. "She certainly does. And normally, a comment like that, however precise, might hurt my feelings. But it's a beautiful day, I'm with my family, my granddaughter, and we're on our way to my stepfather's funeral."

"Dad!"

"Right. We need to stop for lunch first."

"Brigham's off Exit Twenty-seven?" said Phil.

Jim McManus beamed into the rearview mirror at his brother. "Just when the day couldn't get any better. . . ."

The ride over in the minivan was an especially lively one. Anyone who still doubts the properties of pure cane sugar as a stimulant should have tagged along. Ignited by Brigham's sundaes, Jim and Phil swatted around stories about the deceased, the man whose role in their lives had been neither leading nor supporting. Exactly zero of the stories were complimentary or touching, nor were they particularly funny. And they were all woefully out of context. To be someone other than Phil or Jim and appreciate these tales of negation and disinterest, you needed a time machine, not a Dodge Grand Caravan. But the two of them were moved to tearful hysteria and guffaw-beseeching each other for mercy, and their helplessness was rampant enough to get the three girls laughing as well. That is, until Phil invoked the memory of Rickles on *The Tonight Show* and Jim's crack to his father the next morning.

"Yeesh," Janet said.

Jamie shifted Amy into a postgiggling position and wiped her eyes. "Dad, can I ask you something?"

"Sure."

"Two things."

"I bet I know one of them."

"Let's hear it."

Jim smirked at Phil in the rearview mirror. "If he was such a horrible guy, why am I going to his funeral?"

"Right."

"I'm going to be with my mother. Grandma."

"But she can't tell if you're there or not."

"I believe she can. However, if you're right and she can't tell," another rearview smirk, "then I'm going there to be with my brother."

Phil patted Jim on the shoulder, and his brother clasped his hand. He had him. "I knew you'd bring up that family values bullshit eventually," accused Phil, "you right wing *Seven Hundred Club* half-a-Ralph-Reed-New-Testament-thumping dink." Jim McManus, radio gasbag, gave his best on-air laugh.

"You got me," Jim said. "But I know I got you before." Which brought out Phil's first rearview smirk.

"Which brings me to my second question," Jamie resumed. "Is this the reason why we were brought up Catholic?"

"Hah! Excellent question," said Janet.

"Hah!" Amy yelped.

Jim put his right clicker on. "Look, that's a little complicated."

"That's what you always say, Dad. 'It's complicated. We don't have enough time.'"

"Jamie, I say it because it is complicated, and we're almost there. So, maybe—"

"If you don't mind," Phil interrupted, "I think I can explain."

"Go ahead, Uncle Phil."

"I don't know if I want to hear this," Jim said.

"I think you do," Phil cleared his throat. "A fifty-year-old Jewish man is in a hospital."

"Holy Mother of Christ."

"No, Mass General. He's been told he's going to die, he won't last the night, so he asks for a rabbi to give him the last rites. It's late at night. The hospital can't find a rabbi. They say how about a priest? There's one on the floor. He says fine. The priest shows up, but tells the man in order to get the last rites, he has to convert. The man says okay. The priest gives him the last rites. The next morning, the man wakes up. He's fine. The doctors come in, run all the tests. They say, this is unbelievable, we've never seen anything like it. We're going to release you this afternoon. So, they release the guy, he goes home, he walks in his house, sees his wife, yells, 'Sweetheart, can you believe it? I'm alive!' and she says, 'Don't touch any of the food. It's for the shiva.' He goes upstairs, walks into his daughter's room, says, 'Honey, your father's alive!' and she puts her hand over the phone and says, 'Daddy, how many times do I have to tell you to knock?' So, he walks into the next bedroom. His son's playing a video game. He says, 'Son, my son. I'm back from the dead! Come give your dad a hug.' And the kid says, 'Just let me finish this game.' Finally, he walks into his bedroom. The phone rings. He picks it up. It's the priest. The priest says, 'I heard the news. I just wanted to call and say it's a miracle. Praise the Lord! How are you?' And the guy says, 'You're right. It is a miracle. I've been a Catholic less than twenty-four hours and I hate three Jews already!"

You wouldn't think it was possible, but the joke fell flatter with the three girls than the Rickles line, and did better with Jim, who had never heard it.

"That does not answer the question," Jamie said.

"Well, it does for me!" shrieked Jim, and his subsequent pounding on the steering wheel made him unable to follow the hearse and the limo and turn into the main entrance at Mount Ararat Cemetery. The two-mile double-back went a long way toward sedating the man-children in the minivan, but the Brothers Camp made an unspoken concord to keep their heads down or out of each other's horizon line until after the rabbi's benediction.

Phil was surprised at his difficulty getting out of the minivan. Even more than getting into the same minivan at the train station in Old Westbury two months ago, if that's possible. And it was. Here he was, at his father's funeral. Finally. And yet his leg suddenly became a stinging miscreant. Son of a bitch.

Even more surprising was the almost immediate request by his brother once they were all out of the car. "Philly, I gotta take a walk. I need you to watch everybody. I'll be back in a few."

Sure. Go nuts. Go take the walk I cannot take, thought Phil. Instead, he said, "Do what you need to do." He did not look up.

Jim McManus jogged like the ex-footballer he was on a car-and-a-quarter width intra-grave road to the closest area out of earshot. Only then could his walk begin. He skimmed the names on the headstones: *Sobin, Fine, Brezniak, Rodman, Carnovsky,* and four types of *Pearl*. He was far enough away from his brother to look up. He raised his face and shot his eyes to the top of his head. "What am I doing here?" he said quietly.

He tilted his head back. He had not used this particular angle to talk to God in years. Jim McManus, radio genius, usually dialed in on a frequency that ran due south, an open-line connection that could only be made on his knees, with his eyes closed, head lolled off its hinge and hands clasped firm.

"What am I doing here?"

Louder. *"What am I doing here?!?"* No answer. Maybe it was the top of the hour and they were breaking for news.

He picked up one of the small stones lying on a headstone, *Glovsky,* thought about testing his arm, thought better. He placed it back down, lowered his gaze and voice. "I don't belong here," Jim whispered. "What is the point? He's not my father and he never was, even when I thought he was. I got nowhere to go." He kicked at some well-maintained sod. "Stand in this place and listen to that crap? Stand here for what? What was I thinking? Drag me here for what? To show off what a good father I am? Do I even know what that is? Fucking Christ God knows I don't."

It was hardly an opportune moment for Jim to think about his real father, Bob McManus. Not enough time. And much too late in everyone's story. Or maybe there was enough time. There had only been two meetings. That first night in Maryland, before Jim and Mickey were married, when he found what was surely a once-imposing presence of a man at the end of a bar called the Early Times. Jim introduced himself, shared four bourbons and left before Bob McManus could tell him for the dozenth time to "get right with Jesus."

Jim looked back and saw Jamie motioning for him. Harry Camp's funeral was ready to begin. He held up a finger. One more minute. Thanks.

The last meeting with Bob McManus was seven years later—1984. Twenty years ago. VA Hospital just outside Virginia Beach. Who knew he was a veteran? Who knew he'd wound up in Virginia? The hospital contacted Jim through the local radio station that carried his show and told him his father was dying. Jim McManus made it down there two days before the end. Got to tell his real old man he had gotten right with Jesus. Got to hear Bob McManus say, "Tell Him thanks for the fucking cancer," and ask if he'd brought a bottle. "No, Dad," he said for the first time.

"Then what good are you?" said Bob McManus, who squeezed his eyes and the button on his morphine drip simultaneously.

Jim's squeezed eyes were opened by a hand on his shoulder. Phil had made it all the way over against his leg's will. It was as if the pain that was clearly shaking his brother ran along the ground and buffeted his crossing.

"Ready?" Phil asked.

"Yeah."

"You're not going to leave me alone with him, are you?"

They looked at each other for the first time since climbing out of the minivan. "No, Phil," Jim said. "I'm not going to leave you alone with . . . Dad."

The rabbi, a gangly sort named Gabe Erman, was anything but awkward when it came to eulogizing a man he had only heard of a phone call ago. He spoke of the glorious imperfection of our time on Earth and asked that all who would participate in the ritual of tossing shovelfuls of dirt into the grave and onto the pine box do so with care, as one might throw a comforter over a friend who had dozed off and was still slumbering when the temperature dropped. Although neither Phil nor Jim heeded his suggestion (both righteously clinging to the "shove" in "shovel" rather than the "comfort" in "comforter"), they were gripped by the last thing the rabbi said before asking all who could to join in the Mourner's Kaddish. He was trying to impart to the seven who had gathered how the Afterlife is an amorphous, elusive concept hatched in meetings of those left behind on Earth. And like all good men of faith, he said he had searched for the ideal words to encapsulate the distance between here and gone. "It's not that far," Rabbi Erman said, "and it's not too far to send your love. And sometimes, that's the only way to love."

Jim elbowed Phil, but his head stayed down. "He stole your shit," his older brother whispered. Phil smiled, and began mumbling his way through the Kaddish. He figured it would just be him and Gangly Gabe Erman, but he heard another voice. Higher. Softer. Jamie McManus Popken.

Right, she had converted. A couple years ago. Jamie had embarked on that earnest path shortly after she had gotten engaged to George Popken. She had not entered into this lightly. It might have caused more of a righteous stir within her own family, but Jamie's swap of faith was processed almost simultaneously with her parents' divorce. Jamie loved her father, and while it was charming on those rare occasions when he didn't have all the answers, she had always longed for a relationship where the phrases "It's complicated" or "We don't have the time" had no place. She had found that relationship with George. Conversion was the first thing Jamie McManus had done without seeking approval or explanation. And she knew she had made the right decision when her future in-laws, the Popkens, said, "Are you sure, dear?" Yeesh. No wonder the *fifty-year-old Jewish man is in a hospital* . . . joke had died so.

Jamie and George's wedding had been held in some skyscrap-agogue on Long Island, the Bnai Mahal. Jim McManus walked his tall, piety-bedecked daughter down the aisle, then took his place, twenty rows behind his now ex-wife Mickey. Phil had sent his regrets. The date fell only months away from the Trish bomb scare, and he didn't feel like jinxing another templed union. It also fell smack in the middle of radio silence with his brother, and Phil was not about to show up and get thrown against another wall by the father of the bride. He never gave either of those reasons, just FedExed a gift certificate for a week at Canyon Ranch in the Berkshires and hoped it would be enough to herbal wrap anyone's disappointment. It was.

In fact, it worked so well, Phil began regularly sending gifts as his envoys. Over a year before his limp began and he had the plain-to-see physical excuse for not showing up anywhere, he had put this online catalog-armed emissary system in place. It was an especially huge hit with the staff at Carlton-Willard. When his father stopped recognizing Phil, it was frankly a relief. The mind had finally caught up with the attitude. But, in the spring of 2002, when Shirley Camp couldn't tell whether the smiling man walking toward her was her son or an orderly, that proved to be a garment too coarse, too ill-fitting to don. Suddenly, here was baggage that no tidy metaphor could lift. So, Phil stopped coming, but the gifts did not. Today, he had identified a small silver Tiffany pin on the sweater of Magdalene, the nurse and wheelchair driver, and the light blue floral print hanging loosely on Shirley was something a personal online shopper from Bergdorf had helped him pick out for her last birthday. Seven months and two sizes ago.

"May the source of peace send peace to all who mourn," summed Rabbi Erman, "and comfort all the bereaved among us. Amen."

"Amen," said those who could.

"Ahhhh!" said Amy.

Shirley Camp heard it and laughed. That response was encouraging enough for Magdalene to motion Jamie over with the little girl. Why not?

"This is Amy, your great-granddaughter."

"Sure," said Shirley.

Jim, Jamie, and Amy covered her in generations. Phil took it all in, grabbed Janet's hand, and they walked over to Gangly Gabe Erman and asked if he wouldn't mind hanging around a few more minutes.

"What's up?" asked the rabbi.

"Got time for a quick wedding?" Phil said.

"Here?"

"Yeah. Although maybe we should move down a little."

"Are you sure?"

Janet nodded. "We were supposed to be at City Hall in Manhattan today. Right now, in fact. Look, Rabbi, we don't have a license, and this all would be purely ceremonial, but I think he—" She hip-checked Phil. On the left side. He stood tall and did not waver. Like a man who at that moment had nothing wrong with him.

"There are some people here who I'd like to see this," Phil said.

"Folks," Rabbi Erman called out, "one more piece of business. If you could all just follow me over to that little patch of land on the left there, it would be my great pleasure to marry Phil and . . ." mumbling, "need a name . . ."

"Janet."

"Janet!"

The guys with the ropes and shovels stood respectfully in the back, like the world's grimiest ushers. One of them had knocked on the window of the limo, and the driver woke up and grabbed the two single roses out of his backseat and walked them over to Janet.

"This is happening this is happening this is happening this is happening this is happening . . ."

Janet knew the only thing that would stop this mantra was Kleenex. What a break. Jamie had Kleenex, and wipes. And that was more than enough to make her maid of honor. She handed Amy off to Magdalene, who held her close enough to the wheelchair so Shirley could touch her little toes.

Jamie took her job seriously. Shortly before the rabbi was to begin the second, unscheduled, ceremony, she unnecessarily stage-whispered "Uncle Phil!" and handed him her wedding band, a twisted platinum braid of sapphires and diamonds, which would go nicely with Janet's cotton navy suit. Or his cotton navy suit.

Phil was about to put the ring in his pocket, but instead tapped Jim on the wrist with it. He pointed back at the guys with the shovels. "You think any of them are Jewish?" he asked, and before Jim could answer, "probably not. Well, then. Looks like you're the best man." He handed Jim his daughter's wedding band. Jim McManus straightened his tie, then his brother's, then, as he had much of the last hour, stared straight down with bedewed eyes.

The entire ceremony took maybe three minutes. Twelve, if you add in the time it took to herd and resituate the group. Without the aid of a sextant, Phil steered his mother's wheelchair into the optimum coordinates where everyone else could be her shade. They had all moved no more than ten yards from Harry Camp's fresh-topped tomb to a well-dandelioned corner, perhaps the only unbroken ground at Mount Ararat Cemetery, walled on two sides by the simple smoothed backs of recent headstones. Phil never bothered to check the stone he had been standing directly in front of. Shame.

LENNY MILLMAN
1942–2004
Smoking allowed . . . and encouraged

Rabbi Erman opted for poetry over piety, lilting a stanza from Derek Walcott that no one would remember but should have, before heading straight for the vows. When it was over, everyone would have kept hugging, but Amy began to cry and Shirley Camp might have joined her if she hadn't been kissed on the head. By Magdalene. Jamie was handed her daughter and ring back. The limo driver pushed the wheelchair.

Phil, Janet, and Jim trailed the rest of the field as they made their way back up the small slope to where the cars were parked.

"You okay, Philly?" asked Jim.

"Yeah."

"Because I can get the limo guy to drop Mom off and bring the wheelchair back for you."

Phil took three fast steps and jabbed at his brother, who raced up the slope chuckling and didn't bother to look back and check if he was being chased. He didn't stop until he reached Jamie and Amy at the minivan.

By the way, those three fast steps? They were not Phil's idea. That was all his legs' doing. Both of them. Both of them had been in on it. He turned around and looked at Janet, who saw it all and was in mid-sniff.

"Hey," she choked up on the stem of her roses, "who needs a real marriage license?"

"We do."

"But this is enough for now."

"For now? Sure."

The others were waiting. They began to make their way up the small slope, and Phil could feel the flexion start to defect from his left side. Familiar. Could the toothache ass be far behind? Pain. Yeah, inevitable. So, why waste time trying to figure out the inevitable? Why keep waiting for a limp to go away? No, the limp would go away when its business here was done. Any sooner, and Phil might wind up like so many others, who limp on the inside.

"Jesus," Phil said, "when did they put this giant hill in?" He began to reach into his pants pocket, but remembered he'd left the plastic prescription bottle with the M&Ms in the minivan. He almost slowed even more, but felt an arm around his lower back and a hand settle just above his left hip. That would be enough for now.

Epilogue

Bloggage Handling

by Stacey Fleck

(Note: This www.excelsiorpub.com *daily blog is maintained by Stacey Fleck and devoted to news and information about her husband, former Excelsior Publications columnist Marty Fleck, whom she has not heard from since he left, allegedly for Uruguay, last April 21.)*

October 7 / Day 171

Still no word.

Eleven more days until I buy the Pilates machine and turn his office into a gym. I know I said Thanksgiving, but six months is more than fair.

Posted by SF at 10:15 A.M. 44,357 views / 1354 comments

Acknowledgments

And now, please welcome your happy ending!!!

Last April, less than three weeks after my not-from-this-earth agent, Mary Evans, sold this book to David Rosenthal at Simon & Schuster, I went to see yet another doctor, who took one look at a recent X-ray and said, "You need a hip replacement. I'm not saying you should get one, I'm saying you have to get one. This is a no-brainer. You'll be out of pain."

I did. It was. And I am.

When I began writing whatever this would be in May 2005, I had been limping for six months. I was hoping that maybe I could "art" it out of myself. Yak on the page about my halting yet willing journey through the psychogenic and nonconventional medicine wilderness, ideally winding up in a glorious orchard of pain-free fruits. Or some other metaphor less barf-worthy.

A little over two years later, the first draft was done. Phil Camp was better, hopeful. Me, much worse. Once again, I had treated the wrong guy.

And now here we are. I walk among you, like a guy who always did that. It took what it took what it took. Great. Now I'm Popeye.

Let's move on to the acknowledgments . . .

My editor at Simon & Schuster, Priscilla Painton, was thoughtful, careful, clear, succinct, and ego-free. Hard to believe such a mythical creature could exist.

Everyone at S&S, from David to Priscilla to Victoria Meyer to Aileen Boyle to Tracey Guest to Dan Cabrera to Jonathan Evans, was enthusiastic about this novel in a way this novelist could not have imagined, and in the way big-time publishing folk can rarely afford to summon. And the fact that I am now at the house that so wonderfully took care of my uncle, Herbert Warren Wind, for so many years, is beyond humbling.

The same four people read my books as they are being written. And they are never too busy. They are, they just never say they are. Barbara Gaines gives me a gig between chapters. Lydia Weaver asks only that I sneak her father into the manuscript. My brother Tom Scheft is as encouraging as when I was a weak-hitting infielder at summer camp. And my brilliant wife, Adrianne Tolsch, seems to know what I am trying to achieve before I do. Years ago, as I was struggling to finish my first book, she said to me, "This house takes care of artists." So, I ask you, who is the writer in the family?

Alan Zweibel, who introduced me to Mary Evans, is the rarest of friends: Supportive, loyal, and the kind of man who beats you out for the 2006 Thurber Prize for American Humor.

Don Harrell taught a course in Great Jewish Writers that I had the good fortune to attend, and he had the delusional nerve to put my first novel, *The Ringer,* on the syllabus.

Julia Cameron invited me and my wife to a party at her apartment. If this means nothing to you, fire up Wikipedia and take a lesson.

Dave Letterman, who heard my news last April and offered to donate one of his hips.

Justin and Eric Stangel, Tommy Ruprecht, Lee Ellenberg, Matt Roberts, Jeremy Weiner, Bob Borden, Joe Grossman, Steve Young, Gerard Mulligan, Jill Goodwin, and everyone else who walked the picket line with me during the writers' strike.

My brothers, sisters, in-laws, nieces, nephews: Daniel, Dode,

Kevin, Ali, Sally, Jeff, Hazzy, Jonathan, Ella, Huggy, John, Sof, Callie, and Perry.

My mother, Gitty, the original smartest girl in the room. And my father, another Bill Scheft who's finally out of pain.

And the rest of the long crawl (count the doctors, win a prize!): Jonathan Alter, Larry Amoros, Matt Arizin, Tom Aronson, Mary Barclay, Mike Barrie, David Bauer, Tom Bisio, Kenny Bouse, Eddie Brill, Mike Cantor, Gerry Cash, Rob and Jana Castillo, Jane Cecil, James Clarke, Ann Corrigan, Sherise Cortez, Houston Day, Joanna DeMartin, Laurie Diamond, Chris Elliot, Sarah Eyde, Pat Farmer, Barbara Fetner, John Filo, Pat and Jack Flynn, Tom Foster, Lorraine Galler, Marilyn and Frank Gallo, Tim Gay, Gerry Gilfedder, Tom Griswold, Julie Halston, Amy Hideriotis, Kate Horrigan, June Iseman, Howard Josepher, Frank Lipman, Pat and Julianne LoPresto, Kostya Kennedy, David, Ann and Jonas Kerzner, Bob Kevoian, Nathan Lane, Artie Lange, Kristi Lee, Charlie Leerhsen, Harriet Lyons, Ronald MacKenzie, David Malone, Kathy Mavrikakis, Kathleen McCarthy, Brian McDonald, Chick McGee, Pat McGrath, Devin McIntyre, Joe McKinsey, Zack Miller-Murphy, Jim Mulholland, Dan Patrick, Mark Patrick, John O'Leary, Douglas Padgett, Dan Peres, Russell Portenoy, Sylvie Rabineau, Dean Reilly, Davis Reyes, Tommy Richards, Betty Rigelhaupt, Gerry Rioux, Chris Rock, Sheila Rogers, Craig Rubenstein, John Sarno, Frank Sebastiano, Robert Sheu, Paul Shaffer, Grant Shaud, Eric Sherman, Bob Siefert, George and Bette Silverberg, Alex Simotas, John Singer, Steve Skrovan, Kevin Sparks, Jeff Stilson, Kevin Talty, Richard Thalmann, Jeff Toobin, Bill Tolsch, Ben Walker, Reese Waters, Elly Weisenberg, Heather Williams, Gary Wynn, Richard Zoglin.

Enough. My time is up, you've been great. Enjoy the Howlin' Thurstons.

Bill Scheft
New York City
July 2008

Printed in the United States
By Bookmasters